From the Author of Grey Matter Book Series....

City of Sandglass Volume 2:

Beyond the Trenches and the Damascus Sword

Written By:

Anthony S Parker

Copyright © November 2024

By: Anthony S. Parker

All Rights Reserved. Published in the United States by: KDP AMAZON

No part of this publication may be reproduced, distributed, or transmitted in any form or by any means, including photocopying, recording, or other electronic or mechanical methods, without the prior written permission of the Author, except in the case of brief quotations embodied in critical reviews and certain other noncommercial uses permitted by copyright law. For permission requests for the text or artwork in this book, write or email the author, addressed "Attention: Anthony S. Parker," in the subject line to the email address below.

City of Sandglass Series
Regarding Copyrights
Email: authoraparker@gmail.com

ISBN: 9798343104196
Imprint: Independently published

Books › Science Fiction & Fantasy › Fantasy › Action & Adventure
Books › Science Fiction & Fantasy › Fantasy › Coming of Age
Books › Science Fiction & Fantasy › Fantasy › General

First Edition. Vol. 1

Dedication

To those who are defenseless, who fall victim to others. To the nameless victims of tragedy who have suffered, and to those who have passed on. Time is a precious gift to those who value it, appreciate it, and to those who don't take it for granted.

After you receive this book feel free to post on social media a picture of you and this book and tag the author on Instagram

@authoraparker

While you are reading it feel free to email the author @ authoraparker@gmail.com to tell him what you think of this book.

Also, for more information on his books you can look up his others works at www.authoraparker.com

Autograph Page:

****

"Imagine if you wake up every day with $84,600 in your bank account and at the end of the night, it's gone whether you wasted it or not, and then the next day you get another $84,600. If this were to happen, you would do everything in your power to spend it. Because you know, the next day you're getting the same amount again. You don't wanna leave nothing there. You'd want to make the best of it, right? Every day, you get 84,600 seconds. Why waste time? It doesn't carry over to the next day. It doesn't earn interest. Take every day and every moment and make something of it. Do something positive. Be positive and spread love and peace into the world and share it with others around you. Every second counts, time wasted is time lost forever. Don't wait for the perfect moment to live your dreams or to act. Embrace life today, seize every opportunity, cherish each moment, live boldly and passionately. Your Life is happening right now- don't let it pass you by." Director John. XCarey, @success_present

When reading this book series, do remember to keep in mind the time. Many can get lost in reading when the story is most appealing. A curious thing about Bellatrix Kai in this story. She is very much within her own time in experiencing what you are about to read of her experience in life. She has been through so much like us all. But I have found it all quite fun to get lost in if I do say so myself. Happy Reading! Remember to find the bookmark on the back of this book to cut out while reading this book. It will help you keep track of where you are in this timeline of the City of Sandglass.

Special Thanks to:

Nelda Perez

Jorge Almazan

Emily Perialas

Stephen Perialas

Starbucks Store # 29766 - McAllen, Texas

Also, by Author Anthony S. Parker:

1. Grey Matter Series Volume 1: The Story of Mark Trogmyer in The World of the Unknown
Paperback ISBN 9781723022494
MM ISBN: 9781987658781
Hardcover ISBN 979-8873075959
2. Grey Matter Series Volume 2: The Wrath of Nerogroben
Paperback ISBN 9781534993518
Hardcover ISBN 9798875518348
MM ISBN: 9789781722788681
3. Grey Matter Series Within the World of the Unknown Volumes 1 & 2
Paperback ISBN 9781707117291
4. Grey Matter Series Volume 3: Secrets of the World of the Unknown / Fourth Edition
Paperback ISBN 979-8880434091
Hardcover ISBN 979-8882508394
5. Grey Matter Series Volume 4: Mark Trogmyer and the IFRD
Paperback ISBN 9781729565216
Hardcover ISBN 979-8883704344
6. Grey Matter Series Volume 5: The Story of Thomas Joshua McPherson
Paperback ISBN 9781088990247
Hardcover ISBN 979-8320643816
7. Grey Matter Series Book of Illustrations
Paperback ISBN 9781095428160
8. Dreams: An Interactive Journal
Paperback ISBN 9781729745885
9. Dreams: The Official Notebook for Dreams: An Interactive Journal
Paperback ISBN 9781695288881
10. A Step into Self-Publishing Your Own Book
Paperback ISBN 9798623551559
11. A Daily Message of Encouragement and Wisdom
Paperback ISBN: 9798688703014
12. Serie "La materia gris" Volumen 1: La historia de Mark Trogmyer en el Mundo de lo Desconocido (Grey Matter Series) (Spanish Edition)
Paperback ISBN: 9798536496626

13. City of Sandglass Volume 1: The Story Untold Volume 1
Paperback ISBN 9798875517228
Hardcover ISBN 9798884906419

14. City of Sandglass Volume 2: The Trenches and the Sword of Damascus
Paperback ISBN 9798343104196
Hardcover ISBN 9798343102352

15. Guardians Volume 1- TBA (Drafting)
Paperback ISBN
Hardcover ISBN

16. The City of Sandglass Volume 3 – (Planning State) Pending Release NOV 2025
Paperback ISBN
Hardcover ISBN

17. Guardians Volume 2: TBA (Planning State)
Paperback ISBN
Hardcover ISBN

18. Guardians Volume 3: TBA (Planning State)
Paperback ISBN
Hardcover ISBN

19. Mindset Mastery Volume 1: - TBA (Planning State)
Paperback ISBN
Hardcover ISBN

20. A Flame that Flickered – TBA (Planning State)
Paperback ISBN
Hardcover ISBN

21 A Flame Rekindled – TBA (Possible)
Paperback ISBN
Hardcover ISBN

22. A Flame Everlasting TBA (Possible)
Paperback ISBN
Hardcover ISBN

City of Sandglass Volume 2: Beyond the Trenches and the Damascus Sword

Table of Contents

Chapter	Chapter Title	Page
1	Shawna and David Genuit	1
2	Intentions	14
3	Time Council Meeting in the Time Tower	18
4	Leadership Position	36
5	The Meeting	43
6	The Attack of the Night Stalker	58
7	The Big Reveal	77
8	The Four Night Hunters	82
9	The Final Two Weeks	87
10	Aunt Beatrice and Uncle Bernard	93
11	The Secret Six Meeting	103
12	A Hidden Shame Revealed	112
13	The Capture of the Night Stalker	132
14	Verity, The Truth	137
15	The Verdict	145
16	The Celebration of the Life Ceremony	155
17	The Secret Six First Meeting	162
18	Research	169
19	The Mission	177
20	The Trenches	182
21	The Proposal	191
22	The Village of Pequa	195
23	The Passage to the White Wall	204
24	Reprimanded and Consequences	209
25	Repairing the White Wall	213
26	Crossing the Sands of Time	227
27	Take Care of Yourself	238
28	Strengthening Relationships	248
29	Planning for a minute to a Lifetime	254

30	The Daughter we Never had	263
31	The Letter and Election Day	272
32	The Four Hours	289
33	The Clock Chimes	296
34	The Discussion of Time	317
35	Wedding Preparations	345
36	The Wedding	349
37	A Difficult Loss	359
38	The Night Terror	368
39	Old Sins Cast Long Shadows	376
40	The Titus Report	389
41	Stunned	400
42	Overcoming	404
43	The Special Gift	412
44	The Decision yet to be made	418
**	Coming Soon	423
**	Character Chart	425
**	Bookmark	428

Before we begin our story, I wanted to offer you a sort of reflection of sorts. Sometimes when discovering ourselves and things around us in life we only see things at surface value. We tend to forget the details unless you possess that type of photographic or eidetic memory that one hears about.

For example, when going to a nice restaurant, we remember the name, (sometimes), who it was that we go with whether it was family or to meet a friend or even a group of friends, or maybe someone special. But it is rare, that we remember the people who make up the restaurant, the bar tender, the wait staff, the cooks, the bussers, the hosts and hostesses. It takes sometimes what I call a double reflection to remember them. Seemingly we don't just remember them in our experiences looking back as easily. We just remember what was cooked or made for us during the visit and maybe whether it was a good or an unpleasant experience.

It was just like this situation with Bella remembering only the people that she was rescuing from the Time Road, those of whom were captured, and the victims, especially Brent's parents. But perhaps if she were paying more attention to the scenarios and who the people were within the rescue crews, she would recognize or maybe perhaps would have figured out or discovered who the shadow killer was or who was a part of the Time Road when looking back, but I digress....

Previously in The Story Untold...
We went down the stairs to find that it opened to a single stone walled hallway with wooden doors. There were four doorways into the other rooms.
The first door on the left was open already and it had shelves on either side of it with coffins labeled McKobe. No one was in it, so we closed the door and opened the second door on the right.
Just then a flood of people burst out of it as we helped them get back upstairs towards the timekeepers who helped them one by one with medical help. But still Brent's parents were not located yet.
The third door to the left was full of four dead bodies. They didn't make it. To our relief, they weren't Brent's parents.
We all held our breaths in an Erie silence as Brent reached out to the Fourth and final door to the right of us, who saw to his horror five bodies of people who were there just laying down on the ground.
Their bodies didn't move as we slowly went into the doorway.
The room was cold and drafty.
"Mom? Dad?" Brent said with tears in his eyes and was looking at them and then to me in concern as he saw them lying there before us as silence filled the room with everyone in disbelief and in horror at the scene before us...

Chapter 1
Shawna and David Genuit

I saw that the bodies were on the ground and had motioned for James to come over to me and Brent so that I could examine the bodies. James had come rushing over to us just in time to hold Brent in his arms. I had noticed that Brent was shaking visibly and screaming under extreme duress at the sight before our eyes.

Both of Brent's parents were laying on the ground before us motionless. They were next to each other lying on their stomachs. Their hands were touching each other, as if they were trying to comfort each other, as they had felt like they were at deaths door. But they seemed to be strengthened in each other's presence. Brent continued to cry and scream with feelings of anguish and disbelief, in denial, and agony all at once as he buried his face into James's chest.

"Noooooo!" he screamed while hitting James's chest as James tried to comfort Brent. I could feel how broken his heart was feeling at this moment. I empathized for him, as I had felt the same when I had lost my own parents in front of me. The only difference was I couldn't emotionally react to it like he was doing at the time. It would have been the difference between life and death if I had emotionally reacted to Kahn killing my parents screaming loudly. I felt jealous of Brent being able to emotionally let it out at the time partially but even to this day this feeling was not all too unfamiliar. However, I still had hope that Brent's parents were okay. After all these years, after everything that Brent and I went through, all the countless hours of reading and research, they just had to be... his parents had to be alive... I had desperately willed them to be alive...

I was the first one to recover at the situation, and had bent over both Brent's parent's bodies to see if maybe we could have that glimmer of hope that they would be okay. I had put my hand on their wrists one at a time and felt a faint pulse in both their wrists. I noticed, after moving their faces towards me, they still had time left on both their foreheads showing counting down the hours that they had left. His mom's time clock showed: 20:198:16:04:32 and his dad's clock showed 22:164:12:16:42 left.

"They are alive, and they have not been drained of their time Brent," I said calmly standing up in between both their unconscious bodies.

Brent slowly turned away from being buries in James's chest and wiped his tears from his face.

"Well then, what is the matter with them! Why are they lying down?" Brent asked in slight shock through tears, looking down at them wiping his eyes and then looking up at me, "Why aren't they moving or reacting to us being here with them?"

"They are alive, but only just, they are in extremely weakened and stressed-out states due to not having the nutrition that they needed to keep up their strength. They are probably scared too in states of shock because of the terror from being held captive here. But they will be okay," I said reassuringly as Brent nodded, "We just need to get them out of here."

I then walked over to the other three bodies in the room and saw that they had already died, and their time had run out I had assumed. But then something I felt at that moment called for me to double check.

I had checked their history on their time clocks, as I had seen members of the council do on multiple occasions. I was able to see that they were drained of the time that they had left. I kept it to myself, but it looked like someone had tampered and taken the time from them because there was a line next to the transaction – "it was taken unwillingly and possibly unknowingly." I thought to myself.

I made a mental note of this, but didn't want to draw attention to this. I walked over to Brent's parents, and bent down with Terrance who was kneeling over on the other side of Brent's mother's body. He nodded as we slowly stood her up. She was breathing but very slowly and hoarsely. She seemed to be in and out of consciousness. It was then that James and Brent reached down and picked up Brent's father who's voice was faint.

"Brent? Is that you, my son?" he said in a hoarse voice, weakly. I could tell that they had been severely dehydrated, noticing his dad's dry lips.

"Yes Dad, it's me. I am here with my friends, we are here to bring you home safely," Brent said crying through tears of joy. We were all in huge concern of the well-being of both of his parents. They had looked extremely skinny and had both lost a significant amount of weight, they were both dehydrated and looked like they had been there for months.

Brent, James, Socrat and I had helped bring Brent's parents, Shawna, and David outside. Almost immediately, Taylor and Tobey came running over to us, they put their hands on their foreheads and started to say something under their breaths, and a golden mist of light came from their fingers and immediately both Brent's parents were heavily sedated.

"Why did you do that?" Brent asked, anxiously.

"They need to gather their strength up; and need a few days of rest. Once we can get them stabilized with IV and their vitals checked, then we can ensure their continued health. We don't want anything to happen to them during transport."

Tobey said in concern getting them on a stretcher looking bed that seemed to appear out of nowhere.

"Transport to where?" I asked looking at Taylor.

"Well, we haven't exactly thought of a place where we think it would be safe for them yet," Taylor said looking at Tobey as he set up IVs in Brent's mom's and then his dad's hands and placed them on a metal bar that was standing up against the corner of the bed.

"I have the best place in mind for them," Terrance said from behind Tobey and Taylor who both jumped.

"Don't scare us like that Terrance! Where do we have a place for them?" Tobey said curiously.

"The Bookstore will hold them, and they will be safe there," Terrance said as I nodded in understanding thinking about the secret room.

"There is not enough space in there," Tobey said incredulously and in shock shaking his head in disagreement.

"Oh yes, there is, you will see," Terrance said with his eyes twinkling as Brent, Terrance, Tobey, Taylor, James, Socrat, and I all brought them back to the City of Sandglass - Time. It took a lot of maneuvering of Brent's parents, but we finally got to the Bookstore.

The store was dark, and the sign that usually was lit up OPEN was off, so the store was closed. Brent opened the door with his copy of the store key as everyone piled in and opened the secret room. They placed Brent's parents who were in the stretcher beds in the first quadrant on the right with the fireplace.

Tobey looked around the room in awe and started to get visibly upset.

"What is the matter Tobey," Terrance asked noticing he was shaking in slight anger.

"You knew of this place the whole time and the Time Council never has been told of this place?" Tobey asked I surprise as Terrance nodded.

"This is a private store we are not allowed to do anything to this place as this is not owned by the Time Council. It was made for the Genuit Family years ago," Terrance said calmly.

"What do you mean?" Tobey asked.

"I am surprised that you never know that the first watch maker was related to the Genuit family," Terrance said calmly as Tobey shook his head. Socrat, James, Taylor, Brent, and Bella walked over to them.

"I am so grateful we had this place for your parent's to recover in," Terrance said to Brent who nodded.

It was after I heard their conversation that I became worried about Grant. So I left the room to try to find him.

"Grant will be so happy to hear we found his son and daughter in law," I thought to myself. I left the secret room and walked to the bookstore. I walked upstairs to Grant's room and became even more concerned when I had noticed that Grant Genuit wasn't in his room. I had assumed seeing that the lights were off downstairs he would have been in his room. I looked around the bookstore and found to my horror, Grant Genuit lying on the floor in the back in the Kitchen. His clock on his forehead read he only had an fifteen minutes left to live as it counted down. 00:00:00:00:15:32

"BRENT!" I shouted four times and finally Brent, James, and Socrat came running to the Kitchen to see me on the floor next to Grant Genuit who was unconscious trying to resuscitate him.

"Grandpa!" Brent shouted through tears noticing what was going on. Immediately Brent reached for his grandfather's left wrist with the time clock on it and said, "plus temporis."

"What is he doing?" I asked myself

"It means extend more time," came the voice of Emrys in my head as I nodded in understanding.

"Are you okay?" I asked Emrys noticing a sense of discomfort in his voice.

"As spiritual beings, we can sense what is going on with Grant's body and it makes us feel a connection closer to those when they are about to move on."

Brent had repeated it a few more times and slowly I saw more time being added in green to his grandfather's timecard and slowly, I saw Brent's time clock decrease in a red color."

Brent quickly covered his time before I could read how much time he had left as he saw me looking over at him before I had a chance to read it.

"I must tell you that you mustn't do that anymore son," James said shaking his head sadly as Brent buttoned up his shirt and rolled up his grandfather's shirt sleeve.

"Everyone's time does come, and you cannot extend his life forever. It wouldn't be fair if we all lived forever, and couldn't have the ability to move on. You must understand that life is a gift, and we mustn't be selfish with time."

"No! He mustn't move on, not yet! It isn't fair!" Brent said through tears.

"Do you not understand that my grandfather hasn't seen his son and daughter-in-law in years?! It has been since I was ten years old. Now that we finally found them, I want him to have a few more years with us! He is all I had. I have had all these years, and I don't know what I would have done without him!" Brent said through tears, "That is why he can't die, not yet!"

Slowly Grant Genuit opened his eyes and looked around the room with slight embarrassment at everyone who was staring at him, "Brent Daniel Genuit, what have you done?"

Grant looked down at his arm and jumped in shock and noticed that there were five more years added to his time clock.

"Why have you done this Brent?" Grant asked Brent through tears.

"Because we found mom and dad, and I want more years with you and them together for once," Brent said through tears.

"You must understand that this is also very selfish of you in some ways, but also very selfless," Grant said thoughtfully seeing things at various perspectives. He was not sure whether to scold, praise, or thank his grandson.

There was a silence in the room for a few moments.

"I am grateful for the time you have given me Brent, but please do not do this for me again. I believe that my time will come when it is my time. I will not deal or beg or bargain for my time."

There was silence in the room again for a moment before Mr. Genuit continued, "I know I can work for time or sell our books at the store for more time if I need it. I am perfectly happy with the time I have been able to have with you. Now because you have given me time, I owe you my life, and now I am living on "borrowed time."

"No Grandpa, you don't owe me your life," Brent said through tears realizing what his grandfather was saying to him, "Maybe I was selfish because I didn't want you to leave. I need more time with you. I want to learn more from you. I want to create more memories, and I don't want to lose you!"

"Brent, you are so selfless, and you have such a big and kind heart," Grant Genuit said to Brent who was holding his grandfather's hand on the ground, "Thank you!"

"Why were you on the floor?" I asked worriedly.

"When it is an hour left, our bodies go under stress and pressure, and it weakens you more when you are coming up to the last of your time. It is the body's way of saying "Slow down because your time is coming," Grant said sadly, "It's only natural."

Everyone looked at Grant and nodded in understanding as Grant looked up at Brent.

"Thank you my precious grandson," Grant said through tears as Brent helped his grandfather up and they hugged each other and Brent nodded.

I had decided to let Brent have time alone with his grandfather and left the kitchen as the others followed me out. I had walked into the bookstore area, Terrance, and

Tobey and Socrat were looking around the store at the various bookshelves. Tobey was the first to speak.

"The doctors are down there with Brent's parents. Is everything okay in there?" Tobey asked, nodding towards the kitchen.

"Oh yeah, his grandfather had only 15 minutes left to live. Brent helped him out to make sure that his grandfather had the ability to see his son and daughter in law again and so he could spend more time with his grandfather," I explained.

"That was very nice of Brent," Terrance said smiling at me.

I then looked over at Terrance who was eyeing me closely.

"Can I talk to you for a moment?" I asked, looking over at Terrance as he nodded silently as he followed me outside of the bookstore.

"I had a feeling you had wanted a word," Terrance smiling looking at me.

"There is something that I want to talk to you about Terrance" I said calmly.

"Go ahead, ask away my dear," Terrance said smiling.

"I noticed that when getting Brent's parents, there were three other bodies near them," I said slowly thinking back.

"Yes?" Terrance asked with a now more serious face, "What about them?"

"Well, I had checked their histories as you did. Their clocks had been drained of the time that they had left. As my fellow time council member, I wanted to know if you were me, what would you do?" I said cautiously observing Terrance.

"Ah yes, well the very thing that you are doing. You must delve into the past, ask the questions, be the possum with the nose.

Ask the questions and find out your answer! This is very much something that we are still investigating when it comes to the security of the City of Sandglass," Terrance said heavily nodding in understanding.

He walked away from me looking out down the street further noticing no one was about and then he walked close to me.

"We are following a group of people whom we suspect of doing under the radar transactions with Timecards. We just don't have all the details yet. They call themselves Time Dragons."

"Time Dragons?" I asked curiously as Terrance seemed to be internally deliberating whether to explain or not.

He was silent for a moment as Emry's voice came into my head.

"Yes, they are of my spiritual brethren," Emrys said to me carefully.

"Your Brethren?" I asked Emrys to myself as I remained silent in the conversation.

"They are a group of people who pride themselves with their dragon spirit tattoos," Emrys said bitterly.

"Yes, they are people not to be trifled with, time thiefs. They feel the Time System is corrupt and that people ought to live longer than they do here. They are the robin hoods to the Timekeepers," Tobey explained looking around more anxiously, "Let's go inside Bella, I don't want to risk being out here with the night stalker out here that we have yet to be able to find."

"Speaking of that, do you know anything about who this could be?" I asked him as he looked at me thoughtfully.

"This is someone we all know or who we have come across who doesn't like the Time Council. Maybe they have a personal grudge against us?" he said as I followed him and we walked back in. I looked up to see James and Socrat looking up at us.

Chapter 2

Intentions

"I think I am going to go and check on his parents," I said as James and Socrat nodded and said, "We will come with you, We want to see how they are doing as well."

It was then that Terrance and Tobey stayed in the bookstore while James, Socrat, and I went into the secret room to where Brent's parents were.

They were laying on the couches with the IV bags hooked up to them. One of the doctors came up to me.

"How are they?" I asked in concern.

"They were very dehydrated but otherwise they will be okay," said the doctor.

"Oh, thank goodness!" Socrat said happily.

"They should be conscious enough for a short visit within the hour." the doctor said and then he left the room.

We walked up to Shawna, Brent's mother. It was about an later, she slowly opened her eyes and seemed to be responsive.

"Who are you? What is your name?" asked Shawna, Brent's mother, She was the first to recover.

"My name is Bellatrix Kai," I said calmly, and the woman's eyes widened in fear.

"Kai?" she said in concern, "Are you from the council?"

"No, I am not a part of the council yet. I have been considering it though," I said noticing her worry and get slightly anxious, "I am a sister of some of the members of the Council, from the Village of Paska."

"I heard what happened to your village, I am so sorry," she said to me through tears, as I nodded in understanding, "I knew a few people who lived there. While captive we heard it being talked about in the hall outside that... that room. Are we in trouble?"

"In trouble? For what? You got captured and they imprisoned you, starved you, and these captors took time away from people. You have been missing for seven almost eight years and your son Brent has been looking for you for years ever since he learned to walk again!" I said in surprise.

Shawna started to tear up at once and remained silent for a few seconds before responding.

"We were caught in The Underground. We aren't supposed to be down there," Shawna said looking over from me and then to her husband who was still sleeping.

"As to that, it isn't my place to say if you will get into trouble for that or not," I said with slight unsureness as she looked at me in slight concern.

"How is my husband, David!?" Shawna asked, noticing her husband wasn't moving and who was lying in the bed next to us.

"I am not sure, the doctors have looked you both over, and you are the first to revive," I said in explanation.

"Where is Brent?" she asked me.

"I am here mom, with Grandpa," Brent said from behind me in tears.

"Hi Grant!" she said smiling at him.

Mr. Genuit nodded and smiled in tears holding her hand.

"I kept my promise. I looked after your son," Grant said smiling at her as they both nodded through tears.

"Oh, my son, you have grown up so much!" she said smiling noticing Brent was standing behind me.

"Dad isn't awake yet," Brent explained as she nodded.

"He was always stubborn. I am sure he will wake up in his own time," she said smiling and shaking her head at him.

She struggled to breathe for a minute as Brent put the sheet over her.

"You should rest more mom. You will need your strength," Brent said as she nodded and closed her eyes.

It was then that James, Socrat, and I left Brent to be with his grandpa and his parents. I went back to the store front and saw that Terrance and Tobey were still there.

"Now that they are in good hands, we have to take you to the Time Council," Terrance said to me as Tobey nodded.

"Why are you taking her, she should have some rest. We only just barely found Brent's parents and they will all want to spend some time with her," Socrat said in slight annoyance aloud to Terrance and Tobey as James put his hand on Socrat's shoulder and shook his head.

"Bella is needed," James said as I looked from James to Socrat who then nodded in understanding and then I looked at Tobey and Terrance.

"Wait! What? Why?" I asked.

"You will see," they said to me. I followed them out of the store to where the familiar carriage was awaiting for me outside of the bookstore and it took Tobey, Terrance, and me into town to the time tower.

Chapter 3

Time Council Meeting in the Time Tower

Within a few minutes of my arrival at the Time Tower, I was ushered into the Time Council Chambers where the entire council was seated in almost a full circle around me.

"Bellatrix Kai you have been summoned before us because we need an answer to the question that was presented to you before your quest to find the young boy, Brent Genuit's parents. We have been extremely patient up until now given the circumstances and the situation they are in. Now that you have successfully proven yourself to us of being capable and mature in how you manage yourself. You have earned our trust, and we are temporarily rewarding you with the seat formerly filled by your sister Taylor as the second in charge of the Night Hunters," Terrance said. The hall erupted with applause from the council with all but a few nodding their heads and applauding. I shook my head with a serious face as everyone saw my reaction as the applause slowed to a slow stop.

"I am extremely grateful to be given this position, however I am in slight hesitance to take this position as I don't feel that I am being awarded," I said honestly looking around at some of the council members whose faces were in slight shock in surprise at my response.

"Can you give us your reasoning as to your hesitance?" Tobey asked curiously.

"I realize that this position is very crucial and important to be filled but considering the current climate and news of the Time Road and now with this Night Stalker out there, it makes things worse. If I were to be a leader within your council, I would like to see if I could have the unconventional ability to be a leader that of by example within the Night Hunters Organization instead," I asked slowly.

"I see that you are well informed," Tobey said discerningly looking at Terrance who shrugged, and Tobey then asked, "How so?"

"I would like to lead in the forefront of the Night Hunters. I would like to have my own case and a special team of Night Hunters loyally at my side of my choosing to be able to go on adventures as well with me. I don't look forward to the idea that I would need to hide from our own city here within the confines of these walls as a member of this Time Council. Though I appreciate the abilities in which you all lead in here. I do not wish to offend anyone here, but, you all don't know what is truly going on out there being cooped up in here. I don't like this false sense of security that is here behind these walls in which anyone could penetrate easily. I would like to see some change in how this Time Council works before I'd want to even consider being a part of this council fully. The Timekeepers are on the streets daily seeing how the city functions, but what if we traveled with a few of them as our guards so that the public can see that we are all human too?" I suggested.

There was muttering amongst the council.

"I see there may be a need to talk amongst ourselves," Terrance said looking around noticing that both Time Council members Tanya and Taylor on either side of him were trying to talk in his ear as a few of them nodded towards me in whispered muttering more amongst themselves.

"Please wait outside the doors Bella," Terrance said as I nodded and left the room and closed the doors behind me.

Meanwhile... after leaving the Time Council Chambers...

"Do you realize what she is asking of us? Less than a year of Taylor dying out there by some psychotic shadow stalker. Now, she is asking us to risk not only her life and entrust it to the public but also our lives by exposing ourselves to the very people we are supposed to be leading!?" Theresa said with slight frustration and indignation, "These walls are the only things keeping us safe."

"She has a point," said Tommy quietly agreeing with Theresa.

"But our sister is also right, we cannot stay cooped up in here and not know what is going on within the City outside of these walls and pass proper judgements," Tobey said nodding in agreement with Tommy but also disagreeing with them.

"I think I will vote to grant her, her wish to be able to lead as she chooses fit," Terrance said, "Afterall, I think she might need to gain the experience necessary in order to eventually be able to lead the Night Hunters differently."

"You mean? Are you saying?" Tobey said in surprise at Terrance's suggestion.

"Well, you have held this position for years and you seem to agree with her as well that a change is in order for the Night Hunters. Why not let her take the reins for a while. Afterall, we all know that you never gave Terry the chance after everything that she did for you," Terrance said.

There was some muttering.

"While I admit in my younger years, I never afforded this opportunity to take that chance before, times are not the same. We have a killer on the loose."

"Let's take two votes," Tracy said looking around, "All in favor of allowing Bella to lead as part of the Time Council as she pleases?"

Hands raised. Tracy counted them.

"All eleven have voted. One for the nay," Tracy said as she looked and saw that one of the Time Council Members voted nay.

Tracy had seen that Tyrone and Tessa had been talking and Tyrone remained with his arms folded and Tessa had her hand partially up but also didn't seem to be fully swayed. Terrance kept a mental note of this.

"All in favor in being able to leave the tower with protection of the timekeepers at will?"

Hands Raised. Tracy counted them. "All eleven have voted."

"Now I think we need a final vote," Terrance said.

"All in favor of Bella being in charge as temporary leader of the Night Hunters?"

Hands Raised. Tracy counted them. "All eleven have voted."

"Send Bellatrix in," Tracy said, motioning for the guards at the doors to open and usher Bella in.

I came into the room to see everyone staring at me. I had noticed that Time Council Member Tyrone seemed to be eyeing me like a hawk on its prey. I felt uncomfortable and uneasy.

"So, perhaps you are the one that is going to effect change within this Council," Tracy said looking at me and then to all the other council members who nodded at her before looking at me again more seriously, "My only question is now that you are going to be in power, how far are you willing to go in order change things with the council? Are you going to be willing to keep some of our traditions? What is your opinion of time? How is having this power going to change you personally? Some leaders who have power and are put in charge of things are not just leaders simply because of their title. Having this power comes with great responsibility. People follow their leaders not just because of their title but also because of what they do for others and the community. Great leaders are rare, they duplicate that leadership unto others, so that those people they can also lead in the same way that they were taught."

"I must interrupt Time Council Member Tracy," Tyronne said abruptly.

Everyone looked at Tyronne who seemed to be angry.

"You!" Tyronne shouted at me, "Why do you think you deserve my vote to be a Time Council Member? What makes you so special?"

Everyone was in shock and in a stunned silence at first.

"Well, technically she didn't get your vote," Tobey said harshly.

"Yeah well, I needed to have had this conversation with her privately before this was brought up but, now it looks like we will hash this out now!" Tyronne said looking at me beadily as I remained silent and in shock.

There was a moment of awkward silence as everyone on the Time Council looked from him to me.

"Go ahead answer me!" Tyronne said in an aggressive voice slamming his fists angrily on the table.

I remained silent contemplating what to say.

"Where is this anger coming from?" Emrys asked in a whispered tone in my head as I replied in my head.

"I don't know Emrys," I said looking at Tobey who continued to defensively at Tyronne.

"There is no need to push this negative energy towards Bella," Tobey said to Tyronne angrily.

"Are you thinking just because your siblings are leaders within the Time Council that you are entitled or somehow are owed this title? Is that it? Just because you are a Kai prodigal child you automatically get this title as a name sake?" Tyronne said heatedly, "Born with a silver spoon and handed everything in life huh? What a spoiled BRAT you are!"

"You! You have no right to accuse her! How dare you assume...." Tommy Kai said standing up for me, "You don't even know her!"

"That is right we don't!" Tyronne said, "Born outside of this damn city and now she thinks just because she is here, and she has the Kai last name the title of Council Member is automatically hers and she can just waltz into our city and take charge! She doesn't own our city! She doesn't belong here!"

"How dare you!" Tobey said angrily, "We offered her the position to no other Kai! We were all elected by and for our people. Terrance was the one who suggested Bellatrix be a Council Member, need I remind you, NOT by a Kai sibling!"

"Well according to my sources Terrance is as good as a Kai," Tyronne said.

"That is another accusation!" Terrance shouted angrily at Tyronne.

"She thinks you will pick her as a Council member, so she got close to you, and you got a soft spot for her like you did her sister!" Tyronne said

"That is enough!" Tessa said standing up noticing I was putting my hand up.

"I have never assumed because of my name that I was to be a Council Member," I said carefully.

"Why do we need to vote for you then?" Tyronne asked.

I sat there in silence for a moment thinking about what they were all saying, and I replied, "I think I would be a great leader. I don't see this power of a title coming to my head. Time is a precious commodity to me, it is fragile as is all life on

Earth, within all the various City's of Sandglass. The balance of time is necessary to allow for the changing of times. It is also needed transactionally for people of this city to be able to get by to purchase food, clothes, and goods to pay their way to keep surviving. Sleeping helps people earn time too but not as much as a job would to contribute to society. We all need to earn our keep in life and it would be a disservice of me and the people of this City to take this position and think I can take a back seat and not earn my title as a fellow Time Council Member. All our lives here are limited. We mustn't take it for granted. Even though we can be able to change that balance, I also understand that there needs to be law, order, and a sense of direction regarding where we are going, what we are doing and accomplishing as leaders. Within the Time Council there is plenty of room for growth for us all, if we only take the responsibility to do so. By doing this, people would see how we can change the perspective of how people live their lives and improve their quality of life. Some people are working only to just survive and gain the time that they need in order just to feed their families. They do this sometimes with only seconds on the clock left at the end of the month. There are those who gang together to take time from others, and take advantage of kids, and the elderly, who have the time. These vulnerable people don't have the ability to defend their time that they have on them. There are some people who have businesses, who work all the time, and don't get to accomplish their dreams and goals or get to travel to the other City of Sandglass through the underground or explore. Some businesses have made time gains because of loaning excess time to people only to have work double to pay it all back with overtime in various workplaces. This is unfair on so many levels in my opinion. How can people earn extra amount of minutes to pay that off when they can barely keep up now? I wish to make changes eventually as a leader and help people who are struggling." I started to explain and then noticed a change in mood from the council.

There was an awkward silence in the room as everyone in the room remained quiet and still and observed me quietly. I was hoping that someone would say something, anything to break the silence. It was extremely uncomfortable for me as I looked around at all the leaders one at a time until finally someone spoke.

"This idea of you wanting to be able to travel and be…. adventurous… Do you not think this is a dangerous thing for you to do if you were a leader of such an organization like this? Would it not put all our lives in jeopardy if we were to leave these small confines of this tower," Tyrone said eyeing me as I noticed his title.

"Not to be disrespectful in any way Tyronne Mattley, but how can you be a "Leader of Natural Resources," if you don't know the current conditions of them while confined in this tower?" I asked in concern and immediately he gave me a look of even more anger towards me as if I had insulted him. He was immediately talking under his breath to Tyeisha who seemed to be trying to calm him down and then looked around, "Or any of you for that matter? You don't know what they are all going through daily to know what our citizens are going through day after day with seconds and minutes left on their time clocks while worried about how they are going to get through the next day, and to see it in person. Yes, we sleep for eight hours, and our bodies rejuvenate, and we gain 1 hour per hour we sleep but that doesn't help with the rising costs of our resources. Three hours barely gives us one meal and that doesn't include the rest of our day-to-day purchases needed to keep our homes clean and live up to the standards that the Timekeepers tell us to be. You all rely on the information fed to you from the Timekeepers themselves, but that doesn't mean you can empathize with the citizens of the City of Sandglass."

"Empathize? Empathize! Firstly, we never let our feelings of our people affect our decisions. Also, we do not oversee the things that the Timekeepers should be doing," Theresa interrupted, "and we certainly have never allowed intercity travel between the City of Sandglass. This is certainly unheard of. There is a reason the Creator separated the City of Sandglass through the underground into four parts. He certainly didn't mean for any of us to be doing these escapades that you and Brent's parents have been doing lately."

"You say you don't let your feelings of your people affect your decisions Theresa... I mean no disrespect but are you not now allowing your feelings of me affect your decision not to go out in the public and see the people for yourself?" I said looking around at everyone. "I believe in the system we have, but I just feel like if you only knew how much the people are hungry and have poor circumstances in the way in which some of the people you serve live. If you knew, then maybe you all will be more help to them as their leader."

There was a moment of silence.

"Perhaps we have been limiting the people from freedoms that they should be able to do as they please to an extent like being able to have a four-day work week at different times of the week so that they can do things like spending more time with their families, In order for them to live a happier life," Tobey said putting his fingers to his chin and rubbing it in deep thought.

Some muttering happened between the council.

"This City of Sandglass has been functioning with structure as well as the other cities because of their own councils running them. This is something that would need to be discussed amongst the other city councils as well for permissions to enter and allowing for inter-city travel. This is not something that we alone can allow everyone to do without permission from the other cities. We do not need war amongst ourselves," Tina said slowly.

"I say we should try it out," Theodore said smiling at me coming to the table from one of the corners of the room, "Inter-travel would mean more inter-commerce amongst ourselves paving the way for more freedom for all our people and their own. This would also allow for others to see how the other councils are varied and how they run. As you know we are better, and this would mean more growth for us."

I smiled at Theodore and nodded at him as he came in from behind the council in the back part of the room.

"Ah finally the 13th hour decides to give us his time to share his own opinion. How good of you to finally decide to join us and grace us with your presence," Tyeisha said with slight annoyance in her voice. I looked over at Tyrone and noticed he had gripped his hands together on the table in front of him as he saw Theodore come in and sit at the round table in front of me.

"Well, I thought you all could lead and say yes to all these decisions without me but apparently the 13th hour is needed in order to outweigh some of these votes," Theodore said seeing the voting forms in front of him at his seat. He then silently marked his votes and handed them to Terrance who nodded.

"Theodore has cast his votes and now everything is in order. We will have to wait to deliberate on the idea of intra-city travel Bella for the public. Everyone is in agreement because you may offer a new way in which you handle the Night Hunters and because you have shown how capable you are, we are actually going to, with agreement with everyone here I am adding, we are going to give you FULL leadership of the Night Hunters," Terrance said looking around as everyone seemed to agree that they needed to check with the other councils about Intracity travel.

Tyronne remained in silence as he clenched his fists and rolled his lips inwardly together, nodding in anger.

I looked around at all the cloaked council members in surprise. "Full leadership of the Night Hunters?" I asked, looking up at the council where they were all still seated in the high staircase seats above me in a half circle as they all nodded.

"As only a temporary leader until the elections, we want to see what you can do with them," Tobey said, "We want to see if you can manage them. Just remember, as it was once said in Sandglass history, "With great power to change things as they are, comes great responsibility. Welcome to the Time Council Bellatrix Kai. Welcome to the Night Hunters as the Newly appointed ShadowMaster."

I nodded, smiled, and then bowed, "It is an honor to be a part of this Time Council, I will lead the Night Hunters with dignity and strength."

It was then that the Council all stood up, took off their hoods and applauded and came down the stairs towards me to where I was seated to shake my hand. Tracy was holding folded black robes on her forearms as she walked towards me. On top of the robes was the silver Time Council "T" Pin.

"It is an honor to have you on the council with us," Tracy said to me as I nodded, "Your sister Taylor was my best friend, and she was like a sister to me. I hope we can be close too!"

I nodded in silence as she took the robe and placed it on me as I slipped my arms through it. It was comfortable and it wasn't very heavy, but it felt like I was wearing a light weight long rain jacket with shoulder pads. I tied the robe cord around my waist and Terrance put the T pin on me.

"We will be expecting great things from you Bellatrix, and you have a lot to prove," Terrance said to me smiling as I nodded. Tobey was the last of the council members to come down as he walked up to Tracy and Terrance and me.

"Meet me here tonight Bella so you can meet the rest of the Night Hunters, and we can get you settled in," Tobey said as I smiled and nodded as he got up from his chair next to me.

"It is nice to see another Kai sibling on the council, you have a great day Bella," Tracy said as she smiled at me and left the room.

I was happy to be able to be a part of the Night Hunters, but now I am also in charge of them. I had wondered how many there were and what types of missions that they have been and are involved with for the council.

Tobey looked at me as I nodded and bowed. He started to leave but he stopped and turned towards Terrance and me and said, "Brent's parents are both okay and we need to do our part and ensure the safety of the city. You must find out everything that they know, and report back to the council on this information by the next meeting."

I nodded and then bowed, and he left the room as I turned toward Terrance.

"After you," he said as I smiled and led the way out of the room and went into the hall. I looked to my left and saw the door to the way out of the towers and then to my right I saw a long hallway.

"You look tired Bella," Terrance said as I nodded, "Follow me and I will take you to room. We went out into the hallway and up a flight of stairs and down a hallway until we into a room marked 8G.

"This is my guest room," Terrance said handing me a key after he unlocked the door, "You can sleep here for the night because I think the maids are still setting up the room for you with clean sheets. Afterall, your new room will be Room 10, Terry's old office at your request."

I nodded and smiled, "Thank you Terrance I appreciate your hospitality."

Terrance nodded and smiled, "It's getting late and its better for you to rest here for the night instead of heading back to the Bookstore at this late hour. Well goodnight, Bella."

"Goodnight Terrance," I said smiling at him as he nodded and left.

I walked into the room to see it had a four-poster queen sized bed and a window that overlooked the City of Sandglass. I sat in the windowsill and looked out into the quiet streets below with the window open.

"A lot happened today," Midnight said hooted softly in my head. Both Midnight and Emrys came out of me as they stretched out around the room and then got comfortable on the windowsill with me.

"It's different looking from up here isn't it?" Emrys said to me as I nodded. "You know this city and because of that the Time Council is lucky to have you, everyone will see, even Tyronne, you will see. You can't let the negativity bring you down. Everyone will see your value that you bring to the table, as you already know your value."

I smiled and took in a deep breath and let it out slowly smiling and nodding at Emrys.

"Thank you Emrys," I said to him as he nodded.

"Time for you to get some sleep miss," Midnight said as I smiled and nodded and went into the bed and sank in under the covers and fell into a deep sleep.

Chapter 4

Leadership Position

The next morning, I awoke and started to walk down towards the dining hall and had breakfast. After eating breakfast alone, I left the hall and was greeted by Terrance in the hall.

"Good Morning Bella, did you sleep well last night?" Terrance asked me, smiling at me happily, as I nodded and handed him back his guest room key, "I imagine you want to go to the bookstore now to see Brent?" he added as I nodded and smiled again.

"Okay, now if you follow this hall," Terrance said pointing to the left, "and take a right, you will find all the carriages there. There is a cabin there with a wooden door. You just need to knock three times on the caretaker's door and hop in one of the carriages and he will be ready to take you to where you need to go," Terrance said as I nodded, and he took a right as I turned to leave through the Time Tower main entrance. I then took a right and saw a small cabin just as Terrance had described and I knocked three times on the caretakers door and walked into one of the nearby carriages. The caretaker hurried out and smiled at me.

"I knew it," he said excitedly and was smiling widely, "I knew you were going to be one of the council members. Alright, well, I am now going to give you this."

He gave me a coin as I looked at it. It was a gold coin the size of a quarter.

"What is this for?" I asked curiously.

"That is for whenever and wherever you need a ride. You turn the coin three times in your right hand and then rub the top side a few times and then I or my grandson will head out to you wherever you are, the horses will find you," he said smiling at me rubbing some sweat off his wrinkled head and pushing his white hair to the side.

"Oh okay, thank you!" I said, putting it in the front pocket of my robe that was behind the "T" pin.

"Do not lose it, okay?" he said smiling as I nodded and padded my front pocket.

It was then that he got up to the front of the carriage.

"To where are we going miss? Never did catch your name," he said looking down at the carriage to me.

"I am Time Council Member Bellatrix Kai of the Night Hunters and yes a ride to the Bookstore in the City of Sandglass - Time," I said proudly smiling up at him.

"Okay miss, we will get there in a short time. My name is George, and my son's name is Greg," he said smiling as he whispered something, and the horses started pulling the carriage.

"What is the matter Bella," Midnight asked me noticing I was sad while the carriage pulled me along.

"I miss my parents," I said to myself through tears as I looked outside the carriage, "I wish they were still alive. I wish they were still here with me. I wish I could have a conversation with them and tell them about being a newly elected Time Council Member. I wish I could tell them that I am the new Night Hunter Night Master!"

My eyes were filled with tears as I started to emotionally cry for the first time in a long time about them.

"I don't know why I am so emotional about this but if only they could see how far I have come, how much I have grown. If only they could see how hard I have tired to make them proud of me because of my accomplishments," I said through tears.

"I know that they are looking down at you and are proud of you Bella," Midnight said trying to console me.

"You must be strong Bella," Emrys said to me as I nodded and he warmed me.

Within minutes, I arrived at the bookstore. I got out of the carriage after cleaning up my face so no one could tell I had been crying and then I saw David and Sharon outside talking to Brent. It was then that Sharon was the first to react.

"So, the rumor is true!" Sharon said to me smiling, giving me a hug noting my robes and my pin. George waved goodbye and left with the carriage from the bookstore and headed back to the Time Tower.

"I am so proud of you! Are you replacing Tim or Taylor?" She asked curiously.

"I am replacing Tobey. Tobey is taking Taylor's position, but I still have her room," I said to Sharon who put her hand over her mouth.

"You mean? You are fully in charge of the Night Hunters now?" she said bowing down on one knee to me and reached for my hand to kiss it. "I pledge my loyalty to you Night Master."

"Night Master?" I asked taken aback.

"Yes, you are in charge of the whole order now," she said through tears.

"Yes, but I am also changing how the council is running now," I said to her and her face became serious.

"Wait, how so?" she asked.

"Your son will be coming home to see you possibly within a day or two possibly," I said through tears of joy turning to look at David.

"Really?" David said to me as he and Sharon got excited.

"Yes, I told them I didn't want to be a part of the council if we had to keep ourselves cooped up all the time in the tower. I wanted to be on the front lines leading this order and the Time Council. I need to do it properly, seeing things as they are and not as they are reported to me. I want the Time Council to be more firsthand in the community here and to be able to get to know the leaders, and the people, and vice versa," I said calmly.

Sharon nodded at me and seemed to understand what I meant.

"So, what does that mean for us?" Brent asked finally recovering from shock seeing me getting out of the carriage in the robes.

"I wonder who is replacing Tim?" Sharon interrupted curiously as I shrugged, and then turned towards Brent, "We are still together Brent, don't worry."

"So, when is your induction ceremony?" Sharon asked.

"Well, the Time Council kind of just gave me the robes folded and put them on me," I said, "All Tobey said was that I have to meet him back at the Time Tower tonight to meet the rest of the Night Hunters."

She nodded to me as a message was given to her by a passing Timekeeper.

"I think I just got a lead on our Night Stalker. Tomorrow night I should be able to meet or see them. Also, tonight is a special meeting at eight pm," she said showing me the message that seemed to be quickly scribbled on a piece of paper.

"Well, it looks like tonight is going to be a good night after all," David said smiling looking up at the sky.

I smiled and looked at Brent who was quiet and he seemed upset.

"I am trying to see if I can figure out a way so I will be able to leave the Tower to spend time with you," I said to Brent who seemed to relax and nodded slightly after I said this.

"I have come to see if I can talk to your parents at my capacity as a Shadow Hunter Leader now," I said to Brent as he then looked at me hesitantly.

"Um, let me update them so that this isn't all a shock on them all at once when they see you looking like that," he said leaving David and Sharon and me outside.

"David and I are going back to the house to freshen up before the meeting," Sharon said as I nodded, and they had started walking home. Just then Socrat came out with James.

"Wow! A Time Council member!? Already? They sure didn't waste any time, did they?" Socrat said shaking his head.

"Congratulations Bella," James said smiling at Socrat and giving me a hug.

"So, what are you planning for our next adventure?" James asked looking from Socrat who smiled and then they both looked at me.

"For now, the focus is the Time Dragons and the Time Road and ensuring the health

and wellness of those who were captured and held," I said as he nodded in understanding.

"I know that look Bella," James said under his breath to me in my ear as we walked into the bookstore, and I smiled, "We will talk later about this."

"You can come and see them now, Bellatrix," Brent said walking up to us in the doorway noticing that James was whispering in my ear.

I smiled and walked through the familiar doors of the bookstore and took in a deep breath of air smelling the old books coming off the shelves and found it soothing. We walked past the various shelves of books and to the door that was in the back which was ajar.

Chapter 5

The Meeting

I walked down the small hallway and took the first right to the first quadrant where there were two couches, and the hospital beds were originally. They were now folded up against the wall. The fireplace was cackling as Brent, James, and I walked in with Socrat and Michael closely behind. Shawna and David were sitting on the couch talking when we walked in on the couch and were looking at the fire in the fireplace together holding hands and abruptly looked up at me when we walked in.

Shawna, Brent's mother, turned a little more serious when she saw me come into the room. She seemed to instinctively look from me and then to her son who had held onto my hand as we came in and sat across from them on the second couch. There were other armchairs in the room that Michael, Socrat, and James seemed to bring out from the edge of the room and brought them on either side of the couches.

Feeling the warm fire on my back seemed to push me to want metaphorically and symbolically to put a fire under things and get things going. I was the first to speak up in the awkward silence of us coming into the room to get seated.

"So obviously you know why I am here. I am here at my capacity as the Shadow Master within the City of Sandglass.
"Clearly," David said smiling seemingly mischievously looking at his sons hand that was still holding mine, "Tell me what your intentions with my sons are?"
"Firstly, I guess I should clear the air with that," I said turning slightly pink, "Your son, Brent and I have been dating for the last eight years ever since we decided that we wanted to help to locate you, and I wanted your son to start walking again."
"Walking? My son already knew how to walk. His father and I helped him to learn how to walk," Shawna said defensively.
"Your son was not in a good state when Bella first met him," Grant Genuit said from behind Brent's parents coming into the room as Shawna jumped, "After you both left, when he was around ten, he became depressed and eventually become obsessed with finding the both of you. I had closed this room and kept everyone from it. I never told him. He got to the point where he would read for hours at a time in his room. He wouldn't get up but to just use the bathroom. Until eventually he stopped using his muscles to walk around to go to the bathroom, etc. So, for five years until he met Bella, he had never walked since. I had to help him to get from his bed to the bathroom to use it to go to the restroom or bathe. He didn't have the lower body strength to keep going. Every day

he would ask if I had heard from you or if you both had ever mentioned anything to me about anything before you left. I never told him. Until eightyears ago, Bella came into the picture. I imagine he had asked you to try to help him find his parents no matter the cost. Checking places, he wanted you to."

Brent's ears had turned pink, and his cheeks were red from embarrassment as Michael and Socrat and James remained quiet.

"No, I told him if he wanted to locate them, he needed to do it himself and that I would only help him with this endeavor," I said half smiling.

"He was fifteen and finally he found someone else to focus on besides you two," Mr. Genuit said coughing slightly before continuing as he sat on the couch next to Brent, "For three years Bella had helped your son to walk and they spent the last five years researching, reading, and searching more and over time he began to have feelings for Bella. Slowly, over time, she had helped him to begin to walk again. One day, he walked all the way down the stairs on his own to find me, it was then that I knew he was coming back to his old self. Or he was so was determined to finally put in the action to do what he wanted to accomplish most. To find out where you both were. Eventually they learned of this secret room and began researching and learning as much as they could, trying to find out more about where you were going, what you had learned, and where you could have gone. Knowing now what I know about Bella, I couldn't have stopped her even if I wanted to. When she sets her mind to something, there is no stopping her. She may take the time to see things your way, but if it doesn't make sense to her, she won't change course. Her goal was to find you and to help him find peace in his heart and mind. She could tell that this is something that he has been struggling to cope with. He knew that you didn't just disappear without a trace. He had to find you. They did. They have been together ever since. They rely on each other to be ensure each other is happy and they want what is best for each other, even if they get on each other's nerves sometimes." Mr. Genuit said laughing as Shawna and David smiled.

"I am his girlfriend and now I am a council member now," I said calmly as his parents looked at each other.

"We are just not sure if this is a good idea, the relationship between you two and especially after what we did," Shawna said to Brent as he stood up immediately in refute.

"I am 23 years old, I am old enough now to make this decision on my own. I am in love with Bellatrix Kai for everything that she is and has done for our family. If it weren't for her, I would still be in bed unable to walk reading books that wouldn't have even helped me to find you both. We have been together for almost five years now in the relationship and I have known her for eight years! You cannot break us apart!" Brent said in slight defense and anger.

"Though we understand your feelings Brent, you and Bella have been through so much together. Bella has recently got a new position with the Time Council. How is that going to allow you and her to see each other if she isn't allowed to leave the Time Tower?" David said.

"I am the temporary leader of the Night Hunters. I am re-shaping the very way in which the Time Council will be running now. The Council will be allowed to leave the Time Tower at will with Timekeepers as our personal guards now so we can see how things really are in the City now," I said as David and Shawna looked at each other, and then to me.

"So how does your vision work with my son? Will he be allowed in the Time Tower, or will you have to come to him?" David asked me

"We are going to figure this out together as the time comes and all you need to know is that we both love each other and are committed to each other no matter what is put before us. Also, in the meantime, I am here because I need to see how you both are doing?" I said, trying to change the subject.

"We are doing better now that we have had the IV fluids in us. The doctor said it will take a few months, but we are showing promise that we will be okay eventually, which is more than what I can say for others who were caught on the Time Road," David said bitterly, "Have you figured out how extensive this Time Road is?"

"What exactly was it that you were you both researching exactly?" I asked curiously. There was a moment of silence as I looked at both Brent's parent's as they remained silent.

"I am more concerned about what you both were doing down in the Underground in the first place," I said in concern looking at Shawna and David who looked at each other.

"We both just wanted to explore and find out what is down there and why it was that we couldn't go down there according to the Time Council," David said honestly looking at me, "We are also part of the Bear Claw society and that is where the meetings are."

"We were asking questions about the Trenches and the other areas around the underground that apparently lead to the other City's of Sandglass," David explained, "then we got caught for asking too many questions."

"So, what we have learned is the Underground can be unsafe at times. We never went further past the tattoo shop like we wanted," Shawna said.

"What about your son?" I asked looking at them.

"We knew he was in good hands with my father," David said looking at Grant Genuit who had walked over towards us.

"Sorry I was in the restroom," Grant said looking at his son and then to me, "If anything, I am just grateful they are okay. To be honest I was worried that something bad had happened to them and had almost given up hope. Thank you for your help in finding them Bellatrix. Our family is forever in your debt."

I nodded and then bowed.

"Thank you both for your time," I said calmly and decided that this was enough questioning for now for the council.

"Bella, there is someone outside The Bookstore who is asking for you," Mr. Genuit said peering at me wisely with his twinkling eyes.

It was then that I excused myself and went upstairs to the entrance of the bookstore and saw that it was someone I had never expected to see outside.

"Tyeisha! What I lovely surprise," I said calmly reaching out to hug her.

"Yes, I figured that I would find you here seeing these two outside," she said as she was pointing to James and Socrat who were smiling at her and waved goodbye as they went inside.

"Do you want to come inside?" I asked, trying to invite her into the bookstore as she shook her head.

"No, follow me," she said as I followed her past the bakery and up the road. We went down another street and came upon a row of town homes. We walked until we came upon one with a Cherry finish on it. We walked up the steps and she ushered me inside.

"Welcome Bella to my childhood home," she said as we walked into a living room area with off White Walls and photos of various landscapes and plants around the room. We sat down on two love seats across from each other as I watched her intently to begin our conversation.

She disappeared for a moment after she observed me and then came out from what I assumed was the kitchen with a tray of sandwiches and tea and teacups. As you know my name is Tyeisha Bradley and as Representative of the Seventh Hour of the Time Council, I am also the Head of Education and Civil Resources Department for the City of Sandglass. You are the new eleventh hour. It was because of one of our votes today that instead of being the new eighth hour you are the new eleventh hour. I would be lying to you if I told you that I am in full support of you to be completely honest. I have some reservations about you and the type of character you are. I am slightly suspicious of you, but I figured there is no time like the present to get to know you. How is it that you happen to be close to the eighth hour Taylor before she died and then you become leader? How was your relationship with Taylor before her untimely demise? Are you in some way at fault for her death?"

I thought about what she was saying and nodded in understanding.

"While I know that I didn't do anything to personally hurt or kill Taylor. I need you to know that I would never do that to anyone. Life is precious to me. I barely like the idea of having to hurt a fly but if it means life or death, I will take the life that tries to take my own. It is understandable that you are suspicious of me due to my rise of power and the closeness that I had with Taylor before she was killed. I need you to know that you can trust me and that I had nothing to do with her death. I am trying everything that I can to find out what happened and who the Night Stalker is," I said calmly as she looked at me seemingly debating whether there was any truth to the matter.

"Tyeisha, Can I ask you something?" I asked curiously.

"Sure," she said tipping some of the tea in her teacup into her mouth and then looked up at me and taking a bite of her sandwich as I debated whether to ask her what was on my mind.

"I noticed on the voting that you and Tyrone seem close. Why is it that he didn't seem to want to vote for me as a Shadow Master or for me to be a part of the Time council?" I asked, trying to make it seem like it wasn't a big deal or that it didn't bug me when it did.

"Oh, so you noticed, huh?" Tyeisha said noting how observant I am, But then again, with how argumentative he was, it's hardly a secret now."

"Well because Theodore had to vote, if it wasn't for him, I may not have been where I am today. Was there something I have done and that is why maybe he doesn't like me?" I asked uncomfortably squirming in the chair.

"Yeah, I can see why you think that. Tyrone... Tyronne, he is my cousin; he doesn't trust the Kai name well. Let's just say that my aunt and uncle didn't raise him well. Part of the reason he doesn't trust you or your siblings is because he never really gotten around to getting to know you or your siblings. But also, because he has been hurt by the council in the past, during a time when there were different leaders, though. He doesn't trust many people in the first place," Tyeisha explained as I nodded silently, "Now the question I have for you is, can you be trusted?"

"Of course I can," I said smiling, "I intend to lead by example. I know the Council was surprised that I wanted to enable everyone to be able to leave the council as it pleases, but it was also because I wanted other people to get to know them as well and still be able to leave from the Time Tower and spend time with my family, friends, and boyfriend."

"Oh, you have a boyfriend!" Tyeisha said smiling excitedly at me.

"Yes," I explained telling her about Brent and how we met and how this is why the Council seemed to be wanting to consider me because of how I went about researching and looking for his parents when none of the Timekeepers were able to do so.

"You must be very happy to be able to have such an amazing and supportive guy in your life!" she said to me as I turned a slight pink.

It was then that I realized the time and excused myself.

"No problem, Bella, it was good having a chat with you. Now that I have gotten to know you, I will be a little bit more comfortable with you. I must warn you, my guard will still be up as you are only a temporary leader here anyway," she said as I nodded in understanding as I left her house and she closed and locked her door behind me. I grabbed the cloak and wrapped myself around it and pulled out the coin and turned it thrice in hand. Almost immediately the horse and carriage pulled up to Tyeisha's front doorway path and I climbed in.

"Where to Bella?" asked Greg, the younger son of the older driver who looked back at me from in the front of the carriage.

"To the home of Sharon and David Johnson," I said calmly and feeling slightly hungry.

After that conversation we had had, I decided to go home to Sharon and David's house. Within minutes I had arrived and went to the front door and let myself in as the carriage drove away and I closed the door behind me. I made some noodles on the stove and heated some tomato sauce as I was hungry and wanted a hearty meal.

An hour earlier…

A shadowy figure was jumping from rooftop to rooftop in the dark. It was cloaked in dark black robes. No one else could see it. Slowly after passing a few more rooftops, it shimmied down a drainpipe and scooted into a dark alley watching as two timekeepers passed by who were talking quickly and intently amongst themselves.

"Did you hear?" asked one of them

"What? Hear what Tom?" asked the other.

"They are after the Night Stalker; they want us to locate the killer quickly for a prize of three hundred years' time as a reward!" said Tom.

"I am sure we are going to be getting a lot of false tips from people who are hoping to get the reward. I don't know anyone who wouldn't want an extra three hundred years to work with," said the other Timekeeper.

"Who do you think it is Mino?" asked Tom

"I think it's a disgruntled citizen here, or maybe someone from the Time Council or Night Hunters?" Mino said quietly.

"Why do you think it might be someone from the council?" asked Tom

"They just made that girl a Time Council member. Do you think she oversees it to help with the potential restructuring or de organizing of the Time Council to see who or where the corruption is?" Mino suggested.

"Let's just see how well of a leader she is," Tom said as they walked away.

The shadowy figure moved away from its hiding spot and slowly peered down the street from the wall along the edge of the alley way as it watched the Timekeepers turn the corner on the right and disappeared into the night. The figure paused briefly in seeming contemplation and went the opposite direction trying to ensure no one noticed it. No one was there to notice the shadowy figure move stealthily through the darkened night except one person, unbeknownst to it.

"Come on, reveal yourself and remove that mask," Sharon whispered to herself under her breath with a slight anxiety. She continued to watch and observe the Night Stalker from a safe unnoticeable distance with binoculars. Sharon continued to follow the figure through the night to keep tabs and figure out her identity.

It was then that the Night Stalker went into the darkness down another street and seemed to have disappeared.

"No way!" Sharon thought to herself, "That is a dead end!" After waiting for thirty minutes, Sharon came out from her hiding spot and then slowly came to the corner of the street with the dead end. No one was down the street at all. Sharon walked back home shaking her head in disappointment and came into the house as I looked up.

"How did it go Sharon? Was the lead, right?" I asked curiously. Sharon recounted the story of the Night Stalker and how it slowly disappeared, and she didn't know where it went. I then looked at her with a tilted and confused face and asked, "Are there any storm drains in that dead end road?"

"Yes, matter of fact there is," she said thoughtfully, "Perhaps I will attempt to look down there."

"No, not unless you have a force of Night Hunters with you," I said holding my hand up to her at her eagerness to investigate, "there is reward when one is patient and well planned."

Sharon nodded and said, "Whatever you will is Shadow Master."

It was then that I had a random thought come to me, information I wanted to see if it was known.

I walked up to a note pad that was at the door and a pen and jotted down a quick note and then I walked outside and whistled as one of the Night Hunters walked up to me.

"I know you," I said to the young Night Hunter, you were always standing outside Terry's door, weren't you?" I said as the young Night Hunter smiled at me and nodded.

"My name is Titus, I was her head Night Hunter," he said smiling and bowing at me.

"I don't need this done immediately but I need your help, get me all the information you can gather. Leave no stone unturned," I said seriously to him as he nodded.

"Whatever it is my lady, no one will ever know," Titus said putting his hand to his forehead in a solute towards me as I smiled and nodded and handed him the now folded paper as he opened it up and looked at me in surprise.

"Your wish is my command," he said and scurried off.

"What was that about?" Sharon asked me curiously.

"A brief errand," I said mysteriously, and we both went to bed, and I had a well-rested sleep that night.

Chapter 6

The Attack of the Night Stalker

The next morning, I walked into the bookstore to immediately see Brent looking at me seriously as I closed the door behind me, he seemed upset.

No one else was in the main part of the store at the time as we walked between the various shelves across from each other in different aisles

"Did you get the information you needed from my parents yesterday?" he said in slight irritation and attitude through the open bookshelf.

"Brent, I realize how upset that you are, but it was the only way to do what needed to be done. The council needed me to find out this information for them. They both have already been through a lot of traumas, and I am sure they appreciated being questioned there with me, rather than being in front of a whole Time Council tribunal," I said calmly as he nodded as we turned to face each other in the middle of the aisles between the first and second aisle of books.

"Thank you for helping me get my parents back," he said hugging me seemingly being more understanding as to why I managed things the way that I did as I smiled and put my hand on his shoulder. "Please tell me you found that as awkward as I did."

I nodded and then smiled.

"It did feel awkward, but I had to ask them these questions for the council. I told you we would find them, no matter what," I said looking at him as he smiled at me. I hugged him again and he nodded.

"Brent?" I said curiously as he pulled away from my embrace.

"Yes?" he replied.

"I was wondering if you would ever want to be a part of the Night Hunters or on the Time Council or ever considered joining Bear Claw Society," I asked him as he thought silently for a moment.

"Maybe a part of the Night Hunters. Or the Time Council perhaps," he said slowly as I nodded silently and said, "Oh okay."

"Brent!" Grant Genuit, his grandfather said from the kitchen, "Can you help me make food for your parents?"

"Yeah, sure grandpa," Brent said as he kissed me on the cheeks, "Did you want to join us for Breakfast?"

"I was going to go for a walk, but I will be back later," I said as he smiled.

"Don't get into any trouble without me my love," he said smiling as I nodded and he gave me a quick hug before heading towards the kitchen.

"I will talk to you later hun!" I said smiling at him and then he released the hug.

I turned a bright pink, smiled, nodded, and walked outside and started towards David and Sharon's house and decided to keep walking past their house.

"You know you could consult us with this thought process," Emrys said and Midnight hooted in my head as I said to them in my mind, "I just don't know if this will be a good idea for Brent to be a part of these organizations just yet. He just got his parents back."

"It seems like you don't know if you can trust David and Shawna, Brent's parents," Emrys said wisely.

"No, I don't know them well enough to trust them," I said calmly to them in my mind, "So I think it is wise to get to know them first before getting Brent involved with any of the Black Claw Society or the Night Hunters or the Council until I know for sure we can trust his parents."

"What do you mean?" Midnight asked me.

"There was that time that was taken from the other bodies in the room that were in there with them forcibly," I said feeling uncomfortable.

"That is very wise of you indeed," Midnight hooted in agreement in my head and they went quiet as I continued to think to myself.

I wanted to think about things and reflect so I walked around for about an hour or two as flashbacks of my past came to mind as if they were yesterday.

The first thing that came to mind was my parents, growing up with them and reflecting on things that they had taught me. I had started reflecting on the days that my mother had taught me how to sew, clean, and cook. Then I was thinking of my father and when he taught me some leadership skills.

"Remember Bellatrix, when you are a leader, it is more than just the title. Just like the Council Leaders had said, When you are a leader people look up to you, they see your character. If you lead with a loving, caring, and understanding heart, people will gravitate towards your positive energy," he had said to me one night.

"You have a lot to learn still child," my father had said in my mind as a tear came from my eyes down my cheek. I seemed to have gotten lost as I happened across a park with a path that went around a lake. I started to walk around the lake as I would occasionally hear the water hit against the edge of the lake. Various geese were floating around it making noises as kids were playing around outside and various people were also walking around the path around me. It was so peaceful. I hadn't been paying them any mind. Seemingly lost in my memories as I sat down at a picnic table along the lake.

"I know I know," I heard myself say at the time in frustration to my father.

"You don't know what you don't know my child, don't close your mind from being able to expand. It is wise to say you don't know what you don't know because we are all still learning from our mistakes and learning to grow and be better than we were yesterday," my father had said this to me one time when I was frustrated because I thought I had washed all the dishes correctly but forgot to wash the back of one of the plates that he was drying and had pointed out my mistake.

"It is okay to want to grow older and want to grow up quick but at the same time, enjoy being a kid," my mother would say.

Then my memory switched, and I saw it right before my eyes, my father getting killed and my mother being killed right before my eyes! I let out a scream without realizing it.

"Are you okay?" came a familiar voice behind me. It was the last person I expected Kahn.

My eyes were filled with tears.

"What is the matter dear child?" he asked me with concern as he sat across from me at the picnic table.

"I miss them," I said sadly wiping my tears away, "There is nothing I can do to bring them back and I wish they were still here to talk to and to tell them I love them. I want them back Kahn, I want them here with us. But YOU TOOK THEM FROM ME!"

Kahn nodded sadly and remained silent, and he then started to tear up.

"That is impossible. There isn't a day that goes by that I don't think about the atrocious things that I have done and that I must now live in regret for doing. Nothing I did was good. I did what I did because I was following orders. I let the power get the best of me. You must understand that I loved your mother, just as much as I loved Taylor. If I could reverse the things that I had done, I would. But when you mess with time, it has its consequences. Things are as they are, and one must accept them and move forward."

"You are right, if I keep doing this, I am only going to hurt more reflecting on them and it's not going to do any difference by dwelling on them. But you must understand, you took them from me. I still feel like I haven't fully forgiven you for it," I said looking up at him as his eyes filled with tears.

"I know Bella," he said nodding his head, "the day that we first met I could feel that you had hatred towards me and at the time I didn't know why. I understand why you feel the way you do as I hold the same hatred towards the Night Stalker for taking my daughter from me. But you must also understand that there is not ever any good the comes from feeling these negative energies of hatred towards someone."

I nodded and remained silent.

"For what it is worth, I am sorry. I am sorry that I took them from you. But also know, that them being gone, doesn't mean that they are gone forever. If you hold them close to your heart and because of what I had done, you are here today within the City of Sandglass – Time, an event that wouldn't have happened had it not been for me and David. I wish you the best, and I want you to know that no matter what, as your uncle, I am still here for you if you ever need it," he said as he stood up and I remained silent gritting my teeth and tears flowed down my face as I looked out into the water avoiding eye contact from him as he walked away. As soon as he was out of ear and eye shot, I started bawling and crying my eyes out.

I then reflected on the first day I had met Brent and his grandfather Mr. Genuit and the countless hours I spent with them reading various books and helping Brent to learn to walk again and then finally on the day that we found his parents. "Oh, what relief that was that I had felt when we had finally found them," I thought to myself smiling through tears.

It was then that I wiped my face and stood up from the picnic table and started walking back towards my house (David and Sharon's House). "I guess I could consider it my home now," I thought to myself realizing that I had always called it "David and Sharon's house but because for many years now I had been living there I hadn't realized that maybe now I should be calling it my second home now that I will be split living there and the Time Tower and at Brent's home and bookstore.

"I think you need to figure out where you want to actually reside now," came Emry's voice in my head, "you go from place to place, and you haven't been able to settle in one place. I feel like you are becoming a nomad moving house to house."

"Hey that isn't funny," I said to Emrys aloud by mistake as some people walking past me thought I was talking to myself and quickly walked away.

I had walked down the road and reached David and Sharon's house and opened the door to see Michael in the living room cleaning it.

"Hey Bella, congrats! Sharon and David just told me!" Michael said walking up to me giving me a hug.

"Thanks Michael," I said calmly looking up to see another hooded black figure in the room and it was their son and fellow council member was in tears hugging his parents.

"It is so good to see you son! We have missed you so much after all these years! It's good to have you home!" David said holding his son tight in a warm embrace.

"If it wasn't for Bella, I wouldn't have been able to come home to you both!" he said smiling at me.

"Thank you, Bella!" David and Sharon said happily looking over at me through tears as I smiled.

"No problem," I said.

"What brings you home Bella?" Sharon asked me

"It is almost time to go," I said smiling at her as I went to my room to look for something that I wanted to start having on me.

"You seem to have a bad feeling about something happening soon Bella," Emrys said to me.

"What are you looking for Bella?" Midnight asked me.

"My box," I said to myself as I lifted it out from under my bed. I found the long thin red box with Gold Ribbon that was gifted to me by David and Sharon and a cloth chest shield that I had gotten from them as well. It is made with a special material cloth that is practically impenetrable which I put underneath my clothes and robe.

"Are you worried about the Night Stalker?" Emrys asked me as I said, "Yes, though it was my idea to allow us to be more open on the streets, it doesn't mean that we should not take precautions."

It was then that I left the room with the sword at my side in a sheath and hid it in my robes out of sight.

"Let's go," I said to Sharon as David stayed at the house with his son and Michael.

"I see that you are taking the precaution to bring the sword?" Sharon said.

"As David says, "Nothing seems to escape your notice," I smiled sideways at her as we headed towards the tower.

"You allowed for the Time Council to be more open on the streets with the public, but you are still arming yourself even though we have Timekeepers behind us following us and in front of us to make sure we are safe?" Sharon said slowly.

"Yes, the Time council needs to show people not only we are human and have flaws. That we have the want to be around the very same people that elected us. I wanted the people to see that we are also approachable but still protected," I said putting my right hand on the top of my sword as I saw movement in the shadows head of us.

"Bella, watch out!" Emry's said as a fire ball of light came from my mouth and barely missed the figure that out of nowhere came from above us and attempted to strike Sharon down. I pulled out the sword using it in a quick motion to attempt to block the attack. The cloaked hooded attacker kept trying to use their sword against me as I blocked the attacks and countered with multiple moves. Soon the Timekeepers came up to us quickly as the attacker saw that they were soon to be outnumbered and ran away as quickly as it appeared back into the shadows.

"Are you okay Sharon?" I asked slightly out of breath noticing that Sharon nodded slightly and then grabbed her shoulder and blood started coming out.

"Sharon?!" I said again as she fell to the ground in shock.

"SHARON!!" I shouted. Immediately the Timekeepers blew their whistles as I pulled the coin out of my pocket and turned it three times in hand and rubbed the top of it. The Timekeepers checked Sharon's timeclock and saw that her time was reduced to only having two weeks left and was in Red.

Almost immediately a carriage showed up with the driver as I picked Sharon up and brought her into it and closed the door behind us and told the young carriage driver, "Bring us to the doctors immediately!"

We were on the road in seconds as we were brought to an infirmary building.

I lifted her out of the carriage and into the building. Immediately nurses and doctors rushed over to us looking at all the blood that was all over her robes with blood all over them.

"What happened?" asked the doctor.

"There was another attack from the Night Stalker. He attempted to kill us. She was stabbed, I think. It was in her shoulder area and again in her chest, I think. She is bleeding everywhere."

They placed her on a stretcher and brought her to the back.

"We will take care of her, you should let the Council Leaders know what happened immediately," the nurse said as I nodded and left back into the carriage.

"Bring me to the Time Tower please," I said as the driver nodded.

I walked into the hall to see the hall full of Night Hunters in robes gathered around the room.

"Welcome Bella, it is good to see you!" Tobey said smiling and then his face turned serious as he saw the state of my robes, "What happened?"

"I must ask you all for help," I said looking around saying aloud, "there is no time to lose! While on our way here, Sharon and I were attacked by the Night Stalker." We were three blocks from her house and an unidentified person in black was waiting for us. Timekeepers were in front of us and behind us and it still attacked us from above. I need help to investigate who this killer is. Perhaps they are among us, and we don't know. Sharon is in the infirmary now in town and is being looked over. Her condition is serious as she lost a lot of blood and has only two weeks on her time clock left."

"She had 5200 years left," I thought to myself, she lost so much time through losing all this blood."

There was a lot of muttering around the room.

"Now this is an attack on us, not just the Time Council. An attack on one of us is an attack on us all by extension. Not one person is safe," Tobey said gravely as he looked at me, "Let this be your first action as Night Hunter Master. What would you have us do?"

"Comb the streets tonight and look for this person. Anyone caught outside at this hour please bring them to the Timekeepers to hold until morning for questioning. As of right now, after 9pm, we are enacting a curfew except for Timekeepers, and Night Hunters. The Time Council can risk it at will if they choose to go out but under the need of protection to do so past 9pm. We also need to let Council Member #13 and David, his wife, know what happened," I instructed as everyone folded their hands and bowed to me.

"As your will be done Night Master," every hooded figure in the room said and then everyone vanished in thin air.

"How did they do that?" I asked Tobey as he laughed, "Come this way, I will show you."

I followed him down the hall to a room with a big table sized basin in the middle of it and he handed me a large cloth bag. Fill this up with the powder.

I then grabbed what felt and smelled like pink baby powder and filled it up halfway. Then Tobey put his hands around the bag after sealing it and said "Forlossem" the powder turned into a pink and gold mixture.

"Now take a pinch full and put the rest in your pocket and say, "Forlossem" under your breath while thinking about where you want to go and sprinkling it on your feet," Tobey said and nodded for me to do it.

I then thought about David and Sharon's house and said "Forlossem"

Suddenly there was a crack, and someone shouted, "What the Heck!"

David and Michael jumped as I appeared right in front of them.

"Where is your son David?" I asked quickly looking at David.

"I'm right here behind you," Theodore said from behind me.

"Oh, thank God!" I said in concern hugging him.

"Ohkay.... what is going on?" Theodore said slowly pushing me off him feeling awkward, looking from me to Michael and to his dad.

"Sharon and I were attacked on the way to the Night Hunters meeting. She was taken to the infirmary. I wanted to let you know. Also, there is a curfew at this moment for the entire City of Sandglass. We intend to catch the Night Stalker and anyone else caught outside tonight. Sharon is safe. She was stabbed in her chest and her shoulder area. The chest wound I think was too serious as much as her shoulder wound was. She was bleeding a lot, but I know she is well cared for," I explained in reassurance.

"What happened to the shadow stalker after he stabbed her?" David asked in concern.

"The killer got away and disappeared into the alley nearby," I said in dismay and then looked up at David and Michael insisted, "but we will catch this killer eventually."

Everyone in the room remained silent as looks of concern and worry was being exchanged on everyone's faces.

There was a knock on the door as I stood up immediately and walked to the door. There was a Timekeeper there who I ushered in. He stood in front of everyone else who was now also at the doorway waiting anxiously to hear the news of what the Timekeeper had to say.

"We have stabilized Sharon, and she should be back tonight, no mortal wounds were accomplished by the killer. As for the killer's whereabouts, we and the Night Hunters have joined forces but have come up fruitless," The timekeeper said as he then bowed and then left the house.

"Well, this is great news," I said looking at everyone smiling, "at least she will be okay and will be home soon."

"Yes, but the killer has not been caught yet," David said in concern, "When the killer realizes they made a mistake they will be back for her."

"Not necessarily. But then again, we have something that we didn't have before. A live witness who can account for what happened. Maybe Sharon noticed something about this person," I said thoughtfully. It was then that we all turned in for the night and went to bed. It was difficult to sleep but we all knew that there was nothing more we could do now.

I locked the doors for the night and put my sword away in the box on my bedside table and went to sleep.

The next morning, I awoke to a knock on the front door. I noticed no one else was up or near it.

Just then there was another knock, I looked outside the door cautiously and saw that it was Tobey.

"I just heard, I am so glad that Sharon will be okay, she is on her way here in a few minutes using the powder," Tobey said looking at everyone who was now standing in the doorway, "Bella, you are going to be needed. I need you to call a meeting tonight at the Tower around 8pm again. We need to find out what we know and gather our resources."

"Right, especially now that the killer made a mistake. I must see Sharon as soon as possible first though," I said nodded as Tobey looked at me in slight confusion tilting his head, "The killer only maimed/ injured Sharon, it didn't kill her whomever this killer is. May not know yet that they made a mistake."

"Right, well I will see you tonight then!" Tobey said smiling and nodding at everyone and let himself out.

It wasn't until another hour later that we all heard the door open, and we saw Sharon stumble into the house.

"Sharon my dear!" David said rushing up to her noting her bandaged shoulder and gauze and tape on her chest on her right side.

"Hello everyone," Sharon said struggling to get into the house as she then leaned on David who helped her to a seat on the couch.

"How are you feeling?" I asked sitting next to her as David sat on the other side of her.

"Oh, I feel wonderful, just wonderful," she said sarcastically smiling at me shaking her head as she went to sit on the couch in the living room.

"I am glad you survived and were able to come home. It was so dark when we were attacked, I couldn't make out anything," I said in worry, "Do you remember anything?"

"I know who it was..." Sharon said calmly, "I just don't have any proof."

At that moment, the clock struck 7pm and Michael came into the room.

"Who was it?" I asked her quietly and then I looked up at Michael.

"Don't you have to be getting ready Bella?" Michael said calmly, seemingly not realizing what was just said in the room as he was looking at me and then the clock.

"Oh yeah, right," I said looking at Sharon, "We will talk more, I have to get to the tower."

"I will come with you!" Sharon said slowly, getting up.

"How are you going to do that?" David said looking at her with wide eyes, "you can barely walk."

"But I can stand," Sharon said smiling at me as I knew what she

wanted us to do.

"Ok Sharon but only if you want to," I said calmly. I stood up and went to my room and grabbed my sword, put on my robe, and grabbed the bright golden and pink powder.

I went back to the living room to see her standing up by the door.

"I am going to picture the front door of the tower for us," I said calmly as she nodded and grabbed the powder from her bag and attached it back to her side and then covered it with the robe she was wearing and then we both said, "Forlossem" and we disappeared.

Chapter 7
The Big Reveal

We got the entrance of the tower door, and I looked at Sharon before we went into the Tower.

"So, are you going to tell me who you think it is and how you know?" I asked Sharon as she seemed to be slightly scared and nodded and the door opened and followed me in wearing her robes..

"Oh, good, you are early," Tobey said smiling, "Perfect. So, to call the meeting, say "Kār prachum," and you say it while holding your room key up, so the Night Hunters know where to be."

It was then that I pulled my key out of my robe and held it up and said, "Kār prachum"

Within seconds, all the Night Hunters appeared gathering around me and bowed and said, "As you wish at your command, Night Master."

It was then that one of the Night Hunters around me fell on the ground as I ran up to them and lifted their hood. It was Sharon.

"Sharon!" Tobey said in surprise. "Are you okay?"

"I am sorry, I just don't have a lot of strength," Sharon said half smiling at me, "but I am here at your first call of a meeting now, Night Master."

"Your loyalty is commendable, but you need to gather your strength," I said looking over at Tobey who looked concerned, "Do we have a guest room?"

Tobey nodded as he lifted Sharon up and took her away to what I presumed was a room in which she could rest. The rest of the Night Hunters remained hooded and bowed.

"At ease Night Hunters," I said calmly, and they all looked up and stood up straight, and all I could see was a room full of people with their hoods still covering their faces.

"My fellow Night Hunters, My name is Bellatrix Kai, you can call me Bella. You obviously know of my siblings from the Time Council, but you don't know me. I didn't have the same upbringing as that of my siblings within these City walls. In fact, it was only just recently that I found out about my siblings and had a chance to meet them. Nor did I have the same upbringing as all of you and the previous Night Hunter Masters before me," I said addressing the Night Hunters in the room and nodding towards Tobey who had come back into the room joining me in the front of the crowd.

There was silence in the room as I looked around the room.

"Our organization is a unit of intelligence and gathering of information, of warriors full of bravery, and courage, and yet its mystical and enshrouded by secrets and dark history. We are all secret keepers if you will. We are also protectors of those of whom we hold dear to us. Our current state of affairs is at best, seemingly foundationally sound," I stated slowly looking over at Tobey who nodded, "but amongst our city there is a killer targeting us, plucking our leaders of our City off one by one on the streets as if we were "selected" when in fact I believe that the targets are our cloaks that we are wearing. There is no shame in holding fear for our lives. We are all but human, and fear is an emotion like any other. But you cannot let fear, or your emotions get the best of you. I am asking as a friend to you all to reveal your identities to me and to others that are in this room."

There was a moment of silence and Tobey was the first one to break it.

"Bella, hold on, no one do anything," Tobey said incredulously, "we thrive within this organization on secrecy.

"I assure you that no one else will be able to reveal the names of anyone else that they see in this meeting. We have no outsiders here," I said calmly as I whispered some words. Just then the room became slightly darker around us.

"Our cloaks and hoods hide our identities from those around us so that we can collect information secretly," Tobey said with slight frustration under his breath to me.

"Yes, but I didn't select those that are in our organization of Night Hunters, you did. So, I would like to see those of you who are in this organization, just as now, all of you know that Sharon is a part of us here today," I said.

Realizing there was something in what I had said because Sharon's identity had been revealed, Tobey could no longer voice his complaint or concerns at my suggestion.

I remained silent as no one seemed to move, as if debating whether they too felt comfortable.

"Instead, I think, I would like to use the room next to this one," I said calmly, "I would like a one-on-one audience with each one of you. I would like to meet you all in person, and this way you will only reveal yourself to me."

"There are over a hundred of us," Tobey said in surprise.

"That is okay, I will only be a minute with each of you. Please form a line along this wall I said, and I will meet you all," I said looking around, "Unless there are a group of you who want to take off your masks now in front of everyone?"

All the Night Hunters looked at me blankly and then at each other.

"I know this is unconventional, but it is very critical for me and for us to know who we are to each other, for our own security and safety," I said as one by one they revealed themselves. Some of them were from this City but there were some that were from The Underground, and I was concerned, "Those that are from The Underground, please meet me later, so for now those people are dismissed."

More than half the people left the room.

"We need to reveal to each other who we all are so there are no mistakes. I need to ensure that everyone knows who each other is so that we can ensure that we are keeping an eye on one another better than we are now," I explained as I looked around to maybe ten people in the room, "So far, the Night Stalker has not killed or maimed anyone in The Underground, so I am fairly certain it is someone who doesn't travel down there much. Would any more of you feel comfortable revealing yourselves yet now that the room has gotten smaller?"

Six more people uncovered their faces as I nodded.

"You may leave, and thank you," I said nodding towards then again as they disappeared, "As for the last four of you one by one please come into the room."

They bowed as I walked into the room and left the door open.

Chapter 8
The Four Night Hunters

It was several minutes after I placed a chair down to sit on and I had placed another in front of me for the last four people to come into the room to sit at one by one as one came in behind me and closed the door.

"You must realize of course that to me it was quite a surprise that you still wanted to hide your identity even after there were only four of you left," I said looking at the hooded figure who remained still watching me.

"Well? Who are you?" I asked in slight frustration as I ushered the hooded figure forward to sit down across from me.

The figure seemed hesitant and after a few minutes they walked forward and sat down in front of me. I was in shock as the hooded figure pulled off the hood off their head and pulled off the black facemask covering their face and unmasked itself.

"I know you are a bit surprised, but I only just recently just joined Bella," said the hooded figure in front of me.

"Does he know?" I asked as the unmasked person in front of me shook their head.

"No, James does not know," Socrat said putting his head down.

"You ought not to have secrets between you two," I said shaking my head looking down at him.

"I know but he was busy with his father traveling City to City and I want to be able to travel and have a life of purpose too," Socrat explained as I nodded in understanding.

"I will let you tell James when you are ready," I said thoughtfully.

"I am grateful Night Hunter Master," Socrat said through tears looking up at me.

"I am proud of you Socrat," I said smiling slightly, "Now that we are aware of each other, I approve of you being on my select team to be able to go on expeditions with. I have been approved to have my own personal group of Six Night Hunters around me and I want you to be one of my Secret Six members."

"Really? I accept!" Socrat said excitedly, "You won't be disappointed, I was one of the top people to pass the selection tests!"

"I am honored to have you in our organization Socrat. You may put your mask on yourself again and you may go. Please send in the next person," I said as he nodded and re-hooded himself and bowed out of the room, two more hooded figures came in at once to my surprise and closed the door after themselves and one sat in the chair silently and the other stood next to them.

It was then that the hooded figures followed suit to reveal themselves to me at once.

"Well, this is a surprise," I said in exclamation, "Am I to assume everyone I know is already a Night Hunter already?"

"What do you mean?" James and his father Kaide said at the same time in front of me as I shook my head.

"Is that why you didn't want to reveal yourselves to me? Because I already knew you both?" I asked them with slight frustration.

"We didn't know if you would accept us," James said looking at me with a slight shame.

"Why wouldn't I accept you?" I asked as I shook my head. "You both are going to be a part of my Secret Six Team, you may want to talk with your boyfriend James you need to not have secrets between you two, and I don't want to get between that," I said putting my fingers to the bridge of my nose and between my eyebrows massaging a headache that was coming about. "Over time changes happen I guess, one must learn to accept them, you both may leave."

I took in a deep breath and slowly let it out as James stood up, and both he and his father Kaide bowed to me and left the room as the last person came into the room. The figure bowed and sat down. It was then after a few minutes that the figure removed their hood from their face and revealed themselves to me. It was Michael.

"Let me guess, you just wanted to join last minute because they had openings?" I asked sarcastically.

"No, I joined because I wanted to learn more about what is out there than just the City of Sandglass Time. I want to be a part of something bigger," Michael said firmly and quite seriously.

"You will also be a part of my Secret Six Team Michael," I said calmly as he put on his hood and black face mask and bowed and left the room.

That night James got home to see Socrat waiting for him.

"Where did you go?" Socrat asked James suspiciously, "You were gone for hours!"

"Socrat, I need to tell you something," James said hesitantly wincing while trying to speak.

"Great, so do I," Socrat said and then quickly added, "You first."

"Socrat I am a Night Hunter for Bellatrix Kai," James said looking at Socrat who looked at James in a sigh of relief, "Oh, so you are a part of the Secret Six now too?"

"Wait how did you know?" James asked Socrat as he then smiled at Socrat, "So that is why Wren was acting like this during the meetings? He felt you near!"

Socrat looked at James and smiled as they both hugged each other.

"I am relieved to know that we are both on the Night Hunters with Bellatrix!" James said calmly as Socrat smiled and nodded, "So, what were you going to say?"

"The same thing," Socrat said smiling at James as they both laughed happily.

Chapter 9
The Final Two Weeks

It was shortly after I had finished with the one-on-one meetings I went to my room, grabbed the sword, and hid it under my robes. I then walked down the hall and knocked on Tobey's room door.

"Hey Tobey?" I said as he opened the #8 door.

"Yes Bella?" he said slightly tired yawning.

"Can you bring me to Sharon? I just wanted to check in on her," I said anxiously as he nodded and came outside his room and locked the door behind him. I followed him down the hall towards my room and took a left. The door said 11G.

"This is the Guest room for you to use whenever you have someone over and they have their own bathroom as well," Tobey said handing over my copy of the 11G key.

"Thank you, Tobey. That will be all for tonight," I said calmly as Tobey left the hall and walked back to his room. I slowly opened the door and saw that Sharon was sleeping on the bed. It was then that I closed the door behind me and locked it.

I didn't want to risk a chance of anyone hurting her. An immense feeling of guilt for putting her in harms way came over me.

"You cannot blame yourself for what happened," Emrys said

"What was the ball of light that came out of me?" I asked Emrys.

"That is what is called celestial energy," Emrys explained to me in my mind, "Eventually you will learn more of what this is."

Slowly I walked over to Sharon who was sleeping on the bed, and I saw that she only had two weeks left on her timecard. Coming to this realization I felt a myself in a sudden anxiety and it became hard to swallow. After all these years, Sharon had been like a mother to me. Suddenly the image of Brent and his grandfather came to mind.

"I know what you are thinking," Emrys said in my mind, "You are questioning whether it would be right to give her more life left or not. For the average person, this scenario raises some complex ethical and emotional questions. Some might prioritize their partners happiness and choose to transfer some of their remaining time believing it would allow their partner to live a fuller life. Others might feel that their own life, even if short, has intrinsic value and might prefer to live those last moments fully, focusing on quality rather than quantity of life left. This is familiar we spirits have lived to see here in the City of Sandglass, as you have seen people die daily. I suggest you not do anything until you see David about this."

I nodded and slowly left the room, locked the door behind me, thought of home, and said, "Forlossem"

"Bella I was just thinking of you! I was wondering if you could tell me how my wife is doing? I haven't seen her since you both left for that meeting," David said looking at me in slight concern.

"To be completely honest David, she had passed out before the meeting started," I said quite seriously as the color that was left in his face escaped.

"I must go to her," he said hurriedly gathering his coat and hat as I nodded.

It was then that I went outside with him and held on to his hand and said," Forlossem" and we appeared in front of room 11G.

I unlocked the door and opened it as David rushed over to Sharon's side.

"My love!" David said through tears noticing her timecard. He then rolled up his sleeve and started transferring some of his time to her as he was weeping at her weakened body.

As he wept, I had noticed that his time was shortening on his own time clock. After a few minutes Sharon's eye's fluttered awake as she silently looked at David who looked like he aged well beyond his years as she saw that time had been syphoned into her. A tear rolled down her cheek as she put her other hand on David's head.

"David, my precious David," Sharon said as she started to cry.

"You and I are supposed to leave this Earth together, remember?" David said through tears as he moved his wife's hair from her face.

"I'm sorry I was so careless. I just feel so weak, I don't know where he came from, it was out of nowhere," Sharon said.

"He?" David said wide eyed taking his arm from his wife. "Who is it?"

I then motioned for David not to push it looking at David who then nodded in understanding.

Slowly, Sharon sat up noticing the feeling of fresh time coursing through her body.

"What is going on?" She asked, looking up and noticing me standing at her side with the Sword.

"You didn't use the sword, have you?" Sharon said looking at me with hesitation.

"That sword, the time left on it, I want it understood that under no condition are you to use it on us," David said to me seriously.

"Why not?" I said in concern, "I cannot imagine living in this world without your guidance."

"There are preparations for you and Theodore in case of our deaths and Theodore is not to know about this sword. The very mention of how this sword works will cause chaos in this world. You are to sell the house and split the money between the both of you to be able to get a new place together or separately, your choice." David said looking around the room. "This position on the Time council is not permanent and you will need a place to stay when your terms are up."
I then looked at Sharon who also looked at me seriously, "No matter what, you are to let us go when the time comes."
"In the meantime, hun, you must be careful," David said looking at his timecard, they both only had two months left.
"You both only have two months left?" I said in slight anger as I pulled up both my sleeves and held on to both of their hands. "How is that?"
"We have been giving our time up generously to buy things for the house and for food etc. over the last few years, it adds up," David said
"Bella no," Sharon said through tears.
I had given them both five more years on top of the two months left.
"That was not fair of you to make me agree to that," I said to David who shrugged.

"When it is our time to go, that is our time to go," David said, and I told you not to give us more time.

"You said not to give you more time from the sword, you didn't say I couldn't give you time from my own time," I said to David who shook his head.

"Thank you," Sharon said as I nodded my head. "It was a mistake; one slip up, and all that time was lost. I don't even understand how it happened! I just felt myself go weak."

"You are overexerting yourself," David said to her, "Bella and I are going to take you home eventually but for now you need to get some rest."

Sharon nodded as she laid back down on the bed and held onto David's hand.

"I love you sweetheart," Sharon said through tears.

"I love you too my love," David said

I am going to lock you both in here so you will be safe. Sharon has the powder to leave when she has the strength to go back home.

David nodded and laid on the bed next to her.

It was then that I left the room, and I locked the door behind me.

Chapter 10
Aunt Beatrice and Uncle Bernard

I had left the guest room with a slight feeling of happiness as I looked down at my timecard of four hundred years.

"Do you think you should have given them more time?" came a voice in my head, realizing it was Midnight my Owl spirit animal.

"If I had given them more time, they would have felt like Mr. Genuit does with Brent. I didn't want them to feel like that," I said thoughtfully.

"This was very wise of you Bella," Emrys my Pheonix said.

I walked down the hall, and hid my timecard as I turned the corner, I saw Taylor and Tobey in the hall.

"Hey Bella, perfect timing, we were about to look for you!" Tobey said smiling mischievously.

"I can see that as you are standing up against the wall, what are you two up to?' I asked curiously

"No honest, we were, but whatever do you mean?" Taylor asked.

"You two always look happiest, when you are up to no good," I said smiling and laughed slightly shaking my head at Taylor and Tobey.

"Bella, we have someone we want you to meet," Taylor said smiling at me.

"Who?" I said excitedly.

"Our Aunt and Uncle!" Tobey said smiling slightly.

"Oh, I have an aunt and uncle? I didn't know I had more family," I said honestly.

Tobey looked at Taylor in surprise.

"Here let's come to my room so we can talk properly," Taylor said not letting what I said faze him, pulling me in his room with Tobey following closely behind me and then he closed the door behind us.

It was then that I walked into the room to see a roaring and crackling fireplace which lit the room. I looked around and saw a four-poster bed, bureau, a closet, and a desk in the room. It was like Taylors room.

I sat down in a chair which was in front of the fire as my brothers sat in the chairs on either side of me.

"What makes you want me to meet them?" I asked carefully.

"Well, you have never met them, and they are our family," Taylor said as he looked over that Tobey who seemed to avoid his eye contact.

 "I cannot believe our parents never mentioned us or our aunt and uncle to you," Tobey said still seemingly in shock. I sat in contemplation looking at the fire in front of me while Tobey and Taylor remained silent.

"Can I ask you both something Tobey and Taylor?" I said without looking away from the flames.

"Yeah, go ahead," Taylor said as Tobey nodded.

"Why is it that growing up I never had the chance to know of you or any of my other family like Kahn, or any of my siblings for that matter?" I asked, looking from the flames to both who looked at each other. I felt disconnected.

"We know the answer, but this isn't going to be an easy one Bella," Taylor said looking at me as I nodded and then to Tobey.

"Growing up our mom had a grudge against her sister, our Aunt Beatrice. Our Aunt Beatrice and Uncle Bernard took care of us growing up here within the City of Sandglass," Taylor said sadly.

"But why? Why didn't you all get to grow up with me as a kid? Why would they have a grudge to the point that it affects the rest of the family for the rest of their life? Like life is too short as it is. What could have been so bad to the point where they stopped talking? Why make a mountain over a molehill? We were all given a second chance to live a different life here within the city and some, like me and you all, were born here, and we all already know the limitations of life. What was..."

"Easy now Bella," Tobey said realizing I was getting a little stressed, and angry, "Let us explain."

I nodded and waited silently for them to explain.

"Aunt Beatrice, according to our mom, she was a bad influence on me and your other siblings here. She didn't like what Aunt Beatrice was teaching us about magic growing up. Your parents didn't want you or any of us at an early age to succumb to that influence. Your mom, seeing that there was no going back from that with us, kind of gave up on raising us and so Uncle Bernard and Aunt Beatrice took us into the City of Sandglass to raise us as their own. Uncle Bernard over the years begged both our mom and our aunt to talk, and to work things out over the years up until recently. But it was too late for them because of the attack of the Village of Paska. Which is why Aunt Beatrice has been taking things hard lately. We both think it will be a good idea for you to meet them."

I then looked up at them from the fire and nodded.

"In the morning, we will take you, for now you should get some sleep," Tobey said to me.

"Yes, I am quite tired," I said as I stood up and left the room and went to my own for the night.

"Anything you want to talk about tonight Bella before you go to sleep?" Midnight asked me.

"I just wish my mom and dad had a better relationship with the family here within the City of Sandglass.

"People do things for their own reasons and sometimes, its at a cost of consequences that last a lifetime," Midnight said wisely, "Try to get some rest, Bella. The best thing we can do is move forward and get to know them now while we can."

"Goodnight Midnight," I said smiling and nodding as I fell asleep.

The next morning, I was woken up to knocking at my door. I got up to see it was Taylor smiling at me.

"Are you ready?" he asked noticing I wasn't dressed yet.

"Not yet, not dressed like this," I said showing them I was dressed in Pjs.

"Hurry and get ready so we can get going," he said smiling excitedly from the hallway.

I nodded, closed the door, and got changed. Putting on my chest shield and robes then I wrapped my sword at my side close to me, soon I was ready.

Within a few minutes, I met Taylor and Tobey downstairs. Suddenly, I stopped in mid tracks.

"Hold on, I need to check on Sharon and David," I said holding on to Tobey's robes.

"No need, they already left early this morning," Tobey said smiling, "I got them the carriage back home already. Sharon is doing better already."

"Oh good, I will have to stop by eventually to see them at the house," I said feeling like a whole weight was lifted off my shoulders.

"Do they live far from here?" I asked looking at Tobey.

"No, not really," Tobey said

He grabbed my hand and Taylor stood next to me as they both said, "Forlossem" and into the morning air we left.

In seconds we arrived at our destination. It was a creek seemingly on the outside of the City of Sandglass.

"Where are we? I thought you said that they live within the City of Sandglass?" I said looking around.

"They raised us, and we grew up in the City of Sandglass but now they live on the outskirts in the Village of Thurbin," Tobey said smiling

I looked around and saw that we were by a meadow with a creek by it. It was seemingly very peaceful. Certainly, quieter then the streets of the City of Sandglass.

We walked for about a few minutes up a dirt path along the creek. To our right was a house that looked very quaint. There was a gazebo by the lake up ahead and it had a picnic table in it. As we walked up, we saw two people sitting there.

"Hey Aunt Beatrice! Hey Uncle Bernard!" Tobey said smiling as we walked up to them. They were both sitting, and turned around, and stood up immediately to hug Tobey and then Taylor.

"Tobey! Taylor! It is so good to see you!" Aunt Beatrice said smiling up at them and hugged them both as Uncle Bernard followed suit until they saw me.

"Well, who might this be?" Aunt Beatrice said smiling politely at me.

"This is Bellatrix Kai Aunt Beatrice," Tobey said smiling at them and immediately Aunt Beatice's face became serious and sad.

"Young Bella? Is that really you?" Aunt Beatrice said walking over to me and giving me a hug.

"I am so happy that I have finally had a chance to meet you! It was almost 30 years ago that I saw you. You were just a baby when I held you in my arms. I know you don't remember me, but I am your Aunt Beatrice. I am your mother's sister," she said smiling through tears. I could see the resemblance of my mom to that of Aunt Beatrice.

"It is a pleasure to meet you," I said smiling through tears, hugging her back.

"And I am your Uncle Bernard," Uncle Bernard said putting out his hand to shake mine as I hugged him.

"You are definitely a Kai," he said smiling through tears, "You are all definitely huggers."

I laughed through tears.

We had spent much of the afternoon reminiscing how it was growing up and how my siblings were growing up. They had brought out many photographs of my siblings and how things were with my family. It was honestly one of the best things in the world to experience. I could sense that there was a lot of love within the family. Things back then within the City of Sandglass were different then they are today. Things are more developed less time costly, and there are more stores now then there were then. There is a bigger population it seems now then there was too.

"I am so sorry that things got difficult between us and your parents. It was never our intention to have you split from your siblings. It is difficult to make up for lost time especially after all these years. I know this was not fair on you. It is so cruel that your siblings got to spend more time with us then your actual parents or that you didn't get to know us when you were younger. Your mother didn't want you all raised with magic. Magic is in the very fabric of our being. We wanted to raise you all with magic so that it would allow for you to grow with it and learn of its value and uses at an early age. We also wanted you to all to be responsible with it too. Your siblings have knowledge of magic and can use it at will with the power of their spirit animals, but your parents didn't want you having them at an early age," Aunt Beatrice explained.

"Wait, you mean you can use magic with the spirit animals?" I asked as they all nodded.

"Tell me you showed her this stuff already!" Uncle Bernard said in surprise to Tobey and Taylor who both shook their heads.

"We thought she already knew, being raised by Sharon and David the last few years," Tobey said showing them my Owl and Pheonix.

"Oh, I just got them a year ago," I said to Aunt Beatrice and Uncle Bernard as they shook their head.

"They talk to me a lot," I said calmly.

"They can help you do things on your day to day you just have to talk them and can ask for their help," Aunt Beatrice said quietly, as if trying to make sure no one outside of the gazebo could hear us.

"We will show her the basics eventually," Tobey said nodding at me as I nodded in agreement with them.

"Well, we have to get back before we are missed Aunt Beatrice, it was nice seeing you both," Uncle Bernard," said Taylor, getting up from the table nodding to Uncle Bernard. It was then that Aunt Beatrice and Uncle Bernard stood up and smiled and hugged us all and said goodbye looking at Taylor. We walked away towards the path along the creek and after a few minutes they stopped and turned around to face me. Tobey whispered something and three chairs and a table appeared out of nowhere as he placed them on the ground between us to sit at.

"As you saw they were happy to meet you, but behind the smile you could read how much distress she was feeling because of all the guilt," Taylor explained as I nodded silently. "They moved away from the city so that they could be a little more at peace, and away from the busy streets of the City of Sandglass. But they do come to the City from time to time," Tobey said looking at Taylor.

"We wanted you to meet them so that you don't feel like you are the only one left in the family besides us," Taylor said looking across the table at me. "We are concerned that you may feel more alone once David and Sharon are gone, and we want you to know that we care about you and are here for you too."

"Thank you both," I said as I nodded and smiled.

"Time to head back to the City," Tobey said smiling and we then got up and Taylor made the chairs disappear and then grabbed my hand and said, "Forlossem" and we were back at the Time Tower.

Chapter 11
The Secret Six Meeting

"Bella! Where have you been?" I heard Brent's voice from behind me.

"Brent what are you doing here?" I asked looking from Brent to Tobey who immediate put his hands up and started to back away from me trying to nonverbally let me know he was not behind Brent being there. I walked to my room with Brent following me as he tried to continue to talk to me.

"Bella, I am asking you a question," Brent said as I turned around and put my finger to my lips and grabbed his hand and brought him to my room. We walked into my room and closed the door behind him as I pushed him against the door and kissed him.

"I missed you too," I said smiling at him as he smiled back.

"What is going on?" he said.

I had recapped what happened with Sharon at the meeting and how I met Aunt Beatrice and Uncle Bernard.

He opened his mouth in shock and in concern for Sharon and David.

"What do you mean they only have five years left?" Brent said in concern, "I thought that they had thousands left."

"Apparently not," I said in curiosity, "they said they had spent the money on the house but there haven't been any workers there that I was aware of recently. I am not sure how they had spent all those thousands of years so quickly."

I thought about this quietly for a few moments before it was Brent who spoke again.

"I have thought about what you had said, and I think that I want to be either a part of the Time Council or at the very least I want to be a part of the Night Hunters Organization," Brent said looking at me for some sign of reaction.

I was careful not to provide a reaction.

"You want to join the Night Hunters?" I asked looking up seriously at him but still trying to keep a serious face on, letting the change in conversation sink in and said, "Follow Me."

I then led Brent to the meeting hall downstairs, and he looked around the room at the various portraits of people who were part of the history of the walls of the Time Tower.

It was then that I pulled my key out of my robe and held it up and said, "Kār prachum"

Suddenly the hall was full of Night Hunters who were all hooded and standing in rows in front of Brent and I. Tobey came forward towards me.

"What is the reason for your call Master Night Hunter?" Tobey said looking at Brent who was unhooded next to me.

"It was brought to my attention that Brent Genuit wants to join us as a fellow Night Hunter. As I had said in our previous meeting it is my priority to keep those of us in our organization to be aware of each other. It is my opinion that he should be allowed to join in our organization, and I would like a vote with someone else to nominate him first, so it is not biased on my part.

"I would like to nominate Brent Genuit as part of the Night Hunters," came Socrats voice in the crowd.

"I second that motion," came James's voice.

"All in favor say aye," Tobey said

"Aye," everyone said.

"All opposed say Nay," Tobey said

No one said anything.

"Then as Assistant and 2nd in command of the Night Hunters, I hereby accept Brent Genuit as an honorary member of the Night Hunters," Tobey said as he seemed to conjure up some black robes in his arms and handed them to me as I put the robe on Brent and gave him his black mask and hooded him and hugged him as the room applauded.

"You are now part of the Secret Six my love," I said to him in a whisper in his ear as he nodded in understanding.

"The meeting is adjourned," I said looking around the room.

Everyone bowed towards me and said, "As your wish is our command, Night Master."

"Would the Secret Six please stay behind," I said and slowly everyone left the room except for six people who remained hooded including Brent who still stood beside me.

"Now that we are the only ones left," I said looking at everyone, "please remove your hoods so we know each other in the room as my secret team."

I stood in front of everyone and smiled.

"You all know each other so it's okay everyone," I said as everyone seemed hesitant at first. I lit the lights up in the room and made the fireplace burn a bit brighter as everyone saw who each other was.

Brent, smiled at Socrat and James who had nominated him as he hugged them in appreciation.

"Why didn't you nominate Brent?" Socrat asked aloud as I rejoined the group smiling at Brent and then turned a serious face to Socrat.

"As much as I wanted my boyfriend to be a part of our organization, I didn't want it to only be up to me," I said calmly, "I had already called the meeting to order, but also, it would have looked like a conflict of interest if it were just up to me. It would be a little presumptuous to assume he would be voted automatically as well," I explained further and everyone nodded. Brent was smiling as he looked around the room and he saw Kaide, James's father and then Michael.

"You are here? Really? Can I not get away from you?" Brent said looking at Michael scathingly. "What are you here for?"

"I wanted to join because I wanted to make a better difference," Michael said defiantly.

"Haven't you already done enough?" Socrat said in slight discomfort.

"Hey, I am sorry that things happened the way they did. But, I am trying to do better and make amends by being here," Michael said.

"Alright everyone I am calling this meeting as our first meeting to get to know each other," I said calmly.

"Well, I am happy to be here, what will our purpose be here?" Kaide said looking at me and then to his son.

"Well, the Council has afforded me the ability to do things on my own with my own team. I want to gather information like other members of this organization do," I said pointing at the piles of paper in the corner of the room and files and files of folders for everyone in the City of Sandglass. From what I have been told from Tobey, everyone within the City of Sandglass Time has their own binder and the Night Hunters gather information from the Timekeepers on people for the Time Council and that is how they know what is going on within the

City of Sandglass. The Time council gets information that pertains to their departments and makes changes and gives directives accordingly. Let's say, for example, Dan down the road makes a shed in his back yard. The housing department council member can approve or disapprove it. Well, I didn't want our team to be that intricate on the lives of people here. I really want us to expand and explore," I explained as I saw the look on everyone's faces.

"When you mean explore, do you mean going to the other City's of Sandglass?" Kaide asked me in slight concern.

"No, I mean beyond that," I said in excitement, "I will expand more on our next meeting. For now, please stay safe, and keep your ears out regarding the Night Stalker. I want us to catch
him."

"Him?" Socrat said in surprise, "Do you mean to say that you already know who it is?"

"I know how I intend to find out, and who to get the answers from but all in good time," I said smiling.

"Is the timing good Bella?" Brent asked me curiously as I smiled.

"Sometimes it is difficult to find a good time to do things and sometimes it is just a matter of finding the most opportune moment to do things," I said looking at Tobey who came into the room.

"What do you mean?" Michael asked.

"Sometimes when we want things done from others around us or when we have something to ask of others, it is a matter of timing. You can ask anyone for help, but sometimes they only cooperate or help if it is the right opportune moment," I explained looking at Tobey who seemed to want to talk to me.

"Now if everyone can get home safely, we will reconvene in the morning. Brent, would you meet me in my room."

Brent nodded as the Secret six left the hall at the same time, and all that was left was me and Tobey.

Tobey was standing at the end of the table holding a medium sized Sandglass as he flipped it over and watched as the sand slowly went to the bottom of the glass.

"I assume that you are not here to chat Tobey," I said calmly.

"Yes, it is a matter regarding Sharon. It is a matter of you being too delicate on her. We needed answers and yet, you didn't push or allow me to push the matter then, why?" Tobey asked looking up at me for a reaction from looking at the Sandglass.

"The issue is the timing, as I was explaining to the Secret Six just now," I said calmly looking at the sandglass. "You wanted me to ask Sharon at once, while she was slightly delirious from having all that time added into her, about a memory of a recent trauma. She was not in the right state of mind to answer such a question. Something tells me this is something that she will barely feel comfortable in revealing to me alone. As it is, I think this has something that she is ashamed of, or maybe its guilt that is holding her back from answering. I have asked her this question once, but I was interrupted by you in fact, and immediately, she shut down. She started to say it when she was in that state of delirium, but then stopped again when she read the room. This is something that I need extreme uninterrupted privacy with her about in order to find out the answer," I explained as Tobey seemed to be in contemplation of what I was saying.

"So, what do you think is the reasoning for her to act like this?" Tobey asked me.

"I am not sure," I said looking at the sandglass thoughtfully, "But I need some time so I can catch her at the right moment to ask her."

It was then that Tobey started walking to the door in silence and then he turned towards me and said, "I will wait for you, but we need an answer as soon as possible, she is not safe whilst she is the only one that knows. She is in grave danger right now, especially since the Shadow Stalker made a mistake by keeping her alive. You have until that last grain of sand empties before I ask you again and you better have an answer for me. Goodnight Bella."

I nodded and he left the room.

It was then that he left the room and closed the door, and I said," Forlossem," while thinking of my room in the tower and suddenly appeared in front of Brent who was smiling.

"I could get used to this appearing and disappearing out of thin air. Tell me how you do it," he said.

"One minute" I said and came back within minutes as I brought a bag of the sand for him and tied it to his side as he smiled, "You put some in your hand, and think of the place you want to go and say, "Forlossem," and drop it on your feet and then you appear where you needed to go."

"Oh cool," he said smiling and then looked at me, "So if I think of you, will it bring me to you?"

"It doesn't work like that unless you know where I am," I said smiling as him as he looked down, "Don't worry you will get the hang of it."

"I just don't want to lose you with that Night Stalker out there," he said in concern.

"I am not too worried about it," I said happily, "For now, let's get some sleep."

Chapter 12

A Hidden Shame Revealed

The next morning, I woke up and had decided that I was going to make it my firm intention to find the underlying cause of what was going on with Sharon by the end of the day Afterall, I only had until then before Tobey would ask me again. Somehow someway I was going to figure out how to talk to her.

I woke Brent up and said, "Good morning to him as I got up and got ready for the day."

"Where are you going? Are you going down for breakfast?" he asked me as I nodded and he got up himself and started to get ready, "I will join you."

Within a few minutes we were both ready to head downstairs to the dining hall and were surprised to see it empty.

"Everyone has already eaten and is in their rooms getting ready for the day," said one of the Timekeepers as I nodded in understanding.

"Is Sharon by chance available to talk to as of yet?" I asked curiously.

"She is home at the moment," said the Timekeeper who was looking like Brent. I put food on our plates from the buffet that was set up full of breakfast foods. It was after we had both sat down.

"I will be outside if you need anything," he said as I nodded. With that, the Timekeeper left the room.

I ate slowly, eating my breakfast gratefully with Brent and then I looked over at him.

"As soon as we finish eating, we will head over to my house," I said as Brent looked at me in surprise while munching on his breakfast toast and eggs.

"What?" I said.

"That is the first time I have heard you refer to David and Sharon's house as your house," Brent said in a tone of surprise.

"Oh well I figure my things are there and I have been there all these years. I might as well start calling it my house too." I said as he nodded in silence finishing what he was eating.

After a few more minutes we put our dirty dishes in the dish bin at the end of the buffet table and walked out to the carriage house.

I knocked on the door three times as we stood outside the doors hooded with our cloaks.

"Good morning," said the younger driver, "where to today?"

"David and Sharon's house," I said and then we will be coming back here with Sharon.

"Do you want me to just go fetch her for you?" he asked as I shook my head.

"I don't want to scare her," I said carefully thinking logically, "If I send for her with the coach and Timekeepers it looks official, like she is in trouble with the Time Council or Shadow Hunters. But if I go to her myself and ask her to join me, it might let her guard down enough to talk to me."

Brent nodded as I called the Timekeeper back.

"What is your name by the way," I asked the Timekeeper as she smiled walking up to us.

"My name is Shelly, Shelly Kimball ma'am," Shelly said smiling.

"This morning did you by chance see Sharon?"

"Matter of fact I did miss," Shelley said worriedly looking at me, "She was in a right state this morning. Stating that she didn't want to leave without letting you know. To be honest I was just about to let you know right now before you left the hall."

Tobey looked at me and then nodded in understanding at my logic.

"I will go to her immediately. She doesn't know it yet, but her life is in danger now," I said urgently.

"Well let's get going now then," Tobey said frantically as he motioned for us to pick a carriage and get in immediately.

Within a few minutes, we were outside the doors of David and Sharon's house.

The house seemed undisturbed as I walked up to it.

"You stay here Brent," I said as he nodded, "I will be right back."

Brent walked back and waited in the carriage for us to come back.

I walked in to see David looking up at me from the couch in the living room.

"Hey Bella," he said smiling at me, "It's good to see you. What are you up to?"

"I am wondering if I can bring Sharon to the Time Tower really quick, I have something to show her that I need help with," I lied and said urgently.

"Yeah, sure, she is in her room let me get her," he said attempting to get up.

"No worries, I will go to see her," I said walking over to their room.

I walked into the familiar room and saw that she was sitting up in bed and smiled when she saw me.

"Bella, it is good to see you," she said getting up to hug me.

"OH! That's it! That's the reason! Oh my God!" I said aloud and then looked at Sharon.

"Sharon, mom, I need you to come with me," I said through tears.

"Bella, hun, what is the matter?" she asked.

"I need you to come with me immediately to the Time Tower, there is something I need to show you," I lied, as she nodded and walked with me to the front door.

"No problem, dear," she said getting her robe on and followed me to the carriage outside the door.

"Hurry Bella," Brent said looking around and noticing there weren't any Timekeepers in sight.

"What is the matter dear?" she said in the carriage as we took off immediately

"We are in danger," I said looking outside, "Driver rush us faster to the tower."

"Yes, ma'am," he said as we pushed the horses to move faster.

We had arrived at top speed and got there immediately.

I hurriedly pushed her through the Time Tower doors and up to my room.

"Bella, what is going on? You are scaring me," she said, "That was the first time you called me mom."

"You don't have a clue as to how much danger you are in," I

said closing the door behind me as I scurried to my desk and investigated the drawers and still couldn't figure it out, "It had to be somewhere."

"Bella, what is the matter?" Brent said now sounding scared.

"The Stalker. He is in on it. That is why she was killed. She was going to expose him. She didn't want him to do it. She didn't agree with him. She was killed because she was going to tell everyone. But how do you know? How did you know who it was?" I asked her, "Unless you are a part of something I don't know about?"

"Bella?" Sharon asked me in confusion.

I then looked at the desk frantically and saw that there was a false bottom on one of the shelves that was locked from behind when I pulled it out.

Then I pulled out a binder.

"This was what she was investigating. This is what the Night Stalker has been keeping from us. He has been exploring at night and trying to find answers. Tell me. Who is the Night Stalker! I know you know mom! I know you do!" I said through tears looking at Sharon and Brent's mouth was wide open.

Sharon's eyes became watered, and she shook her head.

"I'm ashamed," she said as she started to cry.

"Tell us mom!" I said through tears, "You can trust me! You know me!"

Sharon looked at me in shock as she started to tear up and realized that this was the first time I had called her my mother. I meant it to, no matter what she raised me with David and
they were literally my parents now through thick and thin.
"If you don't tell me, the secret dies with you and more people will be in danger. He must be stopped!" I said through tears urgently, putting my hands on her shoulders. She then started to cry nonstop.
"Mom, you need to tell me what is going on! I cannot read your mind! I need to know who this Night Stalker is, it is a matter of City of Sandglass Security, and it is a high priority investigation for the Night Hunters. Just start from the beginning," I said sitting down across from her putting my hands on her knees in a pleading manner.
Sharon seemed to calm down nodded silently and continued to look down at the ground.
"Years ago, before you came to us, when David was on one of his unit missions and he had been gone for months. I was lonely and weak. I cheated on David. It was only once," she said quickly to me as I was careful not to give her a reaction.
"Continue," I urged and nodded in understanding.
"To this day I regret it. I know who the Night Stalker is because I recognized his cologne. It was the same one he

always wore even when I slept with him. I also know why he is killing the City Time Council and random people. He is on the hunt for something, and he is distrusting of those around him. Especially the Kai family," Sharon said.

"Who is he?" Brent said urgently, "What does he want?"

"Tyronne Mattley," Sharon muttered under her breath.

At first the room was silent in shock and surprise, "He is after the Watchmaker's Watch, he is obsessed with it. He is the other Time Council Member behind the Underground Time Road."

"Say something, please, one of you say something," Sharon said looking up at me and Brent as I closed my mouth in shock and I recovered first.

"Tyronne? Really? He is the Night Stalker?" I said looking at Brent who gave me a grave look.

"He is on the Time Council! We cannot just accuse him or just as easily try to convince the Time Council he is the Night Stalker just because you got a whiff of his cologne! They will want proof! The Time Council will not just believe Sharon at her word when she says it's because she slept with him. They can say either it could be someone else wearing his same cologne or that she is a disgruntled ex-lover wanting him back or to get back at him for something. They will tear this to shreds,' Brent said thoughtfully.

"You must be careful Bella," Sharon said, "He is very manipulative and arrogant."

"Was this the secret project that Terry was working on that Tyronne wants to know? Is that why she was killed?" I asked her and she looked at me blankly.

"You know, I am not sure why she was killed by him," Sharon said looking at Brent. "I am so sorry that I cheated on David, I feel so guilty."

"You know greed makes people do terrible things. Sometimes when people want something bad enough, they will go through great lengths to get there. They will do whatever they can to do and have and get what they want no matter the cost, even if it means killing others," Midnight said wisely.

"But even then Midnight, Tyronne couldn't kill her because deep down, he still has feelings for her. But the reason he tried to kill you was why?" I asked Sharon shrugged.

"Maybe because I was with you at the time? I am not sure," Sharon said.

"You are in extreme danger right now Sharon," I said looking at

her as she wiped a tear away, "For now I would like you to stay

in my guest room."

"But shouldn't I be with David?" Sharon said, "He would be able to protect me there."

"Yes, he could, but he isn't here," I said calmly as I looked at her eyes, I could tell she wanted to be with someone, "Okay I will bring him here."

"But Bella, he must never know what happened! He must never know about Tyronne. I love my husband, and I wouldn't have done anything to intentionally hurt him. It was a moment of loneliness and weakness. A moment I want to truly forget and move on from and regret," she said as I nodded as much as I was disappointed that this happened. I had to understand that we are all human and make mistakes. I couldn't ever see myself doing it to my significant other that I am married to, but at the same time with a significant other who is gone months on end, and never sure when they would return, that would cause me a lot of anxiety and stress.

"I won't say anything to David," I said as I locked the door and said, "Forlossem."

I appeared in front of David and Sharon's house and opened the door.

"David!" I said quickly to him.

"Bella! Hello again! What is going on?" he asked

"Sharon would like you to stay with her tonight in my guest room at the Tower," I said as he nodded and started to pack his bag without question.

Within minutes, he came to the front door to meet me and I grabbed his said and threw powder on my feet while saying, "Forlossem!" and we appeared in my guest room.

"David!" Sharon said walking up to David with open arms.

"My dear, what is the matter?" David said worriedly.

"Her life is in danger. I am afraid I cannot expand more on this, but you must stay here with her. It's the only place that would be safe for her I think," I said looking at David, "I am going to find the underlying cause of who this Night Stalker is. Once we find whoever it is, Sharon will be safe again."

"You don't think that Sharon and I can take care of ourselves?" David said half-heartedly, "You should know there is strength in numbers."

"Close the window David, please," I said as he waived it at me, "You are too worried about us for no reason, just focus on finding out who it is."

I nodded and hugged then both and said, "I love you both!" Sharon smiled, nodded, and I left the room.

I sat back down at the desk and looked at the binder.

"Brent I am going to take some time to read through this binder can you manage the messages that get sent into the room?" I asked as he nodded, and a letter came in the door. He opened it up.

"It looks like the timekeepers think Michael is acting strange by the bakery," Brent said smiling shaking his head, "When is he ever acting normal?"

Brent laughed and put the paper in the trash. Another letter came through the letter slot in the door and Brent bent down to grab it a few more came in. It was then that Brent put a plastic container at the door as more letters came in. Brent opened another letter.

"The bookstore is closed today it seems. I wonder if mom and dad are okay," Brent said looking over at me and shook his head noticing I was delving deep in the binder.

The first part of the binder had random updates on the project from various timekeepers that sent letters in regarding the research she was doing secretly. She kept good records.

The bar tender at the Time Turners Tavern had a lot of hands in many pots, illegal smuggling, and passing on information to other people for money, and she forgot the time road dealings which we knew of, and she hadn't known yet. I had come across a picture of a watch and at the top of the photo it said the Time Turners Watch. *A magical object known to have the capability of seeing the timeline of someone else, but it doesn't give you the ability to change a person's memory or history.*

There were also various documents of meetings from the various other people that she talked to about this mysterious watch. I had wondered why and what was so important about the watch.

After an hour of reading the binder and various information that she had of conversations with various members. I finally came across something that caught my eye. It was an interview between her and Tyonne.

I talked to Tyronne today about the watch. He had said that he knows about a watch that exists like the one I am in search of for the Time Council. He had said that he knows that it is said to be able to not only allow the user to be able to see other people's timelines and what they have seen and experienced but also it is said to have the ability to stop time for the wearer. So, they would never have to worry about losing time even if they had only seconds to live.

"Brent?" I asked looking up to see piles of papers around him organized in various areas of the room.

"Yes?" he asked.

"I think it is time to have our meeting tonight," I said standing up from the desk and stretching.

I walked over to him in the room, and he had piles of papers around him separated by various people.

"Don't these timekeepers have anything better to do then to send us all these papers?" he asked in frustration.

"Any new information on the Night Stalker?" I asked as he shook his head.

"It does seem that there are only two timekeepers who have tabs on Tyronne throughout the day. It may only be the timekeepers that Terry thought that she could trust. What are the names of these Timekeepers?" I asked curiously as he handed me the notes.

I read the names from the notes that were neatly handwritten.

Paula and Eladius.

I then put all the paperwork pile one by one with Brent in the files that she kept and put them in the cabinet for me to review later. After filing the last pile, I pulled out my key to the room and said, "Secret Six" and nothing happened.

"Um Bella," Brent said looking at me, "I don't think it works like that." "Well, I am not calling everyone in the Night Hunters only to say that I only need the secret six. I need to find Tobey."

By happenstance there was a knock on the door and there was Tobey at the doorway as Brent opened it.

"Tobey, what impeccable timing," I said smiling up at him.

"How can I help you?" he said smiling back at me.

"How do I go about calling only certain members of the Night Hunters?" I asked curiously.

"You just say "Kār prachum, and their name," Tobey said

"Well, that is most efficient," I said smiling and then looking at Tobey noticing he seemed bothered.

"What seems to be troubling you?" I asked him.

"I was wondering if you have had any luck with Sharon?" he asked me as I avoided eye contact.

"Yes, I have but I am not at liberty to share any details as of yet," I said wisely.

"May I ask why not?" he said looking at me.

"It is because it is only a rumor and heresy until my suspicions are confirmed. I need to gather more information until either I catch the person in the act, or until I have witnesses, or proven facts to bring forth to cast a shadow of accusation against anyone. This has a lot to do with opportune time and timing. If I warn that person ahead of time of my suspicions, they are less likely to act out. Instead of alarming this person of my suspicions I think I would rather let them think that they are safe from being discovered," I said looking at Tobey who was at first unconvinced and then nodded in understanding.

"At the end of the day, this is your decision. I have the Night Hunters out on the streets, observing them to prevent anything from happening as much as possible,' Tobey said shaking his head, "I just wanted to stop by to see if you had anything to report, so we know whom to look out for."

"Yeah, I don't want to have you chase a wild goose, if it's nothing anyway. But I will follow my lead and see where it takes us," I said as Tobey nodded and left the room.

"You don't trust him, do you?" Midnight hooted in my head.

"You both have gotten to know me so well," I said laughing to myself, "I just don't like to take chances if I am unsure. I had to tell him I had something, so he doesn't attempt to put Sharon through questioning. At the same time, I didn't want to tell him anything for sure because then he would have scared the suspect away if it is him," I said to myself.

"Brent, I would like you to go and find Timekeepers Paula and Eladius and bring them here," I said calmly as he nodded, and left the room.

After about an hour or so of being gone, Brent returned with Paula and Eladius in hand.

"Excellent Brent, thank you," I said smiling at him as he sat on the edge of my bed.

"My name is Bella; I am the replacement for Terry Kai and am now the leader of the Night Hunters. I have a rather curious message from the both of you to Terry regarding Tyronne not leaving his office all day that you are aware of," I said looking at Paula and Eladius who seemed to be timid around me, "Terry trusted me and therefore I believe that I ought not to be mistaken to be able to trust the both of you in turn as she did, am I wrong?"

They both shook their heads nervously.

"Don't worry you both are not in trouble," I said looking at them as they sighed in relief, "I just want to know what kinds of information you were able to collect regarding Tyronne and what is the extent of Terry's distrust of him?"

"Well, she never let her opinions be known with us. We just gave her the information we had in the day and night shifts and gave them to each other when we could during the change of shifts," Paula had said looking over at Eladius who nodded his head silently in agreement.

"Who watched him at night?" I asked curiously.

"We both did, we alternated nights," Eladius said, "We would just work different shifts per Terry's request."

"What came of watching him overnight? Who was on duty on the day that he attacked Terry?" I asked them as Eladius raised his hand, "And what happened that day? Did you specifically see Tyronne all day throughout the shift?"

"To be honest, he was in his room," Eladius said shrugging, "He spends most of the time and his days in his room. I just don't know what he does in there."

"Are there any other exists out of his room besides outside his door?" I asked curiously.

"We don't know, we haven't exactly been in his room," Paula said bitterly and half in sarcasm, "We cannot exactly say, hey Tyronne we are watching you, by the way, can you let us in there and see if there are any other exit from your room?"

"Okay, I get it," I said putting my hand up in understanding, "When he leaves his room, does he go anywhere else? Like where does he travel to?"

"We don't know if he ever leaves this building to be honest." Eladius said.

"You mean, you have never asked the drivers if their services were ever used by Tyronne?" I asked incredulously.

"You guys have that powdery stuff. So, I don't know where you all go with that," Eladius said, and I nodded in understanding.

"Of course, this would also explain how he is able to possibly leave his room without being noticed. It would make it difficult for someone to be followed," I said walking over to the binder of Terry's.

"Maybe he knew he was being watched," Midnight said calmly in my mind.

There was a note and its said "Forlossem" and it was circled. But using that powder would have left a trail even if he left that spot in his room and disappeared. The very use of it is limited to that of those on the Time Council. I must ask, have ever seen this gold and pink powder anywhere on the streets in the city," I said quietly in an almost inaudible whisper.

"Of course," Eladius said poking at the powder from my bag.

"Where? Can you show me?" I asked as they nodded. I then pulled out a voice recorder out of Terry's desk. I found a new tape in the desk drawer next to it and put it in the player and had a feeling in my stomach to press record. I placed it in my pocket bringing it with me as they led the way out of our room. I followed them to the streets outside the Time Tower. No one else was seemingly out on the streets, but then I realized that this Night Stalker would probably only use the powder once to leave the Time Tower and maybe only one other consistent spot to reappear out in the city and the rest of the way, hide in the shadows.

I followed them outside of the towers and down the street.

"Is it far?" I asked as Eladius who pointed to a corner of the next street as we crossed the street two buildings were meeting along the brick road and Eladius crouched over a spot that was on the ally side of the road and looked closely at the brick. Eladius lifted a handful of powder, "This is an area where I have seen that powder here."

I looked at it and saw that the bricks in that area were a discolored bright golden color and it had the familiar bright pink specks in it.

"Residue," Emrys said in my head thoughtfully as I nodded.

"This is the same powder we use to transport," I said aloud picking some up and showing Brent as it went through my fingers and back on the sidewalk.

"So, this is where someone is appearing and disappearing from either from the Tower or to get into the tower without detection. Interesting," I said aloud as Brent nodded in agreement.

I looked around and saw that there was an emergency escape ladder nearby that was down.

"This is what the Night Stalker uses to climb the buildings without being seen," I thought to myself. I then started to climb it.

"Um, Bella, what are you doing?" Brent asked me slightly nervously.

"We need answers and to know what is going on. I know who this Night Stalker is. They are athletic enough in build to be

"Maybe he knew he was being watched," Midnight said calmly in my mind.

There was a note and its said "Forlossem" and it was circled. But using that powder would have left a trail even if he left that spot in his room and disappeared. The very use of it is limited to that of those on the Time Council. I must ask, have ever seen this gold and pink powder anywhere on the streets in the city," I said quietly in an almost inaudible whisper.

"Of course," Eladius said poking at the powder from my bag. "Where? Can you show me?" I asked as they nodded. I then pulled out a voice recorder out of Terry's desk. I found a new tape in the desk drawer next to it and put it in the player and had a feeling in my stomach to press record. I placed it in my pocket bringing it with me as they led the way out of our room. I followed them to the streets outside the Time Tower. No one else was seemingly out on the streets, but then I realized that this Night Stalker would probably only use the powder once to leave the Time Tower and maybe only one other consistent spot to reappear out in the city and the rest of the way, hide in the shadows.

I followed them outside of the towers and down the street. "Is it far?" I asked as Eladius who pointed to a corner of the next street as we crossed the street two buildings were meeting along the brick road and Eladius crouched over a spot that was on the ally side of the road and looked closely at the brick. Eladius lifted a handful of powder, "This is an area where I have seen that powder here."

I looked at it and saw that the bricks in that area were a discolored bright golden color and it had the familiar bright pink specks in it.

"Residue," Emrys said in my head thoughtfully as I nodded.

"This is the same powder we use to transport," I said aloud picking some up and showing Brent as it went through my fingers and back on the sidewalk.

"So, this is where someone is appearing and disappearing from either from the Tower or to get into the tower without detection. Interesting," I said aloud as Brent nodded in agreement.

I looked around and saw that there was an emergency escape ladder nearby that was down.

"This is what the Night Stalker uses to climb the buildings without being seen," I thought to myself. I then started to climb it.

"Um, Bella, what are you doing?" Brent asked me slightly nervously.

"We need answers and to know what is going on. I know who this Night Stalker is. They are athletic enough in build to be able to manage climbing and going roof to roof and shimmy down these escape ladders," I said aloud.

Brent looked up at the top of the ladder and saw that there was a figure at the top of it hooded.

"Bella hurry! Get down here! It's the Night Stalker! Up there!" Brent shouted in fear.

Chapter 13

The Capture of the Night Stalker

"I need to go after him!" I said, "Why would I need to run after him, we already know who it is!"

"You don't know for sure who it is!" Brent shouted back as the figure started to run away.

"We need to find out to be sure!" I shouted back climbing the stairs the rest of the way. I remembered I had the record button on in my robes as I remained confident.

"I am going to get a confession out of him, if it's the last thing I do," I said to myself.

I reached the top of the roof and saw that the figure jumped to the next roof and with their arms folded, stopped and turned around towards me. I ran across the roof, jumped, and barely made it across as the hooded figure ran towards the edge of the building and put their hands up in a fighting stance.

"I am not going to fight you," I said looking at the figure, "I want answers! I know who you are, but I want to know why. Why would you kill Terry!? My SISTER!"

"You do, do you?" said the figure.

"It's you Tyronne!" I said, instantly, recognizing the voice. He then removed his face mask and black hood.

There was a moment of silence between us.

"You stand there and yet you claimed that I was some entitled representative of this city just using my name as leverage, and yet you commit the atrocities of killing people you were worn to protect and you seriously were injuring them too," I said.

"Atrocities that you seem to also benefit from if I am not mistaken. If it were not for me and my actions, you wouldn't - be where you are today would you?" he stated back, "Some might even come to suggest that you had hired someone like me to do your bidding to be in power where you are today," he said in return.

"No one is going to believe you!" I said looking at him seriously.

There was a moment of silence as he smiled at me

"I have records of what you are after and what it was that Terry was secretly investigating. I have proof that it was you who attacked Sharon!"

"You do? Do you?" he said with his head up and laughed, "Was it only her word? Well, that was a mistake I fixed. You will find that your previous Sharon didn't make it through the night."

He was smiling widely.

"You didn't!" I shouted through tears.

"I did!" he laughed, "Right through your guest window to be exact, and it was the best way to make it so that you have something to do with it. After all, you have the only key to your guest room. You are the only one who could have gone in there!"

"I have witnesses of people who have been with me all day," I said angrily.

"Oh Bella, you have gotten yourself into trouble this time, and this time, your siblings will not be able to help you out of this one! The evidence will be overwhelming!" he said as he walked towards me confidently. "You can take me in, but I don't think you will be able to get out of this one once I tell them this lie, I have fabricated. You will be in a prison cell as soon as they believe the lie that I am about to spin and weave for them! Then the name of Kai will never be trusted EVER AGAIN!"

He laughed as I bound his hands and brought him down the escape ladder silently.

"You caught him!" Brent said excitedly.

"You must believe me! I was put up to this by Bella!" Tyronne said through tears.

"What?!" Brent said giving me a look as I shook my head.

"She wanted me to kill Terry so she could be a leader on the Time Council with her siblings, and be in charge of the Night Hunters!" Tyronne said through tears, crying out loud.

"She has been planning everything with me. She even had me kill Sharon today!" he said pleadingly to Brent, Paula, and Eladius.

I started to cry at the thought of Sharon gone.

"You are a liar! You didn't kill her! You couldn't! The door was locked! I locked it!" I said looking at Tyronne

"Which is why you left the guest room window open for me to kill her through it! You intentionally did it so that this way no one, not even her husband David or dear Theodore could come to her rescue!" Tyronne said to me.

"David was in the room!" I said looking at him with tears in my eyes, "Is he alive?"

"I don't know if he is or isn't, perhaps he didn't make it or maybe he did?" Tyronne said evilly watching panic hit me.

There was an ominous crash of thunder and lightning as a foreboding rain came in like a deluge onto the street.

"NOOO!" I screamed in agony as we went to the Time Tower. Tobey and a group of timekeepers were at the door when we walked to the doors.

"We caught the Night Stalker!" Brent said as the timekeepers took Tyronne.

"Bellatrix Kai," Terrance said seriously looking down at me as the rain started coming down from my hood to my face, "You are under arrest for suspicion of murder."

Chapter 14
Verity, The Truth

It was then that the timekeepers took me away. Brent Paula and Eladius started to protest, but there was nothing they could do. Even Tyronne said, "The evidence that he set up against me would be overwhelming."

I felt hopeless as I sat in my room that was locked from the outside.

Two timekeepers stayed in the room with me and two remained out in the hallway outside my door apparently.

I decided to look through the papers in the desk of Terry's trying to find some connection to Tyronne that she may have had to clear my name and at the same time show that this was something that he had been a part of from the start.

After about an hour and a half of searching and the timekeepers keeping close watch on my every move, I found it. It was the link that I needed.

The door opened to the room and a man stood there in the doorway.

"Bellatrix kai?" timekeeper at the door said.

"Yes?" I said looking up from the papers.

"You are needed by the council," he said ushering me out as the other two timekeepers gave me a glare as I passed them with the papers at hand.

When I walked in most of all the Council members were seated at their spots except for Tyronne. I was sitting at a table below them as they looked at me in silent judgment.

"Well, we have heard some difficult information that is difficult to swallow. We need to know what is going on and what happened?" Terrance said as I saw that his ears were redder than his hair. He was angry and I could tell he was upset. Terry was his girlfriend and to have to have this drudged up again was like picking at a scab that was already trying to heal.

"I want it to be known that I saw that Terry was already working on a secret project for the Council without them knowing," I said looking around and pulling out a folder of information, "She was investigating multiple things of which I am aware. Firstly, the day-to-day activities of Tyronne Mattley. I have two witnesses for that Eladius and Paula, who were reporting various information daily in shifts as they watched him. He was in his room a lot and I foresaw that he had the ability to leave the Time Tower of his own volition, and we found Golden and pink Forlossem powder outside of the tower across the street. Nearby, I walked up the fire escape to see Tyronne standing there, and he ran across to the roof of the other building and then tried to fight me."

"Yeah right, and do you have any witnesses to what happened up there on the roof with Tyronne?" Tyeisha said shaking her head, "Witnesses say that they stayed below."

"I have this recording," I said plainly as they council looked at me in disbelief as I played it for them. There was then a few minutes of muttering amongst themselves.

"He is right, how did you know it was him? How did you know that Tyronne Mattley was the Night Stalker? Did you see him hurt anyone? Did you see him attack Sharon?" Tina said with a defensive attitude.

"No, she had told me that she had recognized his scent, his cologne," I said

There was an eruption of laughter.

"Ridiculous! You expect us to believe that Sharon was some sort of bloodhound? That she could tell who this person was just because of a cologne he was wearing? How would she have known for sure it was him?" Tessa started laughing.

I then looked over at Theodore who was silent, but I could tell he was angry.

"Sharon was like my own mother! Her life was in danger, so I kept her in the guest house. I told her that she would be safer here in the room and locked in," I said and then in slight hesitation, "She also knew it was him because he was a former lover of hers years ago."

There was more muttering around them.

"THAT IS A LIE! MY MOTHER WOULDN'T HAVE CHEATED ON MY FATHER!" Theodore said angrily standing up at his chair.

"I call for a memory review," Theresa said aloud in front of everyone, "Tell me Bella, you wouldn't mind us to review your memories for a thorough review so you can prove to us what you are saying would you?"

I shook my head.

"I promised Sharon her husband wouldn't ever find out, I am trying to protect her memory," I said looking at Theodore.

"I don't care, I won't ever tell David, we need to know!" Theodore said as I nodded and agreed.

"How does this work?" I asked

It was then that Tanya came down from the council stands and walked up next to me.

"Think about everything that happened from the beginning and it better be the truth as we will know if this is a fake image of what happened or not," Tanya said as I nodded and closed my eyes. She then put her palm on my head and put her other hand in the air above us as the image and audio of me telling Tobey how I thought that Sharon would only reveal to me the reason she knew who the Night stalker was... then it skipped to me talking to Sharon and her revealing to me who it was, how she knew it was him, and how she didn't want

David to know. Then the image flashed to me researching in my office came to view with Brent in the room sorting paperwork and finding that it was Eladius and Paula reporting to Terry. It then played in my head step by step what happened, me getting David, and leaving them in the room and everything until that very moment when I was told I was arrested. It replayed me telling David to close the window as David waived at me telling me to stop worrying.

There was muttering in the room.

"I really don't have any vendetta against the council or any need to be in power. However, I am grateful to be in the position that I am in today," I said to the council.

"Very well, the council will deliberate your fate after we council with Tyronne," Theresa said as I was escorted from the Chambers and brought back to my room and locked in.

"Don't worry Bella, you have nothing to hide," Midnight said confidently.

"Don't worry," Emrys added, "Tyronne will be exposed."

I nodded to myself deep in thought about how I could have handld things differently with Sharon and David.

Meanwhile, three floors up, Tyronne was bring brought down from the tower to the Chambers of where the council sat eagerly awaiting to question Tyronne.

Tyronne looked worried and concerned as he looked around.

"Where is she?" Tyronne asked looking at the other council members and noticed that the seat that usually occupied by Bella and Tim were both vacant.

"Tyronne Mattley, you have been brought before us under deep scrutiny. Everything that you say and do is going to be judged. You are being accused of being the Night Stalker. Your actions are going to be judged before you today by the panel of the council. What do you have to say for yourself to these accusations?" Theresa asked.

"Who am I being accused by? Aren't I in due of rights to know of my accusers?" Tyronne said looking around at the council members, "For forty years I have loyally been serving and every year re-elected by the people. I have only done what is ever asked of me."

"So, are you telling us that you were told to kill Terry Kai?" Theordore asked aloud as there was muttering amongst the council.

"Yes, that is to say I was," Tyronne said looking at the council pleadingly. "I was told to Kill Sharon Johnson and also Terry Kai!"

"Did you sleep with my mother?" Theodore asked Tyronne as he nodded.

It was then that Theodore got out of his seat and came down and said, "Let us see what you see. Prove your side."

It was then that Theodore came down and put his hand on Tyronne's head and showed the council what was on his mind. It was then that the image showed Tyronne sleeping with Sharon and making love to her. The image was clear, and the edges of the memory were unblemished. And then the seen went to Bellatrix Kai and it showed a private conversation with her telling him to kill them so that she can gain power. Then the image showed Bella telling him that she was going to make sure that she was brought to the tower alone and make sure to leave the window open for him to kill her. "Don't worry, I will make sure she is alone so she can't reveal to anyone that she knows it was you who are the shadow killer." The image was altered and not noticeably clear.

Immediately there was an uproar from the council, "LIAR!" they shouted at him as the image showed him killing both Terry and Sharon and then bragging about it at the bar at the Time Turner's Tavern with the bar tender the day after he killed Terry.

The laughing from Tyronne flooded the chambers as he told the bar tender in a drunken state, "After I kill Sharon and Terry, not a soul in the world is going to want the Kai family in charge of anything anymore!"

It was then that multiple swords were heard being taken out of their sheaths from the Kai Siblings as they came down from the council seats.

"Nooo, Nooo! You weren't to see that!" Tyronne said realizing what was revealed as he put his hands in a pleading way. "You must believe me! I didn't mean for this to go this far!"

"Tyronne Mattley, you are hereby sentenced to death and your term here on the Time Council has henceforth ended. You are guilty of murder and treason against the City of Sandglass and for that the punishment is that you are hereby sentenced to death," Tyeisha said as tears rolled down her eyes as she put her head down not wanting to see what was about to be done

The Kai siblings and Theodore were all about to cut off Tyronne's head in fits of justified anger with their swords at once when the doors opened, and Bellatrix Kai ran in and covered Tyronne with her body and shouted, "NOOOO!"

Chapter 15
The Verdict

"BELLATRIX KAI WHAT ARE YOU DOING?!" Theodore shouted at me angrily, "You are going to get yourself killed!"

"NOOO! YOU MUST STOP!" I shouted as I looked up at Tyeisha who looked up from having her head down and eyes closed. I saw she was crying, and then I turned towards all of the other council members who still had their swords drawn and were still set to kill Tyronne. My own siblings were going to kill someone who had committed a horrible myriad of crimes, even in another City of which he had come from, according to the papers that Terry had collected. They traced back to his hometown and stopped the moment he became a Council Member…. Even with this thought in mind thinking of the hundreds he might have gotten away with killing, there had to be a reason for it I thought. I then turned towards a now motherless Theodore who had tears in his eyes, and his face full of fuming rage.

"He is guilty! You were found innocent. He must pay for his sins, for his crimes against the City of Sandglass! He doesn't deserve to live!" Theodore said through gritted teeth looking at Terrance who seemed to feel the same way.

They both tried to move me away from Tyronne as I didn't move..

"What kind of leaders are you if you kill all those who have wronged you?" I said without budging as I put my hand on Theodore's hand and shook my head as I grabbed hold of Tyronne's hand, "Fear and hatred, they are raw emotions along with revenge. If you kill someone out of revenge you are starting a vicious never-ending cycle of pain and suffering and to what end? This will just make others hurt and cause more conflict rather than resolving it. Do not let your hearts harden because of the evil deeds of others. We do not need to stoop so low to the level of brutes and animals to exact hurt on him and those around him. We must show mercy and forgiveness and yes even restraint even though the need and desire for revenge is strong in our hearts. We must have compassion and understanding and yes love for ourselves and for those around us still when it comes to this," I tried to explain earnestly. But they didn't seem swayed by this.

"If you kill Tyronne now, then what happens? You are just as guilty as he is for killing another. It's not going to bring those that he has killed back. This action would also make those who love and care about Tyronne cause pain and hurt because even though they may not condone or agree with his actions, they still love him as a person. You taking away someone's love for him will entice them to want to exact revenge, and then what type of resolution is this? This isn't going to resolve anything," I tried to reexplain.

"You try losing your mom and try forgiving them for what they had done!" Theodore said angrily and through tears.

"I HAVE!" I shouted and cried as everyone in the room looked at me.

"I am 25 years old now," I said looking at everyone in the room. I had lost my parents fifteen years ago. Still, there isn't a day that goes by that I don't wish they were here. I wake every morning thinking about them. I go to bed every night thinking about them. I go through my day-to-day activities and still try to put a smile on even though I feel like a burning knife is slicing my body every time I look at Kahn! Your parents Theodore taught me how to cope, learn, and grow through love and compassion and understanding. It was them that taught me that killing Kahn wouldn't bring my parents back. It would only have made the situation worse even years after I had learned to fight and pick up the sword. To this day, I still cannot find the strength to forgive Kahn for what he did even though I have told him I have. I understand that he was only following orders. To this day, I hold that anger within me. But to this day, I am grateful I never acted on my feelings and my emotions and lost control over them. Killing Kahn wouldn't bring back my dad or my mom it would only have brought pain and fear to Terry of me had she been alive right now," I cried as I looked around the room and slowly, they all put their swords down.

It was then that Tyeisha came down from her chair, and came down to hug me, as she knew what I had done.

"You are all weak!" Tyronne said laughing at us.

It was at that moment that Tyeisha angrily walked up to Tyronne and slapped him and then she held on to his arm and started draining the time he had left.

"TYEISHA WHAT ARE YOU DOING? NO!" Tyronne said realizing that she was taking time from him. Nobody moved or said anything.

I looked at Tyronne's timecard and it read that he only had a week left.

"You are the weak one now!" Tyeisha said in anger.

Tyronne looked at his cousin in anger and said, "Give me my time back!"

"No, you will get a week when the current week is almost up!" Tyeisha said looking at the council, "With your permission this is going to be his lifetime punishment. He will only have a week of his life at any given time. He will never be able to gain more than that."

"What do you mean?" he asked, looking at her as she looked at his timecard and made an adjustment.

"From now on, you will live your life a week at a time. You cannot gain more than a week and you will continue to be in this weakened state until I see fit that you can truly live an honest and more grateful life. If you kill another soul in this realm of anyone in any of the City's of Sandglass, or any village, I shall know. If you do, you will cease to live anymore. I will be sure of that, for I will strike you down myself," Tyeisha said looking at the

council members who seemed to agree with these terms.

"You can't do this to me!" Tyronne said angrily.

"We just did," I said to him as he looked at me angrily.

"Bella just saved your life Tyronne, you ungrateful slimeball!" Tyeisha said to him as he looked at her in disgust.

"I'd rather have died, then to live the rest of my life in this way." Tyronne said looking at me.

"No death would have been too nice to you," I said looking at Theodore and Terrance who agreed with me.

"Such a wise woman you are," Taylor said looking at me and then Tobey who then both smiled proudly at me nodding.

"As of this moment, Bellatrix Kai, you are reinstated as Night Hunter Master and Council Member. We apologize for doubting your intentions and loyalty," Tobey said to me as I hugged him.

"Thank you!" I said smiling as my brothers gave me a hug.

It was the happiest I had felt finally realizing that we all would be safe again walking on the streets without fear.

It was then that there was a knock on the door to the chamber. I opened it and it was Eladius and Paula who were standing there with David. David looked distraught.

"We wanted to know if we were needed or not. Or if we can go back to our posts?" Eladius said as I looked at Tobey who walked to the door next to me.

"Oh of course, yes, you both may go," Tobey said as he watched Paula and Eladius leave. Then he looked at David.

"We need you to stay David because we need to make preparations," Tobey said looking over at Theodore who still was watery eyed at the situation. David nodded as Tobey motioned for him to walk towards us.

"We have much to discuss Theodore, come with me," Tobey said ushering him and David and leading the way towards his room, "Follow us, Bella."

I nodded silently.

When entering Tobey's room, the walls were covered with golden Floredils and a green background wallpaper. It was filled with various bookshelves of books. He had an office desk with a pantry of various snacks and drinks in a fridge next to it.

He had many plants around his room as well.

He had a bed and a desk as well. And shelving on the wall behind his desk. He had a table and chairs that we all sat down at, and Tobey looked at me, David, and Theordore who were silent.

"I know this is not going to be an easy conversation," Tobey said trying to break the silence looking at us, "but we need to figure out how we are going to honor Sharon and her life."

It was then that David burst into tears.

"I shouldn't be alive right now. Sharon and I were supposed to live together for the rest of our lives!" David said through tears. "I don't know how I am supposed to live my life without her! For hundreds of years, we have lived together, raising you both."

"You must bury me with her," David said and then he looked at me and then to Theodore.

"No Dad! This is not how it's supposed to be!" Theordore said as David grabbed Theodore's hand and gave him his time left.

"I love you both!" David said through tears as his time decreased rapidly as it counted down in red before our eyes. I watched in horror wide eyed as the memories of David and I flashed before my eyes from the moment he rescued me from the Village of Pasqua.

"No Dad!" I cried through tears.

"I love you Bella," David said through tears and then he dropped his head on the table in front of us as tears rolled down his face and then he died at the table.

Tobey looked in shock at what just happened.

I started to cry in Theodore's arms as he looked at Tobey said, "I didn't want his time, take it! TAKE IT!"

Tobey got up and patted Theodore on the back shaking his head.

"We must give them both a proper burial now," Tobey said firmly as I pulled away from Theodore and nodded and tried to comfort him.

Over the next few minutes, we planned a ceremony for both Sharon and David and had figured out where we would bury both of them.

"Well, this is good enough for now, we will prepare for tomorrow. You should all get some sleep," Tobey said finished with the paper he was writing of the plans for the funeral ceremonies of David and Sharon. He looked up at me and Theodore as we nodded.

It was then that Theodore got up and thanked Tobey for his help and shook his hand. He then avoided eye contact with me and was the first to silently leave as Tobey and I stood up with him too.

"Why didn't Theodore say goodbye to you?" Tobey asked me as I shrugged.

"He is still coping in his own way, he just lost both of his parents. I just lost my adopted parents whom I have known since I was taken from the Village of Paska," I said looking down at the paper of jotted notes for the funerals.

"Go get some sleep Tobey," he said nodding at me as he hugged me goodnight.

I left the room and went to my room to see Brent was waiting for me.

"Bella! What is going on out there? What just happened?" Brent asked me. I told him what happened at the Council and the ruling and Tyronne and then David's death.

All throughout the night, it was a restless sleep. I couldn't have felt more alone than I did that night, even with Brent fast asleep beside me I looked up at the ceiling and all I could hear was the traumatizing laughs of Kahn and Tyronne haunting me in my sleep.

I tossed and turned all night until Sharon's voice came into my head,

"Go to sleep child, the morning will come, the day will be anew, and people will be depending on you to stay strong for them."

It was then that I started to cry as soon as I stopped hearing her comforting voice in my mind.

Chapter 16

The Celebration of Life Ceremony

The next morning, I woke up with not only a heavier heart, but dark bags under my eyes.

"Bella? Are you okay?" Brent asked looking at me in concern.

"I'm fine," I lied, wiping my eyes getting out of bed and dressing.

"Bella, I know you all too well to know that things are not okay. What happened last night?" he asked me as I looked at him, "You got arrested and then they escorted me back to the room."

I burst into tears as I told him what happened on the roof as I watched Brent's face turn from concern to anger and then to hatred for Tyronne.

"THAT SLIMEBALL!" Brent said angrily.

Then I continued to tell him what happened after I was arrested and then questioned by the council and that temporarily I had lost Night Hunter Master and Time Council Member Titles while they questioned me and Tyronne. I told him how I had caught him with the voice recorder and played it for him. And then told him what happened with the council after they questioned Tyronne and how they caught him in his lie and were going to kill him.

"WHAT! Why did you stop them!? HE WOULD HAVE DESERVED IT!" Brent said in slight frustration.

"It's hard to say that anyone would deserve this," I said remembering how David had died before my eyes and how my parent's had died in front of me. "I believed that it was far too much to have expected anyone else in Tyronne's life to have suffered if we were to take his life away and then to have to deal with the consequences of those who would have felt his loss. Life is not cheap and to keep it going takes work and we must all improve the quality of each other's life here and be a better support system."

I then told him what his punishment with Tyeisha is and what ended up happening. Brent seemed to be okay with the punishment. So, she took his life, and she will gradually give it back to him week by week so that this way he continues to feel like he is in that weakened state as a punishment for taking the lives that he took from others.

Brent nodded and then he hugged me.

"I am so sorry about Sharon," Brent said holding me in an embrace and then I broke the embrace.

"That isn't everything," I said as I then explained what happened with Theodore and David. Then I told him how David had killed himself in distraught grief while trying to plan for his wife's funeral.

"WHAT!" Brent said in surprise.

"Sharon's death was a torment to us all and the very thought of having to live a life without her even with his own son still here, and me, his adopted daughter, without Sharon, he couldn't manage it. It destroyed him," I said through tears. "Theodore blames me for Sharon and David's deaths even though I wasn't directly involved," I said slowly saying my thoughts aloud.

"What do you mean?" Brent said looking at me, "he cannot do that to you! It's not fair!"

"It is how he feels, everyone deals with grief and loss differently. Some cut ties with people who were associated with the loved ones that they lost. Sometimes they have an internal anger with the Creator for taking them sooner than they should have. Sometimes they get sad and drink at the bar or get hooked on other substances to mask or "cope" or just get quiet and keep the grief to themselves. Sometimes they shop or go cleaning happy all the time. So right now, Theodore is avoiding eye contact with me," I explained thoughtfully as Brent nodded in understanding.

After getting ready and talking to Brent, we had headed down for breakfast to find the dining hall was empty.

"Where is everyone?" Brent asked the Timekeeper at the door.

"Everyone is down at the cemetery by now I'd say," he said looking at his watch.

"You mean we missed the whole church ceremony so far?" I asked anxiously as the Timekeeper nodded.

"Why didn't anyone tell us?" I asked looking at the Timekeeper.

"We were asked to leave you both alone so that you could rest. Theodore didn't really want you there Bella because you remind him of her," the Timekeeper said fragilely, "You might actually make the cemetery ceremony if you leave in the next few minutes."

"Come on Brent," I said hurriedly, "Let's go!"

Brent nodded and we both ran from the dining hall to the carriages and the driver was there.

"Please sir, can we go to the Cemetery?" I asked as he nodded.

"Get in one of them!" He motioned as Brent, and I ran to one of the nearest coaches and immediately we took off.

"I stayed behind because I had not seen you and figured you would need a ride Bella," the George said.

"Thank you, George!" I said smiling

Within minutes, we arrived at the cemetery, as everyone else was arriving.

"Bella! Brent! You made it!" Tobey said happily smiling at us as we smiled and nodded.

"Sorry we overslept," I said apologetically.

"Oh, all water under the bridge, we are just happy you made it to the ceremony for the cemetery for David and Sharon," Tobey said looking over at Taylor and Terrance who came over to me and hugged us.

The ceremony consisted of the Head Timekeeper Teddy Timmons, presiding over the caskets of David and Sharon and then everyone took turns talking about them and about their lives.

"They were inseparable right to the very end," Theodore said looking at the caskets, through tears.

"I loved them as my own parents, and I am proud to have known them and been raised by them," I said as Taylor and Tobey both nodded in tears at me, a few moments later, I had gotten to say after Theodore.

Slowly the caskets were lowered on top of each other into the grave and a headstone, was then placed on top of the loose earth that was pushed over the gravesite.

"United in Love, Together Forever & Always!"

There were several hundred people who showed up and gave their regards to us as they left slowly from the cemetery until the only ones who were left were me, Brent, and Theodore.

Theodore remained with his head bowed at his parents grave as tears rolled down his face.

"I want them back! There must be a way to bring them back!" he said looking at me as I shook my head.

"If I could, I would," I said looking at Theodore sadly, "I would have brought back Terry if I could, but once someone has gone, they have passed on. We must continue to push forward and live fulfilled lives and complete our purpose in our lives."

"I don't want to talk to you anymore Bella," Theodore said avoiding eye contact with me as Brent looked at him, "I know that you didn't kill mom but her death that you could have prevented caused my father's death. I will be selling the house, and the time collected from that will be yours as our parents wanted so you will need to move out as soon as you can. Michael will have to move out as well."

I nodded in silent understanding as Brent stood there with an opened mouth in shock.

"I will also be leaving my post as the 13th member of the Time Council and I might be moving out of the city," he said looking up from his parent's graves and out into the distance of the cemetery of other headstones.

"WHAT! Don't you think this is a little too rash? Aren't all of these decisions that you are making a little too fast?" Brent said in concern.

"I don't think I want to be a part of the City of Sandglass Time anymore, too many memories. Goodbye Bellatrix, Brent," Theodore said as he nodded at Brent avoiding my eye contact and walked away.

Chapter 17

The Secret Six First Meeting

After he walked away there were a few minutes of silence as I admired the headstones of David and Sharon.

"I am going to miss them Emrys and Midnight," I said to them in my mind.

"They both truly ended up loving you and your kind, caring, and loving heart Bella," Emrys said trying to console me as he warmed my body in what felt like I was being embraced warmly.

"David wanted to be with his wife right to the very end," Midnight said soothingly, "Now they are at peace together."

I nodded and took in a deep breath and let it out.

"Are you okay Bella?" Brent asked me in concern as he saw that I was tearing up.

"I miss them and there is nothing that I can do to bring them back," I said as I looked at him,

He shook his head and said, "No there is nothing we can do, but you must also understand that it is only moving forward with your life and continuing, that is what matters and over time, it will heal the wounds of loss and grief. It does not do to dwell on the inevitability of death and forget to live."

At that I turned to walk towards the entrance of the cemetery and looked back towards the direction of the graves.

"Do you know what this cemetery is full of?" I asked Brent as he shrugged.

"Dead bodies, headstones, and flowers?" he responded.

"No lost dreams and unaccomplished lives," I said looking at the nearest headstone, "These are people who have passed on and yet, they may not have had a chance to accomplish what they wanted to the most in life."

He nodded and agreed with me thoughtfully as we reached the carriage.

"Brent, we have much work to do. Let's get some lunch," I said as he nodded, and we went back to the Time Tower.

We got to the dining hall to see that there were only a few of the council members there. Theresa was in a corner closely observing Tyronne and his cousin Tyeisha who were deep in conversation at one of the long tables.

"You owe her your life Tyronne," I overheard Tyeisha say as she stopped what she was saying and looked over at Brent and me who had just come into the room.

"BELLA! BRENT!" Tyeisha said waving us to walk over and sit by them as we filled out plates of cut up halves of sandwiches and chips from the buffet and sat with Tyeisha as Tyronne scowled at the notice of us.

"I am so grateful that you saved my cousin from the council, I was so worried about them killing him," she said as she looked at Tyronne.

"What's the matter with you?" Tyeisha asked him from across the table as he looked at me who was sitting next to her, "I am in a weakened state because of you! You expect me to be spritely about it?"

"You ungrateful piece of shit!" Brent said looking at Tyronne who was sitting next to him.

"Brent!" I said scoldingly kicking him under the table,

"Ow!" Brent said looking at me, "What, I would think that he would be a little more grateful that he was allowed to continue to live for him acting so ungrateful for it is rude."

"That doesn't mean you can talk any way that you like to him," I said harshly towards him.

"Sorry," Brent said to Tyronne who shook his head and ate in silence.

"Tyronne is staying in my guest room still so I can keep a close eye on him," Tyeisha said looking from Brent then to me and smiled at me.

"Oh okay," I nodded and said, "Maybe he can be of help in one of your departments within the Education system or even in the Civil resources Department."

"Oh, that is a great idea. This would also give him purpose and a sense of accomplishment too by helping me out," Tyeisha said approvingly as Tyronne didn't make a face about it and continued to eat the food from his plate in silence.

After a few minutes of eating in silence, Tyeisha was the first to finish her food and her and Tyronne got up out of their seats to put their plates away in the bin.

"I will talk to you later Bella. Thank you again," Tyeisha said gratefully as I nodded and hugged her back as she had hugged me. Tyronne made a little bow towards us and then walked away with Tyeisha.

"I cannot believe that we will still have to deal with him within the Tower and you still are keeping yourself together even after all he had done to Sharon and effectively David as well!" Brent said shaking his head in disbelief as I saw his hands were clutched closed and he was shaking with anger as he watched Tyronne leave the dining hall and follow Tyeisha to their room.

"We cannot hope to find peace where there is anger and hatred for those around us Brent," I said noticing how Brent seemed to calm down, "I realize that this is hard for us to do as I have a struggle with it occasionally, but we must move forward. That is what I had to do for Kahn when I lost my parents. We must deal with the cards we are dealt with in life, and make the most of the new cards and new choices."

"Excuse me Bellatrix," Theresa said from the corner to me as she got up and sat at the table next to Brent looking at me,

"Can I ask you a question?"

"Yes," I said looking at her as I was trying to eat and not get indigestion at her interruption.

"What is it that you plan to do with your share of the Time earned with the sale of David and Sharon's house?" She asked me.

"That is none of your concern," Brent said bluntly towards her, and I kicked him under the table.

"OWW!" Brent said glowering at me as I shook my head at him.

"It is my concern as I am head of the Housing Authority on the Council," Theresa said to him coldly as he rubbed his shins under the table.

"Sorry," he said looking from me, and then to her as she nodded in acceptance of his apology and looked at me.

"I plan to purchase a house of my own eventually for me and my siblings," I said looking at her with her eyebrows raised.

"You don't plan to have kids of your own?" she asked me and then looked at Brent.

"What are you looking at me for?" Brent said

"I haven't thought that far ahead in life," I said thinking to myself.

"Well just keep it in mind when you are purchasing a place," she said smiling and then she got up from the table and looked from Brent and then to me. "It should be sold by the end of the month and then the time will be transferred to you. Theodore said he doesn't want more time from it."

I nodded and smiled at her.

"Thank you, Theresa," I said as she shook my hand.

"It's what I do," she said as she walked off out of the room.

I slowly finished my lunch, and then got up from the table and Brent followed me back to my room. I had decided that I wanted to figure out what I wanted to do for our next adventure.

"Tyronne never did find that watch he was looking for, did he?" Brent said curiously.

"No but what would we do with that?" I asked curiously.

"There is talk that it can be found within the trenches," Brent said looking at me.

"What do you mean" I asked looking at Brent who was looking at a pile of papers at the door that were dropped off by the Timekeepers.

"Word got out who the Night Stalker was and what his true intentions were and many within the City of Sandglass – Time, People are talking about how he was trying to find the magical watch and that he was killing people who had knowledge of it," Brent said handing me papers to read, and then I handed them back to him and he filed them.

"Wait, what else is in that folder on the Watch?" I asked curiously.

Apparently over the years, Timekeepers had handed Terry information regarding the watch and its uses and what people have been saying about it over the years.

There were various drawings of the watch and there are several accounts of how it was used to locate missing items that people had lost over their timelines. It has been used as well as prove points of what actually happened during certain scenarios in the past for people.

"We need to do more research," I said as I got up and left the room and Brent followed me. I locked the door, and we walked to the carriages and Brent knocked on the door three times and within minutes the driver opened the window and smiled.

"Time for another adventure?" the young driver asked me as I smiled and nodded.

Chapter 18

Research

"Where to my lady?" the young driver asked smiling at me.

"The bookstore," I said.

It was within minutes that we were on the road and traveling to the bookstore.

Socrat opened the carriage door as James looked in and smiled at me.

"Bella!" James said smiling at me, "It is so good to see you! We only just heard! How are you?"

"It was a close call, but we survived," I said lightly.

"Barely, and I still want to kill Tyronne," Brent said under his breath as he looked at Socrat who raised his eyebrows in surprise.

"That is not like you Brent," Socrat said slightly tilting his head towards Brent.

"You don't really know me or how I would react to someone like Tyronne! It's not for you to be critical of me about!" Brent said in an angry retort to which Socrat and I were taken aback by surprise.

"Brent Genuit!" I said sternly, "That is enough!"

"I'm sorry Socrat," Brent mumbled and walked away but said under his breath, "Well, you would feel the same way about

Tyronne if you knew the whole story." in slight bitterness, walking into the bookstore ahead of everyone.

I looked at Socrat and put my hand on his arm in support and Socrat slowly pushed my hand off of him and said, "It's okay Bella."

"Forgiveness is a strange thing. It can be sometimes easier to forgive our enemies than our friends. It can be hardest of all to forgive people we love." Midnight said, "You may find it easier to forgive Tyronne and those around you more than others around you."

I nodded thoughtfully.

I walked into the bookstore to see Mr. Genuit and Brent's parents working in the bookstore checking various people out at the register. The bookstore was more busy than usual.

"Business good?" I asked Brent's dad who smiled.

"I will be right with you Council Member," Brent's dad replied as a few people in the room started whispering to themselves in surprise to see me.

"What brings you in dear?" Brents mom asked me quietly coming from behind me.

"I wish to seek your help, I am looking for a private place to study and read," I said with a wink.

"I think that I have just the place in mind," Brent said in a whisper smiling and winking at me as she led the way to a door in the back. She pulled out a key that was around her neck and she smiled at Brent.

"It's good to see you son, you behave back there," she said smiling as I nodded, and Brent winked.

She closed the door behind us as we walked down the familiar hallway and into the first quadrant of the secret library. I found comfort hearing the crackling fireplace and comfortable couches. We sat down next to each other and Brent looked at me curiously.

"Well, what do you want to research?" he asked me curiously as I looked at the tall empty square table and the whiteboard in the room with dry erase markers on it.

"We need books on time and magical watches," I said thoughtfully, "also I need books on the Trenches."

After two hours we had gathered over fifty books on the topics I had mentioned. I looked at the amount of books and raised my eyebrows.

"This is going to take a lot of time. We need help," Brent said as I nodded in agreement.

"I will be right back," I said as I walked to the bookstore. No one was there except Mr. Genuit and Brent's parents.

"Everything okay?" Mr. Genuit asked as I nodded.

"I am calling in reinforcements to help with research," I said as Grant Genuit smiled with a twinkle in his eyes as he smiled wider, Brent's mom came into the room.

"If you need us, we will be in the kitchen we will be making dinner, will you be staying?" Brent's mom asked me as I nodded. "I am calling a few people here so there will be more coming."

I walked outside and pulled out my key and whispered, "Kār prachum, Secret Six."

Just then all six members came forth and appeared out of nowhere in black robes.

"Night Hunter Master," said the six robed figures in unison and bowing to me.

"I need your help in doing some research we have a new mission," I said as they nodded and hurried with me into the bookstore and followed me through the secret room. They all gathered around the table in awe as they looked around the room which had many books. Brent noticed what was going on and closed the book he was reading and stood up from the couch and put up his hood and mask noticing everyone else was doing it.

"Oh Brent, I mean you all can take your masks and hoods off," I said casually looking at all the hooded and masked members. "Not this again, you already all know each other and the room is already hot enough with the fireplace so just keep the robes on."

It was then that everyone took off their masks and hoods.

"How can we be of assistance for you Night Hunter Master?" Kaide asked looking at the books on the table.

"This table is full of information about the Trenches, a magical watch, and about Time. These are the topics that we need to know about if we hope to have any success on the next mission we are about to embark on. We will meet later tonight to discuss what we have all read," I said picking up the last ten books for myself to look over, as everyone nodded.

It was then that the various members picked up five to ten books each and got comfortable in various seats.

For the next several hours all that could be heard was the crackling of the fire in the fireplace and the turning of pages as the various members were reading including myself. I knew I needed the help and the more people who knew about what we were researching the better.

I picked up my first book and was looking through it.

"Time is an important thing to keep each of the City's of Sandglass going. It allows for productivity and as a measuring unit of time, it controls the masses. People don't realize its importance, but if you don't have it or know what's going on, how will people know when to come into work. Over the years,

it has been wasted by many and controlled by the various Time Council members. But overall, the Creator, the original watch maker, wanted it to be used in a manner of responsibility. To show us that we all have a time when we must move forward. Time is a great motivator to do things we couldn't have hoped to accomplish without a goal in mind in time to accomplish our dreams. Time has provided structure and it has endured through time as a constant."

I then put that book down and picked up the next book in the pile to skim over to see if I could get any information from it. The book was called, "A Treasure Like No Other"

"The Time Flex watch is a powerful watch powered by the wearer and uses solar power and the wearer's time to amplify its abilities. Laiden with a golden brass frame, sterling silver band, and on its face blue titanium covered by a clear glass. The wearer can use the watch to travel within their timeline back to the past, and review events of the past. Or the wearer can hold someone else's hand, while wearing the watch, and take that person to review your timeline or their timeline of the wearer's choosing. The watch can increase the ability to double the time when earning time for the wearer for normal deeds like sleeping for example, The wearer will gain sixteen hours for sleeping for eight hours instead of only gaining eight hours. The wearer also can keep living their own life and use *their body heat and the sun to keep their own time going even if they are out of time. The wearer can also bring someone back to life from being dead if only for an hour ONLY ONCE to talk to the deceased person as if they were there again in spirit form. Many have searched for the Flex Watch through the Trenches and have been unable to locate a watch of this power."*

"Oh wow," I said to myself.

"This is a very powerful magical object, Bella," Midnight said wisely.

"Yeah, if you found this watch you could even talk to both of your parents again or even to Sharon or Terry!" Emrys said in my mind as I kept quiet.

I closed the book in quiet contemplation got up from the book and walked around the room. I then walked around to the other quadrants to find the others were separated in each of them. It wasn't until I got to the far-right quadrant that I found Kaide.

"How can I help you?" Kaide said smiling at me.

"I need your thoughts on this," I said calmly looking at him who raised his eyebrows, "You have traveled around to the various City's of Sandglass, and you could see how they are run. Have you heard of such a magical object like "The Flex Watch"?" I asked him.

"To be honest, such magical objects are rare to find," Kaide said heavily closing the book he was reading and showing me the title of the book that he was reading, "Magical Objects of the Sandglass Realm."

I remained silent as Kaide pulled out a tobacco pipe and hit it against the fireplace wall which emptied remnants of old tobacco. Then he pulled out a leather pouch of fresh tobacco to fill his pipe with it and he put it back into his pocket and lit it by the fire in contemplation.

"Magical objects, no matter which one you are talking about are dangerous in the wrong hands," Kaide said wisely as he pulled some smoke through the pipe. I noticed that his time clock had increased in pace counting down. I then looked at my own noticing smelling the tobacco was just as costly, "When coming across these objects we must be careful with who knows about them."

I nodded silently and bowed to him as he bowed back in respect.

"Thank you for your opinion and time," I said looking at his pile of books he had left to read though, "I will call everyone in an hour to meet in the other room."

He nodded and smoked the rest of his pipe before going back to skimming over the books he was reading.

Chapter 19
The Mission

I went back to the first quadrant to finish skimming over the books I was reading and then by the time I was done, the hour was up. I then called everyone back into the room.

"Thank you all for your help," I said looking at all the robed secret six members in the room who nodded and sat down around the table with the books they had looked over.

"James, Brent, Kaide, Michael, Socrat, what have you all found?" I asked as I turned to James who nodded, and he spoke up first.

"Out of the books I have looked over I have discovered a few things. Multiple watches have been attempted to be made over the years by many watchmakers of the past, but few have been successful. The Creator, the original watchmaker, is said to have been the maker of this special specific watch for which you seek. Many have only ventured a guess as to its whereabouts and many have been killed with just the knowledge of it over the years. I have counted at least twenty witness accounts of those who have possessed such a watch and killed out of greed," James said looking around at a few of the secret members who shook their heads in silence.

"Thank you, Socrat, what have you found out?" I asked

"James is right there are multiple accounts of people who have found such a watch and only to turn up missing or tortured or dead just because of the quest to look for its whereabouts from various previous Time Council members," Socrat said looking at James who seemed to get the shivers just thinking about it, "Furthermore I was reading on the power of the watch and it is said that it has the ability to look back in time, stop time, and also allow for the wearer to be able to see other people's timelines and it is run by solar power and off the body heat of the wearer."

I nodded in silence as everyone seemed to be taking in what had been said as far as I then turned to Michael and Brent who looked at each other crossly.

"You first," Brent said to Michael who nodded.

"The Trenches are going to be difficult to get through," Michael started to say looking at me as I nodded.

"No, they aren't its literally just through The Underground," Brent said looking at Michael who put up his hand to stop him from talking.

" This is going to be a dangerous feat," Michael continued looking around the table, "There are going to be all manner of dark magical creatures the likes of which we have never seen before. The Trenches are a great chasm of rocks and there is a dark path straight down the middle of it which is narrow and will make getting away difficult. There are paths that lead away from the central chasm that have pockets where these creatures are said to be hiding along the way not to mention all the plants that grow in there are different from what we are used to seeing."

Everyone nodded silently as Michael continued, "We will need many supplies, food, water, first aid, and common knowledge on how to manage sprains, broken bones, what to do if we get colds. We need to also know how to defend ourselves and make sure that we are well equipped for cold and moisture and hot temperatures just in case."

"It is common knowledge that the two of them don't like each other by now," Socrat whispered looking at me from across the table as I shook my head.

"Time hasn't changed some people," I said looking from Brent to Michael who had crossed arms from across the table of each other.

"Apparently not," Socrat laughed.

"The mission that we are about to embark on will rely on us making sure we not only all get along better, but also get through the tough times together no matter how bad they get or what adversity that we face before us," I said looking at them, "We are to gather more information on the Trenches.

We need to know what secret lies within and past them. about Also, more importantly, what is beyond The Trenches?" I said looking at everyone who was nodding their head. "We will be faced with some challenges and maybe we will come across this watch that Tyronne was looking for. If not, maybe we can at least come back with some information for the Time Council about what we learn along the way."

There was silence along the way as I put on my face mask and hood and said, "Meeting is adjourned. We will meet just before sunlight in the morning at the Church in town."

"As you command Night Hunter Master," everyone said and left the room except Brent who had glared at Michael the whole time he was getting up from the table and leaving.

"I don't trust Michael," Brent said looking at me as I laughed. "He has changed a lot since the first day you met him, you need to give him a second chance," I said shaking my head, "Especially since he is one of the good guys now."

Brent stayed quiet as we left the library and walked up the street with our hoods. There were people on the street observing both Brent and me wearing our black robes as we made our way to the Time Tower. It was late by the time we got there, but it was nice to be able to spend time with Brent walking the streets together. We had gotten to my room without being noticed and got ready for bed and said,

"Goodnight" to each other. We had a big day ahead of us tomorrow morning and I was looking forward to the adventure.

Chapter 20

The Trenches

We awoke the next morning before everyone else did in the tower and grabbed our duffle bags that were in the closet. Brent and I packed clothes, first aid materials, and then went down to the kitchens and packed water, food, and supplies that we may need. We then left for the church without anyone noticing within the hour of waking up. Everyone else came in with their supplies as well including ropes, knives, and flashlights.

"Do you think we have enough?" I asked looking at the bag with three large tents and six sleeping bags brought by James.

"What? Do you think I would have wanted us to sleep on the

cold earth? Some of us want to make sure this trip is comfortable," he said as I smiled and nodded gratefully. We went to the Underground and saw that no one was even up as we slipped past James's mother's café and the familiar darkened warehouse where we had found Brent's parents. We all stopped short of the trenches and looked at them in awe. They towered hundreds of feet above us as black birds seemed to be flying ominously just above them.

Through the center of The Underground lies the unspoken chasm of a shadowy corridor carved from the Earth. The sides of these trench walls are steep and rugged lined with jagged rocks that loomed ominously above casting elongated shadows from the dim light above. The air felt heavy and damp, as we walked closer and it filled our noses with the scent of wet soil and moss that cover the walls in spots throughout the walls. In the opening of the the trench ran a narrow dirt path which many others branched off it that were uneven and marked by the footprints of the few who have dared to traverse through. The path is made of a mix of packed Earth and loose gravel that crunched below our feet. As we moved deeper into the trench, the walls seemed to close in around us, creating a sense of isolation and confinement. Colorful wildflowers bloomed in defiance of the dark abyss. Their petals rioted with color against the monochrome backdrop. Perhaps they draw sustenance from the hidden springs that seep through the rock, nourishing their roots. Every sound echoed throughout as we descended deeper into the trench. The walls closed in more in some parts more than others as their rough surfaces brushed against our shoulders. The unwelcoming air grew colder as we pushed on ahead in silence and it became almost suffocating to me. "Everyone alright so far?" I whispered, trying not to disturb anything that could be around us as I looked at everyone around me who nodded in a scared silence.

Step by cautious step we continued drawn in by an inexplicable force. We didn't know what was ahead of us awaiting our arrival, but I knew in time, the trenches would reveal their truth to us. For now, we moved forward chasing the shadows as the mystery unraveled before us as if by fate. As we walked on there was the rustling of a bush nearby and a wolf came out at us and howled. After it did three more came out as I pulled out my sword.

At the sight of my sword, they instinctively ran away seemingly feeling the power emulating off the sword.

"Wow, I have never seen you pull out your sword before," Brent said looking at it in admiration. "Where did you get it?"

"It was given to me," I said as everyone gathered around it to look at it.

"There is more to this sword than what meets the eye," Kaide said looking at it as he hovered his hand over the blade, "This is not a normal sword."

I nodded my head silently.

"This is the Sword of Damascus," Kaide said in awe, "Who gave it to you?"

"The what?" Brent asked aloud.

"Do not reveal anything else," Midnight said quickly in my head.

"I was given it when I was younger by my parents," I said putting the sword in its sheath at my side.

"You need to treat it well," Kaide said eyeing it in.

We traveled on as I led the way through the chasm, as the day drew on it grew dark ahead and you could hear the crickets and cicadas, and I found peacefulness in these sounds as I pressed on.

Just then I heard a thud behind me as I turned around.

"Ow," Brent said as I looked, he had fallen on the ground and tripped.

"Are you okay?" I asked as he nodded.

"Yeah," He said getting up and started walking again, with Kaide leading the way.

Everyone turned on their flashlights as the dirt path on the ground became full of more tree roots sticking out of the ground, making it harder to see. As we continued there was a path that led to an open clearing to the right of the path, so it was then that I stopped to check it out.

"Everyone lets camp here for the night," I said as the robed secret six members nodded in agreement and followed me into the clearing and started unpacking the tent and the sleeping bags.

"Bella, are you sure that we are going to be safe here?" Brent asked me in concern.

"Well, we will have to take turns keeping watch," I said looking at everyone who nodded.

It was then that we heard howling from what sounded like more wolves. There will be more creatures of the night out right now, and it will be harder to defend ourselves in the dark than during the day.

"What do you mean? It should be daylight out right now," Kaide said shaking his head, looking at the clouded sky.

For some reason, it was more difficult to manage the narrow path when it was difficult to see what was ahead and it made everyone uneasy.

It was in the middle of the night while resting that we were attacked. I had heard screaming from one of the tents. I wasn't sure who was supposed to be on duty but, soon after we were told to come out of our tents by three savage-looking people.

"What are you doing here?" they asked us.

"I am leading an investigation from the City of Sandglass Time to explore these trenches and to find out what is ahead of them," I explained calmly.

"You must come with us," said one of the men.

"No, we don't need to come with you," I said pulling out my sword angrily, "you just woke me up!"

It was then that the secret six fought back as I ended up making one of the savages surrender to us.

"We are going to let you go with your lives, but you are never to cross paths with us again," I said as they bowed to us and backed out of our camp and left us.

"Thank you for your mercy," the one savage said to me as he saw the power of the sword I was wielding.

We went to sleep for the rest of the night without incident, but it still had everyone on edge. When it was my turn to take watch, James was there at the entrance of the encampment off the path hidden behind a tree.

"Hello?" he said looking around and then he took a deep sigh of relief noticing it was me.

"It's only me James. It looks like I am covering the last shift of the night," I said as he nodded.

"I was worried there for a second," he said putting his hand on his chest in concern, "I thought it was someone else trying to sneak up on me to attack us."

"No, it's only just me," I repeated smiling at him.

James stayed with me for a few minutes in silence as we looked up at the sky above us. There were stars out from what I could see.

"James, can I ask you something?" he nodded, "What kinds of things did you discover with the other City's Of Sandglass? What tasks did the council have you and your dad work on?"

"Well, they wanted us to report on each other essentially," James said folding his arms uncomfortably, "you see none of the Council Members from either of the City's of Sandglass like each other."

"Why is that?" I asked curiously looking over at James who kept looking at the stars above us.

"They each try to outdo each other in how they help their citizens and run their City's," James explained, "We would go to each of the City's and tell on each of the City's for the most part and we would try to barter with the Councils by putting one against up against the other."

"That doesn't sound like it was very helpful," I said thinking about it, "Wouldn't it be best if all the Council's got along?"

"Well, our Time Council didn't want one City more powerful than the rest at the time, so we would travel to the various Councils. We would try to work it out so that we made sure that City of Sandglass -Time got the best deals and was not going to be considered the underdogs if you will," James explained as I nodded in silence, "Well I am going to head to bed."

"You said at that time?" I said slowly.

"Obviously, you are the new Time Council Leaders now, so the ball will be in your courts going forward," James said smiling, "I am going to bed now Bella. Goodnight."

"Goodnight, James," I said as he smiled and joined Socrat in their tent to get some sleep for the night.

"That is a lot of pressure," I thought to myself.

"Time is precious Bella, and even though time is limited, as a leader you have the power to make a difference and have the power to change things as they are like others have before you. But how you choose to lead, and the difference you make by being a leader comes down to the choices that you make in your life," Midnight said as I nodded.

I looked around there was a hooting owl that I heard from what seemed like a tree above us. I wanted to know what was ahead of us before continuing our journey in the morning.

"Don't you think about it Miss Bella!" came the voice of Midnight the owl in my head.

"What?" I said to myself, "Wouldn't it be better to know what lies ahead of time?"

"And then what are you going to do if you get into trouble again?" asked Emrys wisely.

I knew he had a point. There wasn't any sense in getting caught and into trouble when everyone else was asleep.

"It's okay to look forward to tomorrow. It will come soon enough," Emry said as I nodded, "Be patient."

After a few more hours of silence, it seemed that the night crickets and cicadas slowly bayed their last tunes of the night. Slowly, the sun seemed to have risen on the bright new day.

Chapter 21
The Proposal

Slowly everyone started waking up, as the sound of birds chirping in the tree above the campsite, seemed to echo below.

"Will you quiet down up there?! Some of us are trying to sleep in!" shouted a grumpy Brent from inside the tent.

I smiled and laughed at the thought of him reacting to nature being disruptive to him seemed to amuse me.

Kaide walked over to me after stretching outside of his tent.

"Any more events happen during the last few hours of the night?" Kaide asked me as I shook my head.

"The night went by as peacefully and swiftly as the night air slips through our fingers," I said smiling at him.

"Ah, this is good to hear," Kaide said smiling as he turned around to see that everyone else seemed to be waking up and folding their sleeping bags and packing up their tents. Kaide walked away to follow suit and start packing up his things. Within a few minutes, everyone was packed, and I had my things packed. I looked around at everyone who seemed to be watching Brent and then he nodded at them and smiled. Everyone seemed to gather around me.

"What is going on?" I asked curiously as Socrat and James side-hugged each other.

"Bella, I want to give you something," Brent said to me smiling, "I meant to give it to you before we left the City of Sandglass, but I wasn't able to."

He then handed me a navy blue box with a black bottom to it. I untied the red ribbon that was tied into a neat bow on top of it. I opened it and a smile crossed my face.

"Brent! This is beautiful!" I said as I pulled out a Sterling Silver necklace of a golden mini sandglass.

"It's only for a minute long," Brent said showing me the sand in the sandglass as I looked at awe at the sands in it. He then put the necklace on me. "I got this for you to signify that even if I have a few minutes left with you, overtime these minutes will last forever if you remember to change the perspective of it. I want to continue to be at your side Bellatrix Kai."

I nodded as he seemed to be shaking and then he walked in front of me as everyone smiled.

It was then that Brent went down on one knee and pulled out another smaller box from his back pocket.

"Bellatrix Kai, will you do me the life changing honor of being my wife?" Brent said through tears, "You have changed my life from the moment you stepped into my family's bookstore, and into my life. Helping me walk again, spending hours and hours helping me to research and eventually find my parents. After all this time, I don't know if I even deserve to have someone like you in my life as my life partner. Bella, you are so selfless, loving, caring, honest, brave, and courageous. It makes me so happy and proud that I have someone like you in my life who makes me smile even when the things around us at times are so dark," he said pointing to the campsite area that seemed to have darkened.

"Aren't you going to say yes?" Emrys said in my head as my body warmed up.

"Say yes girl!" Midnight hooted in agreement.

"YES!" I said through tears as I started crying and he put a matching sterling silver ring on my ring finger.

Everyone around us started cheering as Michael looked at me approvingly.

I was so surprised and happy, to finally have Brent as my fiancé someone who has been through thick and thin with me from the start.

"Weddings there in the City of Sandglass are huge," James said looking at me smiling.

"How so?" I asked curiously looking over at James who had his arm around Socrat.

"You are tied together in and out of the sands of time. Once you are married, no matter what happens in the future you will always be tied through time," James said smiling and putting his head on Socrat.

"You love birds ready?" Kaide said nudging James as he started walking towards the path through the trenches, "The day is young we should get more ground covered while it's still daylight."

I nodded and followed Kaide as we walked on down the moss walled path. As we traveled on there was a dense fog up ahead that we saw that seemed to be pushed in through the winds.

"Stay close everyone! We don't know what we are getting ourselves into!" Kaide shouted behind him to us as we walked closer together.

It was then that he pulled out his sword as we heard rustling of the leaves on the dirt ground ahead of us as they crunched below our feet. We walked through the fog looking like dark figures in the cloud of white fog as we pushed through it. We saw there was a clearing up ahead with wooded walls and tall grass.

"Help me cut this down so we can walk through it," Kaide said turning towards me and James who had our swords drawn. We cut through the grass and the fog started to clear and all we could see was the wooded walls opening to a vast area head of open land.

Chapter 22

The Village of Pequa

We approached the end of the trenches and looked in awe as we saw the vast open valley ahead of us.

"What is that?" James asked as he pointed towards the Village less than a few miles away.

"It's a village," I said shaking my head not understanding what the big deal was.

"No, not that, beyond that, that White Wall," James said pointing towards the village.

I looked further to see what looked like a white blanketed wall. It looked scary but also, I was curious about what it was. What was it was made of? Why did it seem to wave with the wind? What was this, some kind of veil?

"I am not sure, but maybe someone in the Village ahead will know what it is," I said as the others seemed to agree with me. We trudged on forward through the open field walking towards the trenches. I put away my sword, as the others had also done. We didn't want to come across like a threat.

Within a few minutes, we reached the entrance to the village. There were people in the street who were scurrying back into their homes and closing their shutters to their windows so that we couldn't see anyone.

"Not very hospitable people here, are they?" James said quietly to Socrat behind me as he seemed to nod in response quietly. We walked down the road passing many carriages and stores that all seemed to be closed. We walked on through the street passing more buildings and other side streets on the way down the main strip of dirt road, until we reached the end of the road. It had opened to a bridge with water running through it. We started to follow the water after crossing the bridge towards the White Wall. We walked on further down the road as we saw several men riding horses ride up to us fast.

"You are there! You've come far to reach The Village of Pequa, strangers. Few venture this close to the White Wall. And those who do, rarely leave. What is your purpose here?" the Tall slender man sitting tall on his white horse said in a gruff, but wary voice.

"I have heard tales of This White Wall and of its power and what lies beyond it. We are here to see it for ourselves, to understand what it is – and why it exists," I said calmly to the man who shook his head, as I turned towards the village scanning to see if anyone was behind us.

"I am Champa, Leader of the Village of Pequa, now that you have seen the White Wall, its best that you go back from whence you came! You seek answers where there are none to be found. The White Wall is not something that you can simply... explore or just touch with your bare hands or even pass through for that matter. It is a fragile fabric of our reality. It is a boundary, a separation between worlds that should never be crossed. Our world is built of villages and various City's of Sandglass, we are controlled and guided by time," Champa said showing us the time clock on his forehead showing 20 years 10 months 86 days 20 hours, and 4 minutes and 35 seconds counting down, "The rest of the world out there past the White Wall is a different realm, divided by time itself, that wall was created by the Watchmaker itself, the Creator."

"So, it's true then?" Kaide said raising his eyebrows, "Time behaves differently beyond this White Wall? I have heard stories myself from the other Time Council Leaders of the various other City's of Sandglass of such a thing existing."

Champa remained quiet as he looked at us seeing our weapons at our side.

"Well, these stories don't scare us! We have already crossed more lands that are more dangerous than that on our journey here from the Underground," James said in a skeptical voice in agreement with his father who crossed his arms as well.

"You don't understand what you are dealing with. The wall is not simply. Just some a barrier of stone or magic. It's the very essence of time itself, stretched and distorted across our world to keep that which is beyond it from coming into our realm! To cross it or even touch it, it means risking not only your existence, but ours and everyone else's that you know as well. Time bends, wraps and changes… people who have gone through it. They have never come back the same, if at all," Champa said lIfting his chin, gazing unyielding towards Kaide and James.

"You mean people have crossed it?" I asked curiously.

"I think so, I was told by the forefathers, and other leaders before me, that hundreds of years ago someone did go through the White Wall, but they never returned," Champa said wisely.

"We are not afraid of a few stories, nor a village leader, and his small military of village farmers! We have faced worse. We just want to know what's on the other side of that White Wall and why its secrets are kept hidden!" Socrat said smiling coldly looking at Champa and the Soldiers.

"You think that the wall is there to hide something? It's there to protect us all – from the creatures of the dark that are beyond it! Also to protect the time that we hold dear here!" Champa said stepping his horse closer forward towards us as he raised his voice. "That wall was torn once thousands of years ago and they made their choices then, twisting time, bending it to their will, but that came with a price that everyone paid. It is a price that no one should have to pay!"

"What if we want to pay the price?" Brent asked curiously looking at Champa, "What if the power of time itself is worth the risk? We have traveled and come too far to turn back now. Either tell us how to reach the White Wall or we will find it ourselves!" Brent said leaning towards Champa in a more aggressive tone putting his hand on the handle of his sword.

"You think that your weapons will protect you? Against the wall?" Champa said as his eyes were flashing with anger, "You can't force your way through time. Even your strength means nothing there. I have seen entire lives erased; futures snatched away in an instant by the White Wall. People who thought they knew better than I. You will all be lost before you even understand what you are dealing with!"

"We don't want to fight," I said softening my tone and trying a different approach talking to the Leader Champa, "We just want to know what the White Wall is hiding. Surely there must be a way to understand it without risking everything. You must know something more."

"The White Wall is a force of and in time, it keeps the various City's of Sandglass safe trapped in its own loop of people coming and leaving it through their passages of time, "Champa explained crossing his arms with a steady unconvinced gaze at me, "This loop is where the past, present, and future collide endlessly. Some people come to the City of Sandglasses and remember their past lives. If we were to break through the White Wall, we would all be lost in time, and maybe even forever out of time without a road to recovery, I fear. Those of us on this side, once the barrier is broken... we are free from that curse of knowing when we are going to die. But to cross the Wall, and you become a part of that timeless chaos. There is no going back here. There is no way to undo itand you don't know when you are going to die there."

Everyone was quietly intrigued.

"So, it's true," Brent said, "There is a way we can live without knowing when we will die?"

Champa nodded.

"So, it's because of the barrier that we are controlled and consumed by time?" I asked in frustration.

"Can you imagine living in a world when we don't have the pleasure of knowing when we will die?" Champa asked me as I shook my head in awe.

"I feel like we are like ticking time bombs with that pressure of knowing when our time is up sometimes," I said as Brent nodded in agreement.

"In reality though, the timecards are not exact. If you don't take care of your body, it can also make your timecard go quicker," Midnight said quietly.

"This is what the great watchmaker wanted, to give the City's of Sandglass order. The Council's wanted to be the Masters of Time, to control it," Champa sighed as his voice was soft with sorrow briefly reflecting, "Time is not meant to be controlled. The City's of Sandglass, people grow old, yet no one is truly alive forever. They are trapped in an eternal cycle of more souls coming into them. The victories along with the failures of their past lives of the lives they had on Earth are still within them and us all from when we lived on Earth," Champa explained

"No one has ever returned from the other side to know what it's like over there? No one has crossed back through the White Wall?" Michael asked murmuring.

"A few have tired. The ones who have come from the White Wall are, well they aren't alive. Some speak only in riddles. Others have gone mad. Time is a prison there. You will lose yourself in it, or worse – you may never leave from the other side. The ones who have returned are not even able to live longer than a day after they come through. The travel from the other side of the Wall to this side of the wall reduces the life force inside of them. So, we end up burying them," Champa explained pointing to a field of unmarked graves, "They wonder aimlessly out there until they just die."

"I thought you said that no one comes back?" James said as I stepped in front of him.

"No one goes and comes back the same," Champa reexplained as he watched our movements closely, "and the fowl creatures of the dark there are unable to pass through at all because of the wall. It is said that Time is a keeper. Time holds things there like a prison. Once you go there, you either lose yourself or you may never leave."

I had looked back and saw Brent's face. I only have seen that look of determination on him once before when he was trying to learn to walk again.

"We still want to see the White Wall. Whatever the risks. We didn't come all this way only to be turned back by fear! We want to just say we had a chance to visit and look at it," Brent said looking at me, then to Socrat, Kaide, James, and Michael.

"Then I can't stop you," Champa said taking in a deep breath, his tone was heavy with warning, "But remember this: Once you just stand before the wall. Time will no longer belong to you. The past may haunt you. The future may reject you. If you cross, you may never find your way back to this moment to where and who you are now. If you touch it there may be no going back."

"We will take our chance," Kaide said firmly smiling grimly.

""Chance is the architect of our most unexpected moments, while time is the master builder of their meaning," Champa said wisely, "Tread carefully on the path that you are choosing to make.".

He then moved the horse and said the words, "Let them pass," and the group of soldiers moved to each side of the path to let us all through on the dirt path.

"May you find what you are looking for strangers. Heed my words, somethings once lost to time, can never be reclaimed," Champa said with his eyes filled with sorrow, "The path to travel to time will not be easy ahead. Follow the path and you will eventually reach your destination."

We walked past them in silence as they seemed to be uncomfortable with us for our decision.

Chapter 23

The Passage to the White Wall

We walked for a few hours in silence, thinking about what was told to us as we walked towards the destiny that awaited our fate.

"What do you think it's going to be like?" I asked Brent as he was walking next to me.

"I am not sure what to expect," Brent said looking ahead of us as we followed the path through a wooded area.

The path was lined with tall trees as we followed the dirt path. After a while, we finally had come to the wall. It was a shade of bright white, the likes of which I had never seen.

"Do you see that?" I asked, looking at the White Wall. Against the wall I could see Sharon and Taylor alive again trying to talk to me. Right behind them were my parents putting their hands against the White Wall and saying my name looking around the White Wall for me, "I see Sharon! I see Terry! I see my parents! They are alive! Brent, they are alive?! See this is my mom and this is my dad!" I had said pointing towards the White Wall as Brent came to me as I saw them.

"Bellatrix, the wall is lying to you! They are not there!" Brent said insistently, "I only see the White Wall."

"Brent, I see my mom! Dad! I see mom!" James said calling Kaide over to him.

"James, son, your mother is gone, she died years ago," Kaide said through tears, "This wall is lying to us?"

"Do you think this wall shows us what we want to come true so if we open it, it will happen?"

"I am not sure everyone, but whatever you do, don't touch the wall!" Michael said nervously as he saw his worst fear in the wall.

"It's trying to scare us if it knows that we are not enticed by our missing loved ones. It wants us to open it. Remember what Champa said, we might even be facing our worst fears here, and he said not to touch it!" Socrat said shaking his head.

"I want to see my parents!" I said through tears, "What if they are actually alive over there?"

"No magical powers can bring back those that have been lost, Bella," Midnight said.

It was then that I held out my sword trying to see what would happen.

"Maybe if I just put my sword up to it and push it through they can come out," I said as I did this, the wall which seemed to shear at the touch of the sword like a hot blade to a fire. The wall was easily malleable, the sword tore a long hole in the White Wall.

"We did it!" Brent said smiling breathless, staring at the torn wall, "I can't believe we broke through. I can't believe that it worked!"

"Mom! Dad! Terry?" I shouted as I stared through the hole in the wall. There was a sound of a demon laughing as I stared through into the great abyss of complete darkness and nothingness.

Just then there was a howl from a wolf nearby seemingly foreshadowing what was to come.

"What is that? It's like the wall is alive! Its unraveling open slowly. We weren't supposed to – this isn't what I expected!" James said shivering as arctic-like air pushed through. James, now wide-eyed stepped back from the wall in fear.

Then, there was a screeching coming from the other side as dark black long clawlike hands seemed to push through the fabric-like wall. The creature used both of its claws to tear and pull open through the rest of the hole.

"What is that?!" Brent said stepping in front of me to protect me with his sword now drawn out in front of him, "Everyone protect Bella!"

I stepped a few steps backward in shock as the images of my parents came to mind.

"Bella, what have you done?" my mother said to me as I started to physically tear up.

"I'm sorry mom," I said through tears, "I wanted to see you both as my father came into view.

"Bella, we are proud of you that you are a part of the Time Council and a Leader of the Night Hunters, but the Veil of Time is not to be torn. By doing this, it has consequences. You must immediately undo what you have done. The City of Sandglass, everyone, you are all in grave danger now," my dad said as I nodded. Their images disappeared.

I saw dark black and purple clouds of smoke begin to push through the hole in the middle of the White Wall.

Brent and I stepped back.

"Looks like something is coming through! Oh, sweet dear baby Jesus! What did we just release? From what hell do they come from?" said Michael who was now alarmed, pointing at the dark figures now emerging from the great dark abyss from the wall. They bent down and pushed through the wall.

"Those... Those... things, They don't look like anything we have seen from this world!" James said pulling out his sword guarding a now shaking Socrat who seemed scared for his life.

"What the hell did we just release?" I asked looking at Brent who seemed to be standing still with his sword outdrawn in fear.

"They are getting closer! They are not stopping! We must get out of here before it's too late!" Kaide shouted as the winds seemed to be picking up and he looked around at everyone who had taken more steps back.

"No, we can't leave it like this! We must close it! There's got to be a way – something we can do to seal the wall again!" James said seemingly frightened by determined as the winds seemed to pick up. He looked to his father who shook his head in doubt and seemed to be panicking.

"No, it's too late for that! Do you see them? Those things are not slowing down. They are demon giants! We have now unleashed something that is out of our control!" Kaide said shaking as he held on to his sword tighter in front of him.

The creatures were shrieking as they moved standing at least sixty feet in the air above them.

I turned towards the village as I grew worried.

"We need to warn the village!" I shouted at everyone who nodded in agreement as we watched the figures slowly come out one at a time and stretch out along the wall.

"Warn us?! You fool!" What have you done?" came a voice from behind us as we all jumped and saw that it was Champa and his warriors from the village as he looked at me.

Chapter 24
Reprimanded and Consequences

His voice was cold, and his eyes were burning with fury, "Look at what you've done! I told you the Wall was not to be tampered with. Now you've torn it, and these... creatures from that other world are going to be loose in our world!
"We didn't know this would happen. We just wanted to see what was beyond the wall, not unleash... whatever those creatures are!" James said defensively raising his hands towards the large creatures.
"Your curiosity has doomed us all! These creatures are not bound by time or nature. They come from a world where time has no meaning! There life and death merge into something fowl! You have unleashed horrors into our world that should never have been freed!" Champa said stepping forward, reprimanding us and pointing his finger towards James, and then to me in a sharp voice.
"We are sorry!" I said looking at Champa who laughed sarcastically at us shaking his head in anger.
"Sorry?! Sorry doesn't fix this!" Champa said looking at us and pointing then at the beasts and the tear in the middle of the White Wall.

"What are they going to do?" Brent asked in worry.

"They are spreading out along the wall until they surround us and then they are going to attack us," Champa said bitterly.

"Fight?" Socrat asked worriedly as Champa nodded fast and bit his upper lip in frustration.

"Haven't you fought them before?" Kaide asked looking from the creatures and then to Champa who shook his head.

"With what?" Champa asked.

"Then how do you know they will attack us?" James asked

"Because they are not peaceful creatures, they come from that void of hell and they are not here to visit," Champa said looking at James and then the creatures as more came from the tear in the White Wall.

"Then help us fix it! There must be something we can do to close it right? We can fight them off with you, we will," Brent said nervously glancing at the creatures heading out along the wall.

"You have all done enough damage. Your recklessness has brought this upon us. Now my people and your people eventually must suffer the consequences. You are no longer welcome in our Village of Pequa. Leave now, while you all still can," Champa said interrupting Brent in a commanding voice as his eyes narrowed.

"But we didn't mean for this to happen! If you let us help-" I said pleadingly

"Help? You have helped enough! Every moment you stay here, you risk the lives of my people even further. Leave now, before you bring more disaster. My warriors will oversee the defense. You are banished.," Champa said cutting through the chaos of the creatures screeching and roaring. "

"But the creatures will kill you all! We can fight them together! We have weapons we can --" James said looking at their arrows and his own sword stepping forward desperately.

"Your weapons are nothing against them!" Champa said in a voice as cold as steel as he pointed towards them, "You have unleashed things beyond your understanding. There is nothing you can do except leave and hope they don't follow you. Go, before it's too late!"

"He is right! We have messed up, and there is no way to undo this. We need to leave before those things catch up to us!" Socrat said taking a step back, torn between fear and guilt.

"But... the wall. It's still torn. If we don't fix it —" I started to say looking at the even larger tear in the White Wall filled with regret.

"We will deal with the wall. My people have prepared for this day, though I hoped it would never come. We will fight, and we will defend our homes, and our village from these creatures you have released," Champa said grimly, his eyes hardening, "But you—you are no longer our concern. Go, before I change my mind. My warriors force you out."

"He is not going to let us help. We must go," I said pulling Brent's hand and leading the way towards the village as the villagers walked past us towards the warriors in disappointment.

"We came here for answers and all we have done is destroy everything we have touched. We should have listened to him when we first came here," Socrat said as he grabbed James's hand.

"Let's go before we make things worse," Michael said hoarsely to everyone as the six of us nodded and began to retreat as the Villagers of Pequa seemed to be preparing for war.

We had heard Champa shouting at the people who were walking from the village towards us.

"The time has come. These creatures are born of a broken time. But we will stand our ground. Ready the defenses of the village. The wall must be sealed somehow, and we must protect Pequa. We must fight for our very existence now!"

The Villagers started rallying around Champa, weapons raised as the creatures from the void in the wall moved closer.

"We have faced hardship before, and we will face this. The White Wall may be broken, but Pequa will not fall! We fight, for our lives, for our future – for everything!" Champa shouted.

Chapter 25
Repairing the White Wall

We walked away from the Village of Pequa, and we made it to the opening of the Trenches. We all turned around to see smoke coming from the Village as we saw it start to burn as the creatures seemed to swarm to it from the wall. The tear in the wall could now be seen from the opening of the trenches, its flaps waving in the wind.

"This is all our fault, we did this. We must fix it – somehow. We can't just let these people die!" I said desperately through tears, hearing screaming and wailing from the people of the Village being attacked and killed by the creatures who were killing the Villagers of Pequa.

"It's too late Bellatrix. Look at them… look at what we have unleashed. I don't know if this can be fixed," Brent said pointing at the various hundreds of creatures who had pushed through the White Wall barrier.

More screaming and shrilling echoed through the valley and the trenches as we walked further into the trenches.

"We will fix it. We can't just run from this!" Kaide said clenching his fists, his voice was low and frustrated, "There has to be a way – there has to be!"

We continued walking on in silence and deep in our thoughts as we continued through the night. We dared not to stop because we knew every moment was crucial. The people of the Village of Pequa were counting on us even if they didn't know it.

"But how?" Socrat said urgently glancing around at everyone, "We don't even understand what the White Wall is made of, let alone how to repair it. And those creatures…." Socrat shuddered at the mere thought of them, "they are not going to stop coming."

"The White Wall, it's not just a barrier. It is time itself, isn't it?" Michael said thinking of how the wall seemed to pulse with negative energy and the tear itself, "We have torn through time. These creatures –they are things that should never have been. They have crossed into this world because we ripped open that boundary in space and time."

"Yes, captain obvious you have literally just repeated what Champa had told us!" Brent said impatiently to Michael, "Now can you keep quiet and let us think of a way to fix things instead of repeating things and getting on our nerves?"

"Are you looking for a fight?" Michael said with his fists up towards Brent as we continued forward through the trenches.

"Guys, will you both stop? Fighting about this situation is not going to help us all! We need to work together to figure out a plan on how to resolve this issue. Physical fights and arguing is counterproductive at this point," I said to Michael and Brent as I put my hands on Michael's fists that were still up as he looked pointedly at Brent who then put his fists down after a few minutes as he looked at me and nodded in agreement. We walked on as I continued along the same line of thinking, thinking about what Champa was saying to us. I regretted instantly what we did as I felt guilt hit me in my stomach and I grew worried about what was in store for us and the fate of the other City's of Sandglass. This is happening not too far away from us.

"No one even has a clue!" I thought to myself as I saw innocent kids playing at a playground as we reached the underground as we came back from the trenches.

"Do you have any ideas?" I asked Emrys and Midnight.

"These creatures are soulless and do not have a place in our spiritual realm nor in your world. There is not anything that we can suggest for you," Emrys said, "This is not something that we would be able to interfere with."

"Does your magic work against them?" I asked trying to rack my brain of any ideas or possibilities.

"No," Midnight said softly, "But our jobs as spirit animals is to protect the souls we are bonded with. So those that are in the underground might be safe, but those that are in the City's of

Sandglass themselves without the magical spiritual tattoos they are not as lucky. These creatures will feed off those souls and the people will be lost to oblivion in no time."

I then thought again of what Michael had repeated from Champa.

"The White Wall, it's not just a barrier. It is time itself."

"That's it!" I said aloud as everyone looked at me as we headed up the passages to the City of Sandglass- Time.

"What is it, Bella?" Brent asked me.

"That is, it, Time… We've crossed into something far greater than ourselves. That White Wall separates us from the rest of the world –if it's about time itself—then maybe that is how we can fix it," I said.

"Bellatrix you are speaking in riddles. What do you mean?" James asked me frowning, "Do you mean go back? Somehow reverse what we have done? How do we even begin to do that?"

"We cross the very sands of time," Brent said thinking along the same lines as he was smiling at me and at the idea.

Kaide pointed at Brent and his face lit up.

"We cross the Sands of Time," Kaide said nodding his head in thoughtful silence for a minute, "The Time Council has controlled time for centuries, right? If we can make it to the other side of time to the point just before we ripped it open, maybe we can reverse what we did."

"Crossing time? Are you saying we will be traveling through some sort of sandglass or something? That is insane and it sounds dangerous. The creatures came from that other world, does that mean we have to seal the wall from the other side. Or are you saying we go back and somehow stop the wall from being torn open in the first place?" Socrat asked.

"We would go back in time and stop the White Wall from being opened somehow," Brent said looking at Socrat and seemingly getting a headache, "The Time Council may not agree to this. They are very protective of the Sands of Time. It isn't to be used just for fun."

"We don't have a choice," Kaide said shaking his head as we all went up the ladder and got back into the City of Sandglass. "Whatever else is beyond that wall, it ought not to be here and it's going to cause more death, and destruction, the longer that the tear remains there. If we can reverse what happened, maybe we can save the lives that were lost already including the Village of Pequa."

We all nodded and then looked towards the Time Tower.

"This is not going to be easy to beg the council for help," James said as I nodded, "They are not going to be happy with what we have done."

We all nodded in silence and guilt.

"Bellatrix, what brings you here?" Tobey asked smiling at me and then he became serious as he saw who else was with me, "What happened?"

"We need to talk to the entire council; it is an emergency!" I said urgently as I looked at Kaide.

"I am sure this is great news," Tobey said looking at my ring finger.

"No, it isn't about that!" I said shaking my head, "It's a far worse of a situation, we need to meet with everyone as we are all in mortal danger in the City of Sandglass, it is only a matter of time."

"We haven't a moment to lose!" Tobey said then whispered something to himself as the bell towers in the Time Towers struck the normal tune of the need for an emergency meeting. It was then that everyone piled into the Time Council chambers.

"Why is it that every time we have a meeting it always seems to be surrounding you Bellatrix?" Tonya said looking at me in boredom.

"Well, I don't do it intentionally, but drama and trouble always seem to follow me like a shadow on a sunny day," I said smiling slightly and shrugging, "But this meeting is of great importance."

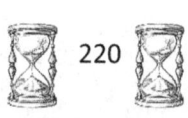

"Tell me what is so important that you had to disrupt my afternoon nap?" asked Taylor slightly sleepy.

It was then that the council doors closed, and everyone was seated at their appropriate Time Council chairs and Brent, Michael, Socrat, Kaide, and James were all seated below at the table.

"What is going on?" Theresa asked looking at me in slight annoyance.

"We need permission to travel across the Sands of Time, "Kaide said breaking the conversation at the Council as everyone looked at him seriously.

"You wish to reverse time?" Tonya said curiously looking over at me.

"Such a proposition has not been brought to our attention in over a hundred years," Tessa said

"I can hardly believe my ears," Tyeisha said, "Bellatrix has barely been on the Time Council, and within months of gaining power, and this position, even as its questioned, she is asking to use something that we protect above all. Time is precious, it is not to be fooled around with or messed with!"

"What is the purpose you wish to Cross the Sands of Time dear sister? Is it for selfish reasons?" Tommy asked me as I shook my head.

"I wouldn't ask this of you all if this was just for me, but also for the protection of the City of Sandglass," I said urgently.

"What on this Realm would you want to protect us from?" Theresa said curiously, looking at me as I remained silent trying to figure out how I was going to tell them.

Theodore came into the Council Chambers, saw me, and shook his head.

"I don't believe it, Bellatrix Kai," Theodore said in frustration, "What did you do this time?"

"Well, it is good to see you Theodore. I thought you were giving up your position on the Council?" I said coolly.

"This better be good, and yes, I am going to eventually once they figure out who they are going to elect to replace me," Theodore said as the council looked at him in surprise at this news.

"Anyway," I said looking from him to the rest of the council as I saw Kaide trying to push me on to explain.

"My fellow council members, I have some foul news to report. Earlier yesterday my fellow Night Hunters and I had gone through the Trenches in The Underground and had stumbled upon the Village of Pequa. Its inhabitants are fierce protectors of this White Wall that is beyond its borders. The White Wall is a fabric of separation of time between our realm and another. The reason we ask for the permission to Cross the Sands of time is because, we dared to tear that White Wall which caused all manner of dark creatures to come through. They are most fowl, the likes of which we have never seen before. We tore it thinking that it would reveal secrets even though we were warned not to. At this moment, the warriors of the Village of Pequa are risking and sacrificing their lives just to prevent these sixty foot tall dark creatures from coming this way. All the while, these creatures are destroying their village. We were told that no mortal weapon nor spiritual being can hurt these creatures that came through the tear in the White Wall."

There was silence in the Chambers as they all looked at us in astonishment.

"We come to ask for your help—no, we beg for it. We've done something terrible. We were... explorers, fools. We tore the White Wall that separates the city from the rest of that world, and now everything is falling apart!" I said in anguish.

The room was full of tension.

"Wow, you tore the wall?" Theodore said angrily, "Do you have any idea of the balance you have disrupted? The creatures of the dark now roam free out there. They were never meant to exist outside of time. Your ignorance has unleashed chaos!"

"We know! We didn't understand at the time the consequences. We thought that we were just crossing a boundary – exploring something unknown. But now the Village of Pequa is under attack and its darkness is spreading. Those creatures are going to destroy everything unless we do something and fix our mistake!" James explained raising his voice a little urgently, while at the same time trying to stay calm.

Everyone muttered at the fact that he was coming off as rude and raised his voice at them. I looked at everyone in concern at the reaction that they were having to James raising his voice at them.

"James's intentions are not to be rude or unkindly. He is simply emotionally stressed and worried about the consequences of what our actions caused. We need to be able to go back in time to just before it happened, so we won't be in this situation anymore as it is a dire situation," I explained as a few of the council members nodded in agreement.

Tonya leaned forward towards me as she motioned for everyone to be quiet so she could talk, "As much as I understand the gravity of the situation you too must learn something today. Time is not a toy to be bent at your will. The White Wall was created to keep our world separated from the other realms and to contain our transactional control over time that we have here. Because you tore this boundary, you have broken the delicate balance that exists between past, present, and future. You have no idea what you have just unleashed."

"That is why we are here and have come to you," Kaide said urgently, We are not asking for your forgiveness – we know what we have done now. But we need your help to fix it, before it is too late. We need to... go back. We need your permission to cross the Sands of Time, to reverse what we have done, before it is too late," Kaide repeated urgently.

"You seek to reverse time? As if it were a mere clock that could be wind backward at will. You are all reckless and fools. Do you genuinely believe you can easily control the flow of time after the damage you've already caused?" said Tyronne said scoffing dismissively.

"It is not a decision that is up to you anymore now is it, Tyronne Mattley," Theodore said angrily.

"We don't have a choice! The creatures are spreading, attacking everything in their path. The Village of Pequa is just the beginning. Soon they will reach the Trenches, then the Underground, and then we are next," Brent said in a desperate and enthusiastic way as the other council members looked at him.

"If we don't stop them—if we don't undo what we did and fix this—it is not just us who will suffer. The entire world will collapse under the weight of what we have done!" Socrat said worriedly, "No mortal weapon affects these creatures."

Just then Terrance, the one council member who hadn't said anything yet spoke up as everyone went silent.

"And what makes you think that you can reverse the damage? You stand here asking for permission to manipulate time, but time is fragile. It resists to change. To cross the very Sands of Time, Do you know what you are asking?" Terrance said in a very stern voice that seemed to cut into the air in the room as Socrat grimaced, "To cross the Sands of Time, is not to merely go back – it is to risk tearing the very fabric of existence apart. You could cause greater destruction than you already have."

It was then that I stood up from my seat at the Time Council stand and locked eyes with all the Council members one by one in a resolute voice.

"We know it's dangerous, we know the risks. But if we don't try, the creatures will devour everything. The Watchmaker built this White Wall to keep our city safe from the rest of the world. We didn't understand that then as we do now, but now that the White Wall is broken, now no one is safe. We must take the chance. Let us go back in time and undo what we did.

We tore the Wall, and we can fix it. I believe in us," I said looking at all the Time Council Members again.

It was then that I sat down, and Tobey stood up to speak and his voice was also filled with skepticism and doubt.

"Fixing time is not so simple. The Sands of Time are not just a pathway to the past—they are treacherous. If you make one wrong step, you could become lost in time forever. Do you genuinely believe you can bear that weight?"

"We must try. If we don't then everything that we have done, everything that we have broken will be broken forever if we don't try. This is our mistake and our burden to bear," Brent said standing up in a quiet but determined voice, "We have to undo the damage, or we'll never be able to live with ourselves."

The council members exchanged glances, the air in the chamber thickened with tension as the weight of the decision loomed over us.

"You seek to cross the Sands of Time and reverse the moment you tore the wall. If we grant you permission, you must understand that this journey will not be easy. Time is not a straight line; it is a labyrinth. The creatures you have unleashed—they are echoes of broken time, and they will follow you. The further you travel back, the more dangerous it becomes," Tommy said calmly.

"If you fail, there will not be a second chance. You must do this right the first time. You may even undo your existence entirely if you are not careful. The consequences of meddling with time are irreversible. Your past selves are not going to be able to see what you have seen so far in your timelines. So, you would need to bear that in mind," Terrance explained.

"We understand," James said nodding firmly, "But we can't let fear stop us. We are willing to risk everything to fix this."

"Just give us the chance. We are ready to cross the Sands of Time, no matter the cost. Let us go back, let us undo the tear in the wall and we can make sure this will never happen again," I said looking around the table.

The council is silent for a long moment, the weight of their decision palpable. Finally, Tanya rose from her seat, her robe was trailing behind her as she stepped toward the center of the chamber.

"Very well," Tanya said gravely, "We will grant you permission to cross the Sands of Time. But heed our warning: the path ahead is dangerous. Time does not forgive mistakes. You will face your own fears, your own regrets. If you falter, you may lose yourselves forever."

Chapter 26
Crossing the Sands of Time

We all stood up at her direction and she raised her hand on the floor in the center of the room.

A towering hourglass rose from the ground surrounding the entire chamber. When it had fully risen from the ground, it had begun to glow with a golden light in the middle of where the two glass bulbs met. The air shimmered with energy as the council raised their hands towards it to activate it.

A doorway appeared as I went to where the others were, and we were all guided to go into the glass bulb.

"Once you have completed your task, say, "End Time" and then it should bring you back in front of the council," Tanya said as we nodded. She closed the glass door, and locked it, and soon the sand in the room started to move around at our feet and around the room.

"The Sands of Time await you. Step carefully, forward, and may the threads of time guide you to the moment you seek to undo," Tobey said as the sand stormed around us for a few minutes.

The landscape is desolate and eerily quiet, the vast expanse of the great White Wall was towering before me, James, Kaide,

Socrat, and Michael. Time swirled around us in a distorted haze. The Sands of Time were churning under our feet as we stood in the exact moment before we first tore the Wall.

"This is it. We go back, we fix the White Wall, and we stop the creatures," Kaide said to everyone feeling relieved glancing at everyone who nodded.

"Let's do this!" Socrat said stepping forward smiling, "No turning back now."

"We can't fail," I said gripping Brent's hand, "Not this time."

"The fate of the Village of Pequa—and the world—rests in our hands so we must undo the moment we tore the White Wall," Michael said confidently as we had begun to approach our past selves.

"Look the wall hasn't been torn yet but it seems to be imminent," I said happily looking at the White Wall.

The air cackled with energy; a strange, unnatural hum was vibrating through the air. We could see our past lives younger, reckless, on the verge of making the same fatal mistake.

"What are you doing?" came a voice from behind us, it was Champa.

He then looked from us and then to our past selves as he understood what was going on.

"You went back in time just before it happened," Champa said wisely, "I understand."

"Champa, we know what we did was wrong in the end. We didn't understand the White Wall then," I said pointing to our past selves, "But we do now. We tore it apart and we are the only ones who can fix it."

Champa remained still noticing that he was watching our future selves and past selves at the same time.

"It's chaos we caused in the future. And chaos we must undo. If there's any chance to repair the Wall from the future. We are here to make sure it doesn't happen in our past, we must manipulate time itself to close it. Please... we don't have much time," Brent said looking at Champa.

"I am sorry for how we were behaving earlier," I said looking at Champa as he nodded, and backed away as he ushered us to stop our past selves, "We don't know what we don't understand."

"If you think that you can fix this and undo what you have done, then you must go," Champa said softly after a long pause, "But if you fail, you will doom not just Pequa, but the entire world. Remember that."

"We understand. And we'll make this right," Kaide said nodding, and then he looked at everyone, "Let's do this together!"

"There we are, just before it happened. We were so... careless." I said with a tight voice, as I stared at my past self looking at the others as they also were watching their past selves.

"We thought we were just explorers. We thought we were invincible," James said through clenched fists and regret, "But we had no idea what we were about to do."

"We were so hungry for adventure, so blind to the consequences. If we don't stop this—if we let it happen again," Kaide said in a voice heavy with emotion.

"Pequa will fall. The creatures will overrun everything. The village, the people—they will all die because of us," Socrat said finishing Kaide's thought.

"We must stop them. We must stop ourselves," Michael said staring at the wall, his voice was quiet but determined.

"This is it; This is where I used the sword to tear the rift into the White Wall," I said through tears, "We can't let it happen again."

"We have to stop them —now!" Kaide shouted urgently.

We all took a deep breath, as our hearts were pounding in our chests. The energy in the air pulsed as our past selves had reached the White Wall and we were just mere seconds away from repeating our own pasts.

"NO!" I shouted to my past self just in time before I had pulled out my sword.

Suddenly, our present versions of the group surged forward racing towards our past selves. The air around us distorted and warped but the timeline had not yet been locked—there was
still a chance for us to intervene.

"Don't do it! You have no idea what you are about to unleash! You think this is just another adventure but it's not—it's the end of everything!" James said grabbing his past self by the shoulder. James's past self-looked at the present James with wide eyes.

Past James froze and was just staring at his future self in shock and confusion.

"Who are you?" James stammered and was confused as he looked at his future self.

"I am you in the future. I'm here because we messed up—we destroyed the Wall! And now, creatures... monsters are killing everyone. You must trust me—don't touch the Wall! You are about to make a mistake that is going to ruin you." James said to his past self pleadingly.

At the same time, Kaide rushed past his past self and pulled him back from the wall as the others followed suit.

"You think you're strong. You think nothing can stop you. But you're wrong. If you touch that Wall, it all falls apart. Everything. You must listen to me," Kaide said to his past self, gripping his arm with his voice trembling. Staring at his future self, disbelief in his eyes. "This... this isn't real. It's a dream."

"It's not a dream. It's a nightmare. We caused this, but we're here to fix it. Please—don't let this happen," Kaide said shaking his head, eyes filled with regret.

Meanwhile, I stood before my past self with tears streaming down my face as I watched myself start to reach for the sword again.

"NO!" I shouted, "Stop! You don't know what you are about to do. I was you – I know what you are thinking. You want to prove to others that you can be a leader, flawless, wise, strong, and explore. But this... this will destroy everything and everyone we love!

"I... I don't understand. This is supposed to be... a discovery," my past self said to me my past self, hands trembled in fear around the sword that was being held near the wall.

"It is not a discovery—it's a mistake that you all will make." I said shaking my head and stepping closer with a voice of urgency, "If you decide to do what you are about to do to the wall, there is no going back and that is why we have come back, it was our last hope to stop my former self with the Time Council's permission, using the Power from Crossing the Sands of Time to use. Trust me. I know how much you want this, we

don't find the watch doing this, you must let it go. Please... for the sake of everyone we care about and for your future with Brent," I said nodding towards Brent, who was standing not too far away from us with his past and
future self at the same time as well.

Michael and Socrat were standing together staring at their past selves in disbelief as the younger versions of themselves glanced back and forth between them and then everyone looked at the wall.

"You can't do this. If you do, the dark creatures will come. They will tear apart everything. This is the only wall of protection that we have against them as no mortal weapon can kill them. You must let go of your pride, of your ambitions. Please, we have come this far—don't let it happen again as it did for us, don't let this be another regret that you all have in your lives!" Socrat said calling out to everyone in a strained voice.

Past Socrat lowered his hand, trembling, fear in his eyes.

"What do we do?" the past Socrat stammered looking at his future self and the others for direction.

For a moment, everything is still. The past versions of themselves hesitated, caught between their curiosity and the future warnings they now face. Then, slowly, they begin to lower their hands, stepping back from the Wall.

With sighs of relief from everyone we smiled to each other and nodded in gratitude.

"Place signs up along this wall, and warn everyone that the wall is a protection for this world, not to touch it because it will unleash creatures that are unknown to man and no mortal weapon can harm them so that this doesn't happen again," I suggested to my past self and to the past selves who nodded in agreement.

"Thank you, you have no idea how much this means to you," I said breathing out in a soft voice filled with relief.

Suddenly the air around us began to shimmer and warp and the timeline seemed to correct itself. The Wall, which had been pushing out negative unstable energy the entire time being a greyish color, started to glow into a soft, steady white again.

I looked over at the future James who seemed to be smiling as we all watched the Wall as it seemed to restore itself, as he looked at me and jumped giddily, "It worked, we did it, we stopped it!"

"Yes! We stopped it!" Michael said in a voice full of wonder smiling brightly.

"We… saved them," Kaide said letting out a breath, his voice heavy with emotion as I knew he was thinking about the Village of Pequa.

Tears rolled down my face in heavy emotion as I whispered, "We fixed it."

"Gather around everyone," Brent said motioning everyone's future selves to join in hands. "On the count of three, One Two, Three!" The ground beneath our feet began to shift as we all shouted, "End time!"

We held onto each other's hands as we were whisked away by time, while we held onto the relief and the hope that we had restored balance. The grainy-looking Sands of Time swirled around us one last time, pulling us back toward the present. We were by the Wall again this time there was no tear in as it stood before us whole and strong as if nothing ever happened.

"We fixed it!" I said with tears still streaming down my face as I looked at the wall.

"The wall is whole again! The creatures, they are gone. We... we did it!" Socrat said looking around shaking with relief and smiling happily at everyone.

"It's over, we changed it," Michael quietly said staring at the White Wall as it stood tall, unbroken.

We all stood in silence for a moment, the weight of what we had accomplished was sinking in. The world around us shifted and the Village of Pequa, and everyone in it was in one peace, safe, and whole, untouched by the horrors of what they had nearly unleashed. No lives were lost at the end of the day, and that made all the difference, and the feelings of the regret that they had felt though diminished, remained fresh in our hearts as it is what could have happened and could have been. We made signs and spread them along the wall to warn others not to come close to the wall due to the gravity of the situation of how it would change time itself. We advised no one to touch it or communicate with anyone who pushes through the White Wall. After the signs were posted we gathered and started to head back to the City of Sandglass.

"We changed time, and it worked out right the first time," James said turning toward everyone.

"We undid the damage," Kaide said nodding in approval of our efforts.

We walked down through the Village of Pequa as people watched us pass by without realizing what had happened.

"They aren't ever going to know what almost happened because you changed time to make it so that it never happened," Midnight's voice came into my head as I was trying to understand why people were not cheering at us for what we had done and then I nodded in understanding.

"What's the matter?" Brent asked me as he noticed I nodded

"We aren't going to get any cheers or congratulations or words of approval or affirmation," I said aloud to everyone as they looked at me as we walked toward the trenches.

"Why is that?" James asked curiously.

'Because we changed time so no one will know what once was or what could have been, not even the Time Council will know because by going back to undo what was done, it's as if it never happened," I explained smiling.

"So, we won't get into trouble with the Time Council because of what we did?" Kaide said looking at me as I nodded my head.

"What did we do again?" I asked laughing half-heartedly as everyone laughed.

We walked through the Underground as we passed the kids who were playing in the playground before.

"We saved them, and ourselves," I said aloud as I wiped tears from my face away as everyone nodded in understanding and gratitude.

We all arrived in the City of Sandglass and made it to our respective homes safely that night and slept soundly knowing that for now at least all was well and right in the world.

Chapter 27

Take Care of Yourself

I woke up the next morning in my room next to Brent who was sound asleep in my bed still, trying not to wake him. I decided to go on a walk. As I walked down the familiar street, I saw that James and Socrat were sitting on the side of the road looking stunned.

"Socrat, James, what is going on?" I asked walking up to them. James pointed inside the bookstore and was shaking as his voice was breaking, "He's... gone. I—I can't believe it. He was just... right here. How could this happen so fast?"

"I don't know baby. I don't know. It's not fair. It's. It's not fair at all. I'm so sorry," Socrat said with tears welling up, gently placing his hand on James's back, and rubbing it.

"We woke up this morning, and he had plenty of time!" James said almost angrily. "WHY?! Why did this happen?"

"Were you attacked last night or this morning? Was the house broken into?" I asked as Socrat shook his head.

"Well, who died? How?" I asked as no one seemed to answer me.

"I – I didn't even get to say goodbye properly. He was here one minute, and now, he's just... gone. What am I supposed to do without him?" James said choking back sobs.

"Why are you both sitting out here?" I asked curiously.

"We were staying here at the bookstore because James's dad's place is being worked on. We woke up this morning and came downstairs to see James's dad, Kaide dead on the floor," Socrat explained.

"How?" I asked as Socrat shrugged, "If he had years on him what happened them?"

"One thing you need to understand Bella is that just because you have the currency of time on your hands doesn't mean you have time to live forever," Emrys said in my mind softly in his deep voice.

"What do you mean?" I asked aloud not realizing it.

"Well, we don't know—" Socrat started to say and then I interrupted.

"Oh sorry, I was talking to Emrys," I said aloud looking at Socrat.

"Oh, what did he say?" Socrat asked.

"He said that just because you have the currency of time on your hands, doesn't mean that you have the time to live forever," I said softly as James looked up at me.

"What the hell does that mean?" James asked slightly angrily.

"You can have all the time left but if your body isn't in shape, it makes your time go faster, it shortens your life," I explained. "Now James, you don't have to do anything right now. Just…

just breathe. I am here. I am not going anywhere, okay? We will get through this together, I promise," Socrat said motioning for me to talk to him later, wiping his tears as I nodded.

"I loved him so much Socrat. He was my rock, my everything. I don't know how to handle this. I feel like my life around me is falling apart," James said sobbing and crying harder clinging to Socrat.

"I know baby, I know. He loved you so much, too. You were everything to him. I saw the way that he looked at you—so proud. He would have wanted you to remember that, even now," Socrat said holding James tightly as tears were streaming down his face.

"I just—I didn't think that it would happen like this. I wasn't ready to lose him. I thought we had more time," James said with his voice trembling.

"No one is ever ready for these things, there never is enough time," Socrat said sobbing softly thinking of his own family, but holding James close, "But you... you gave him so much love, James. Every day, he knew how much you cared, he knew, and I know he was proud of the man you are and have become."

"Do you think so? I just... I keep thinking I should have done more. Been a better son, told him I loved him more often,"

James said looking up, his eyes were red and swollen from crying and tears.

"You were more than enough. He knew exactly how much you loved him, trust me. You were there for him when it mattered, and that's what he will take with him. He wouldn't want you to think you weren't enough. You were a perfect son to him," Socrat said holding James's face and looking into his eyes.

"I don't know how to do this without him," James whispered breaking down, "I feel so empty."

"You don't have to do it alone. I'm right here. I will be with you every step of the way, even when it hurts like this. I will cry with you, scream with you, whatever you need. I love you so much, James," Socrat said to him as tears were falling down his face as he held James tighter and closer to him.

"I don't know what I would do without you," James said crying into Socrat's shoulder. "I just... I'm so scared. I've never felt this broken before."

"I'm scared too, but we will get through this," Socrat said with a soft but steady voice, "You are not broken, James. You are grieving and that is okay. You are allowed to feel all of this. And when you can't hold yourself up, I will be here to carry you, even if we both fall apart for a while."

"Thank you, for being here for me, for everything. I don't know how I would make it through without you," James said in a muffled voice against Socrat.

"You never have to find out what it's like to be alone going through this, because I'm not going anywhere. Ever. I love you, James. We will take this one moment at a time. Together," Socrat said to him as I smiled at Socrat, and nodded through tears.

"I love you too Socrat, so much," James said nodding and sobbing quietly as he was holding Socrat.

I walked into the bookstore to see a white sheet on the floor and turned towards the doorway to see Brent standing there.

"I had wondered where you had gone and was told you went into the City on your own," Brent said seemingly out of breath, "I only just heard and was worried about you."

I nodded towards the sheet on the floor through tears. I bent over the motionless body, pulled up the timecard of Kaide, and saw that he still had over fifty years left of time. I pulled the time out of Kaide and then went over to James who was sitting on the street and held his arm.

"What are you doing?" James said noticing time was being added to his timecard.

"That was your father's time," I said calmly, "It was either going to be given to you from me or one of the Timekeepers when they come to pick up your father," I said looking at Socrat who nodded in gratitude to me.

James used his other arm to wipe his nose as he nodded towards me.

"It seems your father didn't die from lack of time, so Emrys was saying there are other ways people die here in the City of Sandglass?" I asked as Socrat nodded towards me to walk inside.

Brent came out to comfort James, as Socrat talked to me in the bookstore.

"James's dad told me once in passing before we left for the Time Council on the night we were at the campsite," I said, "He had said, You may have time currency but if you don't have your health, your time currency is worth-less because it runs faster."

There was a moment of silence and then I continued, "He knew he was dying; It must have been his heart. He was saving more time for his son, which is what he wanted to make sure was done if something ever happened to him."

"Thank you for giving that time to James," Socrat said smiling at me as I nodded.

"You mean he knew and you knew?" I asked as Socrat nodded through tears.

"Why didn't he ever tell James that he was dying?" I asked Socrat.

"Some people don't want to be swooned over when they are about to die. He wanted to die in dignity doing what he loved, spending time with his son. I was never to tell James I knew," Socrat explained softly as I nodded.

"We will bury him properly," I said calmly as Socrat and I slowly

picked up Kaide's body and brought him to a cart that was outside with the Timekeepers who had just arrived.

"Where to Night Hunter Master?" asked the Timekeeper.

"To the cemetery of the dignitaries," I said calmly as Brent, Socrat, and James looked at me wide-eyed.

"But sire, that cemetery is reserved for—" said the Timekeepers looking at me in concern.

"I know what it is for, and he was one of them. If it weren't for him, we would not be alive today. If you only knew," I explained harshly as they quickly nodded and saluted me.

"Are you sure Bella," James asked through tears as I nodded, "Of course!"

"I am so grateful to have you all as friends!" James said through tears who was now balling in emotion.

By that evening we had the burial for Kaide. It was a small ceremony, but everyone felt it was the right thing for Kaide that we did this for him.

"Thank you, Bella," James said as Brent, and I got up from our seats at the cemetery as the ceremony ended.

"Of course, James. You have a good night, try to get some sleep," I said calmly as I said goodbye to Socrat and James.

Brent and I walked home back to the Time Tower in silence as the night crickets and cicadas chimed in their peaceful chorus of humming tunes.

Brent grabbed me lovingly by the hand and smiled looking at me as we walked on, and I looked at him and smiled slightly.

"What?" I asked him

"Today may have been a rough day with losing Kaide, but at least we are still together." Brent said as I nodded, and he continued.

"We are healthy and support each other no matter what," Brent said smiling at me as I nodded and smiled again.

He leaned on me as we stopped to see the sunset in front of us, "Can we let time stand still long enough to enjoy this time we have together?"

I smiled as I patted his head lovingly and then looked at him, "Time stands still for no one," I said looking at him as a small breeze of wind pushed past us as he nodded.

We then walked on down the road towards the Time Tower with his arm around my waist.

"What do you think happens to us after we have lived our time here?" he asked me curiously, seemingly thinking about Kaide.

"I think we move on to bigger and better things, peace, a place of no worry, and unconditional love," I said looking ahead as we came up to the tower within a few more minutes in contemplative silence.

"When do you want to have the wedding?" he asked me as I smiled as he looked at the ring on my hand.

"I wanna make sure we are okay together more first, I am in no rush," I said calmly looking at him.

"I wanna get married soon!" he said, turning towards me as we stopped at the doorway.

"Why soon?" I asked curiously now holding both his hands.

"Isn't Kaide's death proof enough?" he asked me, "Heck we may die tomorrow but we don't know for sure. We are one choice, and sometimes one small interaction or transaction away from leaving this world and we never know for sure," he said worriedly.

"My dear Brent," I said looking at him kissing his hand that was in my hand, "Our lives here are never guaranteed for tomorrow. Even as we are talking right now, someone may be minutes perhaps seconds away from breathing their last breath and yet we still move on, as we all must. We need to learn that we must not take things and people in our lives for granted, for it is their kindness and their love that matters in the end. It doesn't always mean there is an ulterior motive for what others do for us, just like there shouldn't be one for our acts of goodness and kindness for others."

I kissed Brent's forehead as he remained silent and then nodded his head in understanding as we opened the door to the Time Tower, and he continued to hold my hand as we walked towards my room.

"You never cease to amaze me at how much wisdom you have within you Bellatrix Kai, and each time I learn from you," Brent said as we walked on down the empty hall, "I fall, more and more, for you every day. I feel even deeper in love with you."

I blushed and smiled in silence as I pulled out my key and opened the door and closed it behind us.

Then, Brent started to get ready for bed for the night as I picked up the various envelopes that had come into the room, organized them in my hand, and put them on my desk.

I then went to lie down in bed to go to sleep. Within minutes Brent was snoring in his sleep with his arm around me as I lay on my back with my hands behind my head thinking about the day's events, unable to go to sleep.

Chapter 28

Strengthening Relationships

"Marriage," I thought to myself smiling while watching Brent snore in his sleep. I could tell he was tired as he had yawned on the way home towards the Time Tower that night from the Cemetery.

"That is a heavy word," came a voice in my head, it was Midnight.

"I'm sorry if I startled you," he said hooting softly in my mind, "I just figured you would want to talk to us since you seem to not be able to sleep with today's events still fresh in your mind."

"You know what I like to do when I can't sleep," Emrys started to say as Midnight interrupted.

"We don't sleep so don't you even start with that!"

I laughed to myself.

"I know listen to us fighting like an old married couple," Midnight started to laugh at his own joke.

"Haha, very funny," Emrys said seriously back.

"Midnight, Emrys, I need your guidance. Brent and I just got engaged and I can't stop thinking about what marriage means and how it will change our lives," I said with my mind full of anxiety.

"Marriage is indeed a significant milestone in life, Bella. It's a commitment to be with someone through thick and thin, to love and support each other, to grow together, and to share a life together," Midnight hooted happily

"Yes, marriage is a sacred bond that should be cherished and nurtured. It's not just about the wedding day or the fancy rings, but about the love, respect, and understanding that you have for each other," Emrys said wisely.

"I want to make sure that Brent and I are ready for this next step. I want our marriage to be filled with love, joy, and understanding. How can we ensure that we are prepared for this journey together?" I asked laying on my back with my hands behind the back of my head as I looked at the sky outside the bedroom window.

"Communication is key, Bella. Make sure that you and Brent are open and honest with each other, and that you listen and truly hear what the other is saying. Trust and respect are also vital in a successful marriage," Midnight said encouragingly.

"Remember to always be there for each other, to support each other's dreams and aspirations, and to be each other's rock in times of need. Marriage is a partnership, a team effort; together, you can conquer anything," Emrys added

"Thank you, Midnight and Emrys, for your wise words. I feel more at ease now, knowing that Brent and I have your guidance as we embark on this new chapter in our lives. I will cherish our marriage and make sure to enjoy every moment of it," I nodded in agreement with Midnight and Emrys.

"We will always be here for you, Bella. Trust in your love for each other and in the strength of your bond. Congratulations on your engagement, may your marriage be filled with happiness and love," Midnight said happily.

"And remember, Bella, marriage is a journey, not a destination. Enjoy the ride, embrace the challenges, and celebrate the victories. You and Brent are a team, and together, you can conquer anything that comes your way," Emrys said encouragingly as a warmth came over me.

"Thank you both. I am going to get some sleep now," I said feeling my body settling to get rest.

"Goodnight Bella," Midnight and Emrys both said after another as I nodded and said, "Goodnight."

I closed my eyes and fell asleep for the night smiling at the thought of a wedding with Brent.

Meanwhile, Socrat was trying his best to support and comfort James as this was the first night that they were going to sleep without Kaide being alive and Socrat was nervous for James. The room is dimly lit, the soft glow of the moon casting gentle shadows across the space. James sat on the edge of the bed, his face pale and drawn with grief. His eyes are distant, still reeling from the loss of his father, Kaide, whose death has left a gaping hole in his heart.

Socrat stood quietly beside him, his gaze tender and filled with concern. He watched James in silence, understanding the weight of the moment, feeling his boyfriend's pain as though it were his own. He stepped forward, slowly kneeling before James, his hands gently resting on James's knees.

"James, I'm here. You don't have to go through this alone," Socrat said in a soft voice filled with love.

James's eyes well up with tears, his hands trembling as he reached out, resting them on Socrat's shoulders. His grief is palpable, raw, and overwhelming, but in Socrat's presence, this is an anchor—something for James to hold onto in the storm of his emotions.

"I don't know how to do this... how to be without him. It hurts so much, Socrat," James said as his voice was breaking.

Socrat's heart ached to see James like this. James was so vulnerable, so broken. He cupped James's face gently in his hands, his thumbs brushing away the tears that fell freely now down James's face.

" You don't have to do it alone. I'm with you, always." Socrat whispered.

Their eyes locked, the air between them thick with emotion. Socrat leans in, his lips brushing against James's in a soft, tender kiss. The kiss was slow, full of unspoken promises, and shared pain. The kiss deepened, becoming more intense as James clung to Socrat, James need for comfort, and connection was now overwhelming.

"I need you... I need to feel something... anything other than this pain, loss, and grief." James whispered against Socrat's lips.

Socrat pulled James close, holding him tightly as they sunk back onto the bed. There was a sense of urgency now, not out of lust, but out of a desperate need to be close, to find solace in one another. Their hands roamed over each other's bodies, not in search of passion, but in search of comfort, grounding each other in the present moment.

"I love you, James. I'm here... I'll always be here," Socrat said in a voice of emotion.

They continued to move together, their touches slow and deliberate, each one filled with love, with a desire to heal the wounds that ran deep. Their connection transcends the physical—it's a merging of souls, a shared understanding that they are each other's safe harbor in this storm.

As they lay together afterward, their bodies entwined, James buries his face in Socrat's chest, his tears soaking into his shirt. Socrat runs his fingers through James's hair, his touch soothing and gentle.

"I don't know what I would do without you," James said in a muffled voice.

"I am not going anywhere my love," Socrat said holding him closer to him.

They stayed like that, wrapped in each other's arms, their breathing slowly evening out. In this moment, amid the pain and the loss, they found a small measure of peace in their love, knowing that if they have each other, they can face whatever comes next as they fell asleep for the night.

Chapter 29

Planning for a Minute to a Lifetime

It was the next morning that I awoke to see Brent watching me and smiling as he seemed to have been up for a while first. "What is it?" I asked him curiously wondering why we was smiling at me silently.

"I am just happy that you said yes to marrying me yesterday to spend the rest of our lives together," he said smiling gratefully as I smiled at him back.

"We must get serious about the wedding planning! There is so much to do, and when did you want to get married? I was thinking we need to figure out our budget," I said looking at Brent who only smiled at me.

"We can get married anytime," Brent said after a few minutes of silence, "We can get married six months from now or a year from now, or even if you want to elope, we can get married tomorrow."

"Elope? Tomorrow?" I said in surprise, noticing how laid back he was being about it.

"I am just kidding. Let's shoot for some time this year," he said noticing my reaction about getting married tomorrow.

"I'm sure that you wish David and Sharon were here?" he asked me curiously.

"Yeah, but I know if they were here, they would be happy for us," I said sadly.

He nodded his head in understanding.

"What kind of budget do you want to spend?" I asked trying to think realistically.

"Right, budget. I was thinking we just throw a number and try to stick to it. Maybe 10k hours?" he said calmly.

"You can't just "throw a number" out! We need to break it down. The cost of where we will get married, the food, the clothes, decorations, music, flowers, place settings and centerpieces for the meal and the reception afterwards... everything adds up," I explained.

Brent seemed to be lost in thoughts of what I was saying.

"I was thinking we could spend about 40% on the venue and catering, 15% on photography and videography, and—wait, am I overwhelming you?" I said looking at him as his eyes got larger.

"No, no, I'm with you. We need a plan. How about we start with the guest list first? I also already have the venue set up," Brent said as I nodded in agreement.

"Good idea, well the Time Council, and the Night Hunters for sure, and the Timekeepers, and then your parents, and James and Socrat, grandfather, and then Michael. So that's maybe 150 people total?" I said looking at Brent who nodded.

Brent seemed to be thinking for a few minutes and then he said, "I also have some more family that you haven't met yet that I would like to come so maybe 200?"

I nodded in agreement.

"So, 200 invitations, announcements, and also 200 plates of food and drinks, and also the venue would have to be able to hold 200 people as well," I said thoughtfully.

"Great!" Brent said smiling at me.

"Where did you want to get married?" I asked him as he looked at me quietly, "Unless we could look to see if the church could host us? Unless you want it done outdoors? Or at another location?"

"We have another idea," Brent said smiling as he got up and started getting dressed.

"We? What are you doing?" I asked him as he smiled at me mischievously

"Get ready Bella," he said smiling at me as I got up, and got dressed to get ready to go.

Within minutes we were walking down the familiar road in the City of Sandglass, and we arrived at the bookstore.

"Honestly James there is not enough room here in the bookstore for over 200 people, not even in the secret room," I said shaking my head.

He then smiled and put out his hand for me to grab it and then we walked into the house.

"Hey Brent," his mom said smiling at him and then to me, "What are you up to?"

"Mom, Dad," Brent said smiling proudly, "I have officially asked Bellatrix Kai to be my wife, and she said Yes!"

It was then that his mom and dad gave us both congratulatory hugs and shed tears of happiness for us.

"When do you want to have it?" Brent's dad asked, smiling at him.

"This year," Brent said holding my hand up to his lips as he kissed it.

"This year!" Grant Genuit said happily smiling at his grandson as he came into the bookstore area, "I am so happy for you both!"

"Thank you, grandpa!" Brent said, smiling proudly showing them the ring I was wearing, "We were talking, and I told her. We would like to hold the wedding here."

"That room is a library and its updated daily, I wouldn't want to disrupt the process in which it updates itself," I said in concern, "We could use the church like everyone else does."

"You are not everyone else to me Bellatrix Kai, you are going to be my wife," Brent Genuit said firmly, "I want everything to be perfect for us. Besides, I wasn't talking about that room."

Brent looked at his father who smiled and then said, "Ah, Oh."

Brent looked at his grandfather as they both smiled and looked at each other mischievously.

"Boys, what are you up to?" Brent's mom said curiously.

"Well, honey, one day when we were studying Brent and I stumbled across another secret room here in the bookstore," Brent's dad explained to his wife who had her hands on her hips.

"And when may I ask were you going to tell me about this?" she said in slight disappointment.

"The right time never came up until now," Brent said trying to save his dad from his mother's fury.

"Humph," Brent's mother said shaking her head at her son.

"Anyway. Bella, follow me, I have something I want to show you that I have been working on," Brent said winking at his grandfather smiling at me, taking my hand as his parents and grandfather followed us to the kitchen.

The memory of his grandfather being on the floor in the kitchen hit me as we stopped at the exact spot where it had happened. Brent opened the pantry door that was against the wall and knocked three times on the wall and then suddenly the pantry came to life and opened even more. The door revealed a huge room even larger than the hidden library. The room was already decorated with twenty tables of ten place settings the centerpieces were all set up with flower vases with hour sandglasses set up in them and there were two candles on them with decorative plates and white tablecloths. There was an area in the front of the room set up for a live band to the left and in the middle was a podium and an area where we could say our vows in front of rows of benches for people to sit at.

"I figure we could have the wedding here and the reception here as well," Brent
said smiling at me as I looked in awe at the room and the decorations that were already set up.

"You did this already for me?" I said through tears as Brent looked at me with both of his hands on his hips proudly smiling at me and giving me a side hug. The room had already been decorated with fresh flowers of assorted colors as I looked around the room.

"We just need a caterer, and we need to set up a vendor for an open bar. I was thinking maybe make it a buffet set up, so people have options," Brent explained as I nodded in understanding and kissed Brent on the cheeks.

"I wanted to help with what I could so far. I replace the flowers every week just in case," Brent said smiling at me, "It just took forever for me to pluck up the courage to ask you!"
I turned a slight pink in the face and said, "This room looks amazing!"

"There is another way to get into this room too," Brent said showing me a set of doors. We walked through them, and I recognized that it opened into an alleyway that led to the church.

"I figure we will tell people to come in and out this way from the alleyway so that this secret remains a secret, and no one will use this secret entranceway during the wedding and that can be kept between us," Brent said as I nodded.

"As far as the ceremony goes do, we use the traditional vows, or do you want us to write our own?" he asked me as I looked at him seriously.

"We will use the traditional vows," I said looking at him, "Through sickness and health and for richer or poorer."

He smiled at me as I noticed he seemed to enjoy talking about the wedding and upcoming nuptials.

His parents were smiling at us and shaking their heads as they saw how well we were working together to plan things out.

"You don't need to have it all planned out this minute," Brent's Father said laughing at us, "you act as though you are getting married next week."

Brent looked at his dad seriously at first.

"Not that that isn't okay either, it's up to you both," He said realizing Brent wasn't saying anything and then Brent laughed then said, "We are both prone to rash decisions, but no, we are thinking next year."

He then turned to me and asked, "Did you want us to find out own officiant or priest or someone we know? Or should we hire someone?"

"I think I know someone," Grant said.

"Thank you grandpa!" Brent said nodding to his grandfather.

It was then that Brent's parent's gave us both hugs and Brent's mom said, "This is going to be like a fairytale wedding to rival all other weddings that have happened here in the City of Sandglass! We are also buying the 8-tier cake for you both and the catering you just must let us know who you want to be your caterer or what kind of foods you want available for the guests!"

"That is going to cost a lot of time Mom," Brent said worriedly.

"No hun, it's not going to be that bad," Brent's mom said reassuringly.

"Well, we are both very excited for the both of you," Brent's dad said looking at his wife as she and he left the room and went back to the bookstore.

"You have been planning this for a while, haven't you?" I asked him with a look of accusation as he nodded guiltily.

"Grandpa and I have been planning this for six months so far and putting this room together as soon as we found it. He knew my intentions with you have been serious so he has been getting people in to decorate, set up the tables and chairs and decorate them and then I have been continuing to renew the flowers weekly because I haven't been sure when I was going to have the chance to propose after I had gotten your ring," he explained as I nodded in understanding.

"That's why your grandpa was smiling the way he was when you told him you wanted to have it in the other room. Even your parent's didn't know what you two were up to?" I asked

Brent shook his head and then smiled and added, "We had a few close calls when they could have found out, but they never did."

"I would like to go to David and Sharon's house really quick," I said looking at the ring and then around the room.

"I didn't need to get permission from them to marry you when they were alive did I?" he asked worriedly

"No not them but you should have asked permission from my siblings at least from the Time Council," I added smiling jokingly.

"Oh no!" he said putting his hand to his forehead, "I knew I was forgetting something."

"It's okay," I said smiling at him as we left out of the room onto

the alley way by the church. I led the way towards David and

Sharon's house.

Chapter 30

The Daughter We Never Had

When we had gotten to their home, there was a for sale sign in front of the house for 30,000 hours. It was dark and gloomy looking as I let myself in.

"Is Theodore here?" Brent asked nervously looking around. "I don't think he likes me."

"No, Theodore has already gone through the house," I said remembering a note from him in the room that was left for me from him. He had told me to look through the house to see if there was anything I would want since he took what he wanted already before it is sold as is."

Brent nodded.

"So where is he living now?" Brent asked me

"From my understanding, he still resides in the Time Tower for now but plans to move out of the City and into an outlying village," I explained looking around the room.

I started to tear up as I looked in the kitchen.

"This is where I would always find Sharon," I said through tears, "I looked around the kitchen and was reminded of multiple memories of her talking about life lessons and teaching me, giving me cooking lessons, and watching her prepare dinner for David on many occasions.

"You cut the cucumber with your fingers bent like this so that you don't cut your fingers and your knuckles rest against the blade, so you have better control of your cutting," Sharon's voice came into my head.

I wiped the tears from my eyes as I walked into the room to see there was three envelopes on my bed addressed to me.

"What is that?" Brent asked me as I turned to him after I realized what they were.

"They are letters that were left for me. Theodore must have found it amongst his parent's possessions and this one is from him," I said holding up all of them as I started to cry, "Please leave me be for a while."

Brent nodded silently and respectfully left the room and went to sit in the living room.

I took in a deep breath opening the envelopes one by one that were left on the bed. One was from David and the other clearly a lot longer was in the formal handwriting of Sharon addressed to me.

I read the first one written from David first.

To my Dearest Bellatrix Kai,

If you are reading this right now, obviously something terrible must have happened to my life and therefore am no longer around. I have found it difficult to write this farewell letter as I am not sure what to say or what it would mean to you for me to write this to you. I know that we must move on from this world as you know we all must on our own time. Ever since that day that we met, when our unit had stormed the Village of Pasqua, I still remember the scared little girl full of innocence staring at me in fear. I had realized then that you had seen your own parents get killed in front of you. Not a day has gone by when I haven't thought of that day. I have felt the need to protect you since then and shield you from the horrors of this life ever since. You have been the daughter that I never had. I am not sure what to say other than ever since that day, I have had the feeling that in a way you resent me. For not doing more, even though you never said it, your eyes have told me, I have owed you an apology. An apology for not only for "only doing what I was told to do and to follow orders without question," as Kahn had said. But I owe you an apology for not doing more that day, possibly stopping the events that happened that fateful day from happening. Perhaps I should have tried to do more to have prevented the deaths of almost everyone you knew and cared about. It would be wrong of me to say that I am happy that things happened the way that they did as I would not have wished the deaths that had occurred that day. But I am happy that even with the events that had occurred, that I got to save you. I'm grateful that you were able to come into me and Sharon's life. Since that day, I have

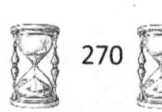

vowed to myself that I would protect any other lives lost by our unit's account from ever happening. If I am no longer around, we may not have had a choice other than to protect ourselves at the time of my demise. It is with regret that I have written this letter to you in a way because I would have liked to have had a chance to see you and Theodore grow up and live your lives. I so wish that things would have been different so that maybe we could have met you under different circumstances and your parents would be alive. Some part of me felt like you wanted me to have done more that day to prevent the loss that had occurred from those in the Village of Pasqua and for that I am so sorry. But all Sharona and I want more than anything is for you to be happy, to live your life to the fullest, and to find your purpose. Be happy, and ultimately find love and hold onto it tightly. I know maybe even you and Brent would make a beautiful couple. I am so proud of you and what you have accomplished in your life and the beautiful, strong, independent, courageous, and loving, caring woman you have become and grown to be. I will always be in here, in your heart and I am so proud to have been able to be like a stepfather for you, I love you!

Forever,

David Johnson

I started to tear up halfway through the letter because I knew in my heart, I needed to hear this from him in person. Knowing he was gone and that I couldn't hug him hurt even more. I folded up the letter and put it in the envelope and then I looked at the other envelopes and noticed one was written in the hand of Sharon and then the other I assumed was Theodore's.

I started to read the one from Sharon wiping my eyes of tears as my hand started to shake as I took two deep breaths to calm down.

My Beautiful Bellatrix Kai,

First, I want to tell you how proud and honored I am that you were a part of our lives. I am so proud of the woman that I have seen you grow to become even though at times you never knew it, I have always been watching you. Seeing you growing to become the woman you are today has brought such extraordinary joy into our hearts. Ever since you came into our home on the first day, in a basket of rice. I have sensed a great strength in you, there has been a strong resilience within you against all odds of adversity that was against you from the start of losing your parents. Seeing you deal with Kahn and get over your fear of swords, it brought to us a sense of pride to see how courageous and brave you are. We are so proud of you seeing how you are holding up even after seeing death and loss and calamities in the world going on around you. I am so proud of you, especially when I saw you push through internal feelings of anger with Kahn, while ensuring it didn't affect your character, and your own integrity, and who you are as a person, it has brought great inner strength in David and me. As much as the temptation was to exact revenge on him, you persevered, and you overcame it. When David and I saw that, we knew then that no matter what we all face together, we can get through it all together.

Even though I have passed on from this world, and even if I am not here physically, if you remember me and smile, I will continue to always be in your heart. From the moment you came into my life, you brought a light that I never knew existed and I never knew I was missing. You filled a space I my heart that I always longed to share, and in you, I found the daughter I never had. Watching you grow and triumph over obstacles has been one of my greatest joys of my life. I am so proud of the incredible person you have become. You have taught me so much about love and generosity; I will always be grateful for that. You were the daughter we never had, and your presence around David and I was the light of our house. I remember when you were helping me in the kitchen doing dishes and cooking dinner when you told me how anxious you were for Brent to learn to walk again and that you wanted it more than anything so I could eventually meet him. I smiled because I could tell even then that you had within you a strong motivation to help those around you be successful and that you weren't going to give up on Brent that easily. It made me smile that day and I started to love you even more like a daughter. You were a part of our lives every day filling the void David, and I had felt when Theodore was absent. You bring such immense joy and love to those around you. Even though you have been through so much loss, seen so much death, and have felt so much grief and even though you have had to face the challenges of adversity, it is amazing to see how much love you still have within you. I have seen your fierce, fiery, caring tenacity. Your perseverance of burning love, and bravery within you burn so brightly in your aurora. It is so full of positive intentions that it energizes those around you and attracts people to want to be near you just to feel it.

As we say goodbye, know that this isn't an end, but a new chapter, a new beginning for you. Chase your dreams, embrace the world and never forget I am cheering you on from afar. Our bond transcends distance, you will always be a part of my heart. Remember the laughter and memories we have, the moments of vulnerability and the dreams we painted together. I will cherish those memories forever, especially of you being my Night Master and my Time Council Member. You have changed how things are just with your very presence around others. I am so excited about what adventures await you. You have so much to offer this world, and they are ready for you! Take care of yourself, my dear Bellatrix. You are loved more than you know and could ever imagine, and I will be waiting for the day that we meet again. With all my love,

Sharon Johnson

I burst into tears and started crying. It was my fault, my fault that they were both no longer here. They were such a significant impact of the foundation of my life and now the memories of their once existence stay imprinted on my heart. In the dimly lit bedroom of Sharon and David, Bellatrix Kai sat on the edge of the bed, my heart heavy with the weight of the farewell letters I had just read. The words from my adopted stepfather felt like a distant echo, filled with well wishes but lacking the warmth for which I had hoped. In contrast, my stepmother's letter was a tapestry of memories, woven with affection and understanding, each line stirring a bittersweet mix of nostalgia and sorrow.

Tears brimmed in my eyes as I recalled the moments shared—cooking together, laughter echoing through the halls, and the gentle guidance that had shaped me. They were a loss that felt profound as if a part of my heart were being pulled away with their departure.

Just then, Brent, entered the room, sensing the somber atmosphere. His presence was a comforting contrast to the emotional turmoil inside me. He approached me cautiously, his eyes filled with concern.

"Bella, what's wrong?" he asked softly, kneeling beside me.

I looked at him, my voice trembling as I shared the weight of the letters. Brent listened intently, his hand finding mine, offering silent support. As I spoke, the warmth of his touch slowly began to ease the ache in my heart.

"It's just... they meant so much to me," I admitted, wiping away a tear. "I feel lost without them."

Brent squeezed my hand gently. "You're not alone, Bella. I'm here for you. We'll get through this together."

His words, simple yet profound, wrapped around me like a warm blanket, reminding me that even amid heartache, there was still love and a connection to be found, as I nodded and smiled at him as we held each other in a warm embrace.

It was then that I broke off the hug as I remembered there was still one more letter that I had left to read.

It was from Theodore as I looked at Brent and he nodded towards me as I opened the envelope that was marked, Bellatrix Kai.

Chapter 31

The Letter and Election Day

I took a deep breath and slowly let it out as I opened the envelope and unfolded the letter that was addressed to me. I looked at Brent as he nodded at me in encouragement with a serious face but a half smile. I could tell he was nervous about what it might say. I read it to myself in silence as Brent watched my face and reactions.

Bellatrix Kai,

I want you to know that I just read the messages that were left from my parents, and I know from their love from you that you wouldn't have hurt or tried to get them killed intentionally. I would like to believe that you did what you thought was the right thing to do at the time. My parents thought of you like their only daughter and therefore you truly had a tender place in their hearts.

The fact of the matter remains, they are not here and yet here you are. I don't know what truly transpired between my parents and you as I was not there and nor do I trust what Tyronne was saying about you either. But I cannot find it in my heart now to forgive you for what you could have done. Nor do I think I will ever forgive Tyronne for what he chose to do as he too had the freewill to choose to kill my mother and father or not regardless of him being ordered to do so.

I need to have some time to myself and therefore am leaving the house to you. I already talked to Theresa, and she is okay with this as this is my will to want to leave behind the fond memories that I have of my parents here and move on with my life. I have taken all my things from here as I know you noticed. I will be moving on to either another City of Sandglass with the signed letter of approval from all the other remaining Time Council Members or with an outer lying village. Maybe one day I will come back to visit and choose to revisit memory lane here, but for now I must go, and clear my mind and find inner peace of my own. I think of you like a sister as my parents thought of you as their only daughter. I am happy that you were able to come into my parent's life and bring them so much happiness.

Please continue to lead as a leader on the Time Council with integrity, love, compassion, and courage and live your life bravely. Please remember that though sometimes we are told to do things in our life by others around us, sometimes with good intentions or hidden intentions, I need you to remember to be your own boss. Lead the ship like a captain of your soul in the ocean of unwavering waters of your life. Don't be misguided to believe that there is only one way to accomplish things in your life.

Smile, be positive, find happiness, and continue to thrive and be yourself.

With Sincere Regards and eventually forgiveness

Theodore Johnson

I read it again aloud for Brent and then looked up at him.

"So, he hasn't forgiven you yet for not being there for your adopted stepparents?" Brent said as I shook my head and looked at him.

"Eventually he said in his letter that he will find it in his heart to do so," I said half smiling through tears.

Brent looked around the room and then said, "So officially, this house is yours?"

I nodded and looked at him.

"It's down the street from your bookstore," I said looking at him.

"I want us to start a family eventually, maybe we can eventually get a place of our own," he said looking at me as he smiled and then kissed me.

"Michael just got a place with his girlfriend I think too," Brent said as I nodded, "I forgot to tell you, they are holding elections this afternoon."

Brent then handed me a paper which read Time Council Elections begin today.

"How does this work again?" I asked trying to remember the last elections and couldn't.

"Oh, this is your first time?" Brent asked me as I nodded, "Oh that's right you never grew up here."

"So, follow me," Brent said smiling as he pulled me hand outside, and we started to walk down the street.

As we walked closer towards the middle of town by the square, it was packed with everyone in the City of Sandglass. Some of the people that were in front of us moved over to make way for Brent and I. There were thirteen large wooden boxes all labeled with the different various departments labeled in the front of them. On the table in front of the box was a number representing each of the hours of the clock and on top of the numbers was a pile of index cards with pens next to them.

Brent pointed to a poster above the table, and it had a list of the current Time Council Members and what they oversaw and below that there was listed a bunch of names, also to be considered below each department. Tim's picture had an "X" over it along with Terry and Tyronne's as names were listed below them.

"You see there you are!" Brent said pointing to my name smiling at me and then his face turned more serious.

"What's the matter?" I asked him as he pointed again.

"My name is listed as a potential member of the Time Council," he said nervously looking at his name in a serious face, listed below one of the hours.

I looked at the Time Council Box for the first hour representation where Tim McKobe used to be and there his name was Brent Genuit as clear as day. There were no other names there that had been elected thus far as several people came up to us whom I hadn't recognized.

"Hey Brent! I knew you were going to be elected onto the Time Council eventually! I trust the spot you are at especially with your girlfriend being in charge of the Night Hunters," said a guy with red hair and freckles, "You definitely have my vote to be Head of the Safety and Security Department of our City!"

I smiled at him, as Brent seemed to have unshaken himself out of a daydream and smiled at the man, "Thank you Jerry, it means a lot!"

At that at least twenty people added their names in box marked Hour 1.

"Well, maybe some people on the Time Council think you have what it takes to be a member. I know that with the both of us working together we will keep this City of Sandglass safe," I said smiling at him and a few people put their names in the boxes marked Hour 3 for me and Hour 1 for Brent. I then looked at him seriously realizing that he was looking at me feeling unconvinced, "What's the matter?"

"I am not sure if being a part of the Time Council is something that I could handle," Brent said seriously, "It is a lot of responsibility to be a leader of this city and there is a lot of pressure in order to be run things right and to make the tough decisions."

"Yes, in any role of leadership, it comes with a lot of responsibility. If you are unwilling to take on this type of a challenge, and to be willing to fail and fail again, how can you hope to be able to grow as a person interpersonally, and be successful?" I asked him as he frowned.

"Why do you enjoy being on the Time Council?" Brent asked

"Though I just started as a temporary leader in this position, I have learned so much, and we all have been through so much together," I smiled and explained looking at Brent who remained silent, "These people are precious to me. We all share a home, and we share a life and though we may not share ties of blood, the people of the City of Sandglass are all precious to me. They are like my extended family!"

"So how does this work?" Brent asked me as I shrugged silently.

"Well, if your name is the only one on the list then you are the only option for people to pick unless someone signs someone else's name on their paper. People can either print the name of someone on the list, or nominate someone else. Then in the back of the paper they must print their name and address and phone number down. As the ballots come into the box, the spotters come in and take the folded pages and mark how many votes people got and ensure that no one has voted twice for the same people. So, if there are five people then everyone of those people were given thirteen ballots each to write down who they choose or nominate on the index cards," James explained as we all jumped because he appeared out of nowhere behind us.

"So, because I am the only one on the ballot so far, I am the only one people have picked so far?" Brent asked nervously.

"Yes," James said as Brent nodded.

"What about when there are more than one person running up for the same slots," I asked curiously

"Then there is a second vote for everyone to vote for one of the two highest votes for that position tomorrow," Socrat said smiling looking at James as I nodded in understanding.

"I hope I get voted onto the council!" Socrat said smiling, "I nominated and voted for myself for Head of Social Injustice and as another judge for social and criminal cases," Socrat said.

"Do you have experience with the laws here?" James asked him curiously as Socrat shook his head.

"But I think I can manage being Head of Social Injustices," Socrat said confidently, "It has always been a dream of mine to be a leader here in the City of Sandglass."

"I don't know if it's a good idea for you Socrat," James said thoughtfully, "They may want someone who knows and follows all the laws here. I am afraid you will not succeed in that area, no offense, especially with no experience."

"But" Socrat started to say as I raised my hand for him to stop talking as Socrat and James looked at me thoughtfully. I then turned to Brent.

"If you don't want to be a Time Council Leader, What is it that gives your life a sense of meaning and purpose? If you don't know what it is that you showed up here to do, if you don't know why you are here, I encourage you to find out what your purpose is. Some people doubt themselves when chasing after their dreams when experiencing hardships. They like to complain but don't want to do anything about the situations that they are in. You must keep growing and stretching. Some people don't want to accomplish their dreams because of fear of failure – We all have inner fears inside ourselves, there is the fear of failure. Then there is the fear of success. What if you take on this roll of leadership and things don't work out? Or what if you do it, and you become successful and you can't handle the success and you fail? -These are not risk takers. Most people allow their fear of failure to out-way their desire to succeed. When you are willing to fail repeatedly. When you make up your mind to become unstoppable, then that will give birth to a part of yourself that you don't know even about you right now," I explained wisely as Brent nodded.

"I think that I want to accomplish my dream no matter what," Socrat said smiling at me happily, "You are right. I may not have experience in law, but I know what it's like to be different that the rest of society and treated differently. I know what it feels like to be treated like an outcast for being different, especially when it comes to family."

I remembered all too well what Socrat had faced coming out of the closet with his family and how much pressure was on him growing up. There was a level of perfection that he said he felt he had to have in order to get along better with his family, trying to be the best he could be.

I nodded at him in understanding.

"Socrat, Brent, I know you both will be great leaders! You just need confidence and encouragement," I said wisely, "Maybe the Council would allow you to split the Department with Tessa, and she could go on to still being a judge and you can be in charge of the Social Injustice Department."

It was then that I placed my voting cards in the boxes, and we sat at one of the tables nearby in the square and ordered drinks and food at one of the restaurants for a late lunch while we waited for the results. After three more hours the sun came to set, and the Time Council leaders appeared at the tables and cleared out the last of the votes. The counting of the votes started by the various current members for the boxes. I was called to the Hour 3 box and was told to start counting them.

After about an hour of counting and recounting votes, everyone was supposed to have one thousand votes in their boxes total and tallied for each of the nominations.

In my box, I had eight hundred votes plus there were still one hundred votes for Tobey in the box. I assumed it was because not every one of Tobey's former supporters was convinced even that I could handle being the leader.

It was then that Tina came over to me and said, "Looks like you got the majority votes for the spot still."

"What about your slot?" I nodded and asked her as she smiled.

"Everyone seems happy with the job I have done," Tina said smiling.

"Well, I am glad for that," I said happily looking over at her as I stood up.

The results were finally posted the next morning on an electronic billboard at the City entrance.

	Welcome to the City of Sandglass from the newly elected Time Council members:	
1	Head of Safety and Security Department (Timekeepers)	Brent Genuit
2	Head of Discipline for all citizens	Tina Marrowe
3	Head of Night Hunters	Bellatrix Kai
4	Head of Financial Dept	Tommy Kai
5	Head of Education and Civil Resources Dept	Sarah Bradley VS Sandra Davis

6	Head of Natural Resources	Hope Senitis VS Shania Towers
7	Head of Job Security and Placement	Laura Fidel VS Michael
8	Head of Health and Well Being Dept	Terrance Kindle
9	Second in command of financial Dept	Taylor Kai
10	Second in command of Night Hunters/special projects	Tobey Kai
11	Head of Social Injustices / Judge for Social and Criminal Cases – Special case 2 Leaders	Socrat and Tessa Stormberg
12	Head of Housing Authority	Tonya Diavecca VS Tierra Sondra

13	Duties Unknown/ 13th Hour Voting	James Tucker

"So, for the Hour slots that have two people listed on them we will have a second round of voting?" I asked Tommy Kai who was standing next me at his 4th Hour Box.

"Yes, for the fifth hour its Sarah Bradley VS Sandra Davis. For the sixth hour it's Hope Senitis VS Shania Towers. For the 7th Hour it looks like it's Michael VS Laura Fidel. Finally for the 12th Hour it's Tonya Diavecca who is Theresa's Sister VS Tierra Sondra." he explained. I curiously noticed that Tina had called people who were tied in 5th, 6th, 7th, and 12th Hour Boxes.

"Now that it is between the eight of you left, we will hold another round of elections. By tomorrow evening, we will see who amongst you are the newly elected Council members. Good luck to you all," Tina said as everyone bowed towards her, and left.

"Tina?" I asked looking over at her as she smiled at me acknowledging me, "What is involved in your department?"

"It is up to us to ensure that all the rulings that Tessa does in the eleventh hour are fully followed through with regarding all the punishments for the crimes committed. Our department ensures that the law takes its course with the help of the

Timekeepers and if they give us issues it will be up to Brent to ensure the Timekeepers are kept in line as well. Especially if some don't obey our rules of this City or report things properly. It's a checks and balances system, so no one department is give more work and we prevent corruption within the city and Time Council departments as well."

I nodded in understanding as she walked off clearing the unneeded hour boxes off the tables and bringing them into the Time Tower.

I looked at the remaining four boxes left in deep thought. "It's more than just boxes you know. They come with their fair share of weight and responsibility," Brent said looking over at me as I nodded, "What it comes down to is principles."

"What is the consensus of the City from what you have heard?" I asked Brent.

"Well for the 12th hour, Tonya Diavecca is the sister to Theresa and as you know when Theresa was leader, she didn't do much but stay in her room the whole time getting messages in and barely responding to messages from various Timekeepers and citizens. She was hard to reach to. Tonya, her sister is insistent that she is not her sister. That she can get things done for the people and improve the quality of life at the various homes that people live in. A lot of our homes have been run to the ground and need a lot of work. Tierra is using

Theresa as an example of how her sister ran as leader will be the same as how she will be as a leader. Tierra Sondra literally is saying, "Well her sister didn't do anything, what makes you think that her family can do anything to help everyone out? The apple doesn't fall far from the tree, and one bad apple ruins the bunch."

"These arguments are not going to help each other win," I said shaking my head in frustration as Brent went on to explain nodding his head in agreement with me.

For the seventh hour, you have Michael and Laura Fidel which of the two I am not sure which one will win that one. Michael has been using how he and Socrat took weeks to get placed into a job and how it really affected their quality of life being without a job and have access to food here without being able to get themselves established. And then Laura Fidel, I am not sure what her intentions are for the position of Head of Job placement and Job security other than she is Tanya's sister. Tanya herself hasn't even endorsed her sister which even though they have led private lives, they are not that close," James explained as I looked at him with a frown.

"Why didn't the town elect Tanya again?" I asked curiously

"Tanya has already had four elections as a leader. She could have run for another position on the council, but she can't have run for the same one again," Brent interjected.

"Next you have the sixth hour fighting for the Head of Natural Resources position Shania Towers who is popular but only for being evil and controlling and is always out to hurt those around her. She thinks she will win because everyone knows of her, but not in a good light. Some feel with her being known to be evil no one will be able to get any resources from us with her bulldog-like attitude towards people and life. And then there is Hope Senitis who wants to have the position, but she is fighting tooth and nail for it. Everyone loves an underdog like her too. Hope, well poor woman, she has had a rough upbringing. She is not very wanted or well-loved, not even by her own family who are very selfish people. She is not like her family though; she is determined to be successful and prove herself to be number one to everyone in her eyes. She pushes hard to be liked by the people around her, but in a way has lost her own identity, but she desperately wants to be the one to make her mark on the world," Brent explained nodding to James to explain the last Hour.

It was then that Brent and I started following James and Socrat to their home.

"Well, finally, we have the 5th hour, Tyeisha's former position," James said looking at Brent for help.

"Sarah Bradly and Sandra Davis both are fighting to be Head of Education and Civil Resources Dept," Brent said looking at

James who understood that James didn't have much to say on the matter, "Well the feud has been rough between both of them, quite practically mudslinging each other and not talking about where they stand on the positions."

"It will certainly be interesting to see who wins in the end," Socrat said smiling at me as I nodded silently as we arrived at their home.

"Well goodnight, Bella and Brent see you tomorrow," James said smiling and hugging us as he and Socrat said goodnight and went inside their home for the night Brent. I turned towards the Time Tower and decided to go to bed. We got home without any incident and crawled into bed for the night. I turned to my side facing the window in the bedroom and smiled. I know everything is going to be okay."

Chapter 32

The Four Hours

Brent and I had woken up late the next morning and headed downtown to vote.

"Well look who finally woke up and decided to place their votes!" Michael said smiling at us, "You are all voting for me, right?"

"Well, you desperately need us to vote for you this time!" Brent said lightly.

"Now boys, I am sure Michael will be grateful if you would place your votes for him," Michael's girlfriend said from behind him putting her hand at his waist, "I have all my friend's voting for you darling."

Michael nodded in gratitude as I looked at the four boxes left on the table.

I walked up to each of them and placed my votes in each box and walked away as more people crowded around the table to fill out their tallies and put them in the boxes.

As the hours pushed on, more of the votes came in as all the candidates seemed to get anxious and full of anxiety. It was then decided that each of the candidates were getting five minutes to talk each about the reason people should vote for them.

Within a few more hours, the sun was set and the final votes we're being counted individually.

"I don't know who is going to win," I said anxiously as I looked at the electronic board to see the blank spots for the numbers 5, 6, 7, and 12 for the leader spots.

"Did you hear that Shania Towers was out late last night?" Michael whispered to us.

"Really?" I said curiously.

"Yeah, word is she was so drunk that she lost a lot of her supporters at the bar she was at because they saw that she couldn't handle the position. She was plastered! She was talking so badly about Hope, that people wanted to vote for Hope now because they knew of how evil Shania could be."

"Oh wow," I said in complete surprise as I looked up and saw that Tina was trying to get everyone's attention.

"Alright everyone let's settle down now! Everyone has been waiting and the time has come for us to see who the new leaders are representative hours for the hours of 5,6,7, and 12 are. For the Head of Education and Civil Resources Department..." Tina said pointing at the electric board, which had pictures of all the already selected members with their corresponding department and hours they represent.

"Sarah Bradley!" Tina said as the board lit up with her name on it, "Next we have the representative for the 6th Hour, as

Head of the Natural Resources Department." Tina said as everyone seemed to anxiously be looking at the board.

"Hope Senitis!" Tina said and there was a lot of muttering in the crowd as Tina looked around in a slightly worried face, "Yes, this was a close race but be reassured we triple counted these votes!"

"Impossible!" Shania Towers said aloud to the crowd, "Are you saying that I lost to HER? This must be a fraud! This election is rigged! I demand to count each of these votes for each of us! I want another vote from everyone."

I observed Shania and she seemed to be in a half drunken stupor standing in front of everyone next to Tina who seemed to be a little angry.

"No, you lost Shania!" Tina said

"Do you know who I am?" Shania said, "My family owns the very Tower that the Time Council stays in. I deserve a seat non contest."

"That is not how it works Shania, We are a democracy here and vote for our leaders as a country. That's that," Tina said

"Was there One thousand votes?" Shania asked as Tina nodded.

"Just to make sure this is correct I will personally separate the cards and put them next to each other and we will all see that they are all from people with different names and addresses on them. There are no duplicates," Tina said defiantly as Hope turned a bright red in embarrassment.

It was then that Tina separated the voting cards out and put them on a pile next to each other. The exact number count on each side was the same three separate times 200 votes for Shania VS 800 votes for Hope. In the end, Shania nodded in understanding that there was nothing that she can do to gain the votes that she needed to have won.

"What happened to the people who originally voted for me?" she asked Hope in slight anger.

Hope shrugged.

"Look at yourself!" I said aloud, "You are drunk, and you claimed to be better than your running mate. Just because everyone knows you, doesn't mean people will vote for you. That is not how we decide. We decided based off who we think had a better chance at running this country and guiding it. You think that being evil, manipulative, and popular is good. Well, it's all fine and good to be known by others, but what is the reason that people know you. Is it because of the good you do for others? Is it the morals and values that you have that have helped people decide to vote for you? Or are you strictly relying on the family heritage?"

"You horrid little twerp, Who do you think you are judging me? You are just a poor village girl, sister to the other Kai

Council Members, you are no different then me! Earning your spot in the council because of your last name! No one cares about you! Nor do they care about your character. They just look at your siblings and think, she collaborates well with them so we will vote for her," Shania said to me angrily.

"SHE IS MORE THAN HER FAMILY HERITAGE!" Brent said angrily.

"Oh, look the little and embarrassed boyfriend, here to defend your girlfriend? Don't make me laugh. You are taking the place of the one who is at fault for the terror that was put on the Village of Pasqua? Such a name to live up to in ensuring our security for this lame City," Shania said aloud.

Just then there was a lot of booing from the crowd at Shania who walked away in slight shame in how much she had lost by.

"Alright everyone now for the next Council Member position for the representative of the 7th Hour for the Department of Job Security and Job Placement," Tina said motioning for people to look at the board which now listed Michael as the newly elected member, "Congratulations Michael!"

There was applause for him as he smiled happily at everyone, proudly thanking everyone around him.

"Alright everyone, now the moment we all have been waiting for, the newly elected representative of the Head of the

Housing Authority for the 12th hour is," Tina said looking at Tierra and then to Tonya who was on the other side of the crowd.

"Tonya Diavecca!" Tina said proudly pointing to the now full board with the new council members listed.

"WHAT!?" Tierra shouted angrily at everyone, "What is the matter with you people? Her sister didn't do anything the whole time she was a council member! Do you think that she will do anything? Her sister was lazy and didn't do anything! What makes you think that she will do anything? Don't you think I could have done a better job?"

"I am my own person, Tierra Sondra!" Tonya shouted angrily at her, "I am going to do a fantastic job at this position! You watch and see!"

"All you did is spend five minutes up there bashing Tonya!" Brent said to Tierra who shot a look at him, "You didn't exactly explain to any of us how you plan to lead this city or what you envisioned for us!"

"You and Bella, I swear!" Tierra said angrily pointing at us, "You keep out of this if you know what is good for you!"

It was then that Tierra walked off away from the crowd.

"There you have it everyone, the newly elected Time Council members! Can I have everyone come up on this stage here?" Tina said carrying out folded robes in the signature Time

Council colors and the silver "T" pins. One by one in order of the hours we represented, came up on the stage and one by one as she placed new robes on us with a new pin and we all bowed and said the following oath to the City together:

"As your newly elected Time Council Members we promise to uphold our duties that we are sworn to lead in our own departments. We will lead with respect, pride, integrity, and honesty. Above all we swear to protect this City of Sandglass from corruption, and we will lead with love of the people we are sworn to protect and strive to be better leaders daily by continuing to learn and grow as one."

And the crowd applauded and responded:

"We trust you and believe in you. We will be depending on you all to keep us safe from harm and dutifully lead us honestly."

It was then that we walked off the stage and immediately were put into the carriages which were packed with the belongings of the newly elected leaders, and we were lead in procession to the Time Tower and Brent led the way to the Time Tower Chambers where we all quietly took our new seats.

Chapter 33

The Clock Chimes

As I took my seat in the third chair on the horseshoe shaped stand, I could hear the carriages being unloaded.
Brent looked around the room and I nodded at him as saw that everyone had also sat down.
"I call to order on this day our first meeting of the new Time Council!" Brent said loudly and every one of the members banged their gavel one by one from Brent down to James who sat on the other side of the room. James nodded at him and Brent smiled proudly. Just then the bells above us started to chime. I smiled at them above us because it symbolized a new beginning for the council and a new way that we all could help contribute to the inner workings of the city. It was then that the Timekeepers one by one started to come in and pile notes in front of us respective to the departments that we represented.
"These are the recent notes gathered from various people in the city that they need help with or wish to get our advice on," said the Head Timekeeper to Brent who nodded, "As our new

leader it will be our pleasure to be of assistance for you Brent. My name is Harrison."

"Thank you, Harrison," Brent said as he looked at me and then seemed to get a little jealous looking at me for some reason. Just then there was a whisper behind me, "Night Hunter Master, there are some messages here from us as well of things that need your immediate assistance. My name is Miguel."

"First off Miguel," I said hotly realizing why Brent was acting like that towards me, "I need you not to whisper in my ear like that ever again. Second, if you have something for me from now on, please just hand them to me quietly."

It was then that Miguel nodded quickly, bowed apologetically, and then quickly said aloud, "I am sorry miss."

He then stood against the wall blending into the darkness as quickly as he got out of the darkness.

It seems that Brent seemed a little happier with my reaction as everyone seemed to be reading the messages that were sent to them on notecards quietly.

I opened my large envelope and immediately at least a hundred note cards came out

I organized them one by one, so the writing was on top and then, I had started to read them.

In front of us there was a large metal trough that was put in front of us with oil in it which was lit by the timekeepers as I understood what we were supposed to do. One by one I read the cards.

"Bradley from Village of Ailes"

I know this may be of little meaning to you possibly, but I need to know what is going on in my Village. People are dying daily. There is a killer here. Time is not being taken from anyone, but someone is getting a thrill of killing others in the dead of night. Last night we lost six people. The night before it was only four."

I put the card aside as I continued to read my next card.

"Henrietta from the Port Village of Thalmia"

I know you may be busy, but I wanted to let you know that recently there was an oil spill here and people are not able to depend on fishing for making a living to get by anymore as much of the fish have died. We need help cleaning the spill.

I then put this card on top of the other.

Tweadle from the Village of Bingley

"I only have a month left to live and I was wondering if there was any chance the Time Council or the Night Hunters might have extra time to give or if there is any way, we can earn extra time?"

I put this one on top of the others.

I then looked around and saw that the room was stirring with anxiety.

"All these people need our help, and we need to coordinate to figure out how to help these people," I said aloud looking at my cards and everyone remained silent and looked up at me. Tommy put his card in the fire in front of him.

"What card was that for can I ask?" I asked Tommy.

"That is strictly the business of my department," Tommy said snidely to me as everyone looked at him and then to me. Everyone seemed to be on edge as they felt the temperature in the room get icy.

"I'm sorry Tommy, I didn't mean to have it look like I was overstepping myself I was just wanting to help," I said noticing how defensive Tommy had gotten.

"You just focus on you over there, okay?" Tommy said now looking down at his cards.

"My, people sure do like to complain!" Hope said looking at her cards trying to break the unsettled silence.

I nodded at her and smiled. I then decided to try an experiment. I wrote down on a page number 1-13 and then looked at everyone, one at a time.

"What are you doing?" came the voice of Midnight in my head.

"Ah, I see what you are doing," Emrys said, "You are reading the room. This is incredibly wise of you."

I looked at Brent down the row from me and he eventually looked up at me from his card he was reading and smiled.

I put a smiley face next to number one.

I then looked at Tina who seemed to have not paid any attention to anyone else in the room while reading her cards. I left it blank for the time being.

I then looked at Tommy who was sitting next me and put a star next to his name.

I then looked at Sarah Bradley who was sitting next to him and she seemed to be focusing on her cards. I couldn't get a read on her, so I left it blank.

Next, I put happy faces next to the ones I knew for sure were okay with me. I knew that Hope was okay with me for number 6, and I knew Michael was okay with me for Number 7. I knew Terrance for Number 8 and Taylor for Number 9 were okay with me. Then I looked at Tobey who smiled at me who was seated at Number 10. I then looked at Tessa and Socrat who were both seated at Number eleven. They seemed to be talking together and getting along fine. They noticed I was looking at them and they both smiled at me, so I added two smiling faces from Number eleven and then Tonya seemed to be trying to focus deeply on her cards but was disturbed by the whispered talking between Tessa and Socrat. She then looked up at me angrily and rather annoyed, so I added a star next to her. And finally, I looked at James who was sitting across from Brent who continued to look at Brent and didn't have any cards in front of him. I added a star next to his name and looked up at the list.

"Interesting odds you have there," Midnight said calmly as I counted, "Three possibly four out of the bunch you are unsure about?"

"Even your own brother?" Emrys asked me curiously as I responded in my head, "I am not sure why he is acting like that."

I then took out a piece of paper and printed the following names:

Tina Marrowe (For or against me?)

Sarah Bradley (For or against me?)

Tommy Kai (Why is he acting rough against me?)

Tonya Diavecca (For or against me)

I handed the paper behind me to Miguel and whispered, "Get these answers to me as soon as possible to my room."

"Right," Miguel answered and nodded quickly, and he threw pink powder at his feet and disappeared.

James then looked over at me and smiled noticing I was watching him as he waved nervously and then got up and walked over to me.

"Bella, I just wanted to say congratulations on making your new position permanent. I am sure that we are all expecting great things from you!" James said smiling at me, "Any news on wedding plans yet?"

"Ah that is still being set up, but the date is set for a few months from now," I said smiling.

"If you survive being in charge of this department long enough," Tommy Kai said under his breath.

"Whatever do you mean Tommy?" James said curtly to him, "What has gotten over you?"

"You perfectly know well what I mean with her and her new rules," Tommy said curtly.

"New rules?" James said looking at me curiously.

"It's nothing, just that I want the City to get know their leaders," I said calmly looking at Tommy who shook his head in disagreement.

"You are going to get us all killed with targets on our back," Tommy said in slight frustration.

"Well, don't get killed, and remember, we have the Timekeepers as our guard and besides Tyronne isn't roaming our streets anymore. He has been locked up with house arrest now that Tyeisha isn't on the Council anymore."

"Yeah, but her sister, Tyronne's other cousin is now on the council," Tommy said in almost a sinister voice.

"Now that is quite enough Tommy, let your sister be," James said in slight anger, "Go get yourself in a better mood."

It was then that James walked back to his seat in slight irritation and glared at Tommy for the next few minutes as I looked back down to my cards.

From the City of Sandglass – Time

This is Kaide, I know by now my son has made it to the Time Council. This was a prewritten message. I don't want you to think I am back. I instructed a dear friend of mine who is a Timekeeper to give this message to you at this exact moment. Firstly, I knew I was going to die soon, way before our mission to the Trenches, but I wanted to give myself a chance to enjoy being with you all and my son. I know he is going to ask for Socrat's hand in marriage and I whole heartedly give my permission. I am so happy for him. I have one last bequest of you and Brent. Within the Trenches, I have hidden a special artifact that is ancient and rare. You need to use the word "Goethe," and it will appear. You will find it in the wall above the old wooden table that is there along the path. This artifact is a special wedding gift for you and Brent. Use it to your will. Be careful in returning to the trenches.

All my love and regards,

Kaide.

I looked up at Socrat, and then to James, and then to Brent with teary eyes. I then took the rest of the stack of cards in front of me in hand and left the room.

"Where are you going? You must decide on these cards now," said one of the Timekeepers who was blocking the exit to the chambers.

"It's okay, let her go," Brent said from behind me. The Timekeeper bowed and opened the door, and I left to my room.

There was about thirty other cards that I went over in my room asking for help from the Night Hunters to catch certain thieves that have started targeting various stores in the city and then there was a gang that seems to be causing trouble stealing time away from kids in a daycare and other older people who were at a local nursing home.

I wanted to help them all and I knew I could organize everyone for the tasks to ensure that everything was handled well. So, I had made the decision to call a meeting for the Night Hunters that night as our first order of business to get things a little better under control.

Just then there was a knock at the door.

"Bella?" came Brent's voice as I opened the door, "Are you okay?"

I nodded and then ushered him into my room.

I walked over to my desk of the three cards that I put aside and handed him Kaide's letter which he intently read for a few minutes and then looked up.

"So, the secret five is going on an adventure?" he asked me curiously.

"Eventually maybe after the wedding, which is coming up around the corner," I said smiling at him as he nodded at me.

"Yes, that is very important," he said to me smiling, "So what made you upset?"

"Kaide's letter?" he asked

I was silent now and then a voice came into my head, "You should tell him," Midnight said wisely.

"I have possibly three maybe four people on this new council I am not sure that I can trust," I said looking at Brent intently as he nodded.

"I noticed that interaction with your brother Tommy today. That was a little uncharacteristic of him, but I don't think that you can say that you cannot trust him," Brent said calmly.

"I have my guard up now," I said calmly, "I just wanted you to be aware."

"Who are the other people?" Brent asked me quietly.

"I have the Night hunters looking into this for me," I said realizing that it might be best to keep open communication with Brent as a sign to him that I am putting my confidence into him, "Tina Marrowe, Sarah Bradley, and Tonya Diavecca."

"And your brother Tommy you are unsure about I am assuming," Brent said as I nodded slowly and silently.

There was a knock at the door, and it was Socrat and James.

"Hey there Bella!" Socrat said smiling at me, "I was having a tough time remembering what number you and Brent are to figure out which room was yours. I'm afraid we bugged everyone coming to this room tonight."

Brent laughed at Socrat's foolishness.

"I am not so sure I am cut out to following this dream of mine of becoming a Time Council member. No one ever tells you what is involved with being a leader until it's too late it seems," Socrat said worriedly.

"Don't worry you will get the hang of it," James said smiling.

"What do you care? You have the easiest job in the world!" Socrat said crossing his arms, "being number 13 and all."

"Actually, my job is secret and it's a heavy burden," James said secretively, "I can't even tell you."

"What do you mean?" Socrat said trying to mickey it out of

him.

"Per the notes, I got I am not to say a word to anyone," James said.

"You didn't get any notes though," Socrat said quizzically.

"I actually did," James said looking at me.

"Not really, you came over to me and talked to me because you didn't have any notecards," I said looking at James.

"My messages were given to me just not in the same method as everyone else," he said looking at Brent and then to me.

"You are so mysterious James," Brent said smiling at him and he just smiled back.

"So, what is the matter, Bella? What made you leave early?" James asked me as I hesitated.

"There was something that was given to me, but I will wait to share it with you after the wedding," I said to James as he nodded in understanding.

"I trust you," James said nodding at me in understanding.

"So, when is the wedding?" James asked trying to quickly change the subject before Socrat can push the matter anymore for which I was grateful.

"Ah yes, we are thinking sometime maybe next week," Brent said quickly as I shot him a quick glance.

"Next week?" James said in surprise.

"Brent, I was thinking give me at least a month more," I said looking at him.

"A December wedding?" Socrat said smiling in approval.

"Yeah," Brent said in agreement, "Grandpa and I have been planning this for years!"

"Really?" James asked me as I nodded.

"Apparently, I was the only one that didn't know that this was in the works. Shortly after I was also told about another secret room.

"Oh, so that is where it will be?" James said smiling as I nodded, "Strange that you have been living there all these years and you hadn't discovered this?"

"Yeah," Brent said smiling excitedly holding my hand.

"I am so happy for you both!" Socrat said looking at James, "So when are you going to put a ring on my hand?"

"Eventually, when I know we are more stable," James said smiling at us, "Well anyway, I just wanted to make sure that you were okay, we are going to look at our new rooms."

"Wait we don't share a room anymore?" Socrat asked nervously as James looked over at him and shook his head.

"As members of the Time Council we don't get to share rooms, our positions come first hun," James said seriously, "You cannot come into my room and nor can I come into your room overnight. Our duties are to the City of Sandglass first."

"Bella that means I cannot sleep in your room anymore?" Brent asked as I shook my head, "Now if you sleep in my room its considered a conflict of interest."

"But we both have a guest room each," I added smiling at Brent who seemed to catch on.

"I love it when you think of loopholes," Socrat said hugging me and saying goodnight to us.

"Goodnight you two love birds," I said laughing jokingly at them.

"Who are you calling love birds? You are both getting married before we do anyway!" James said laughing back as I nodded in agreement.

"Goodnight Brent," I said to him as he realized I was going to get to sleep. Brent nodded as I handed him the spare key to my guest room, "Here is my key that opens my guestroom door. If I get a chance, I might come into that room tonight. I do have some work to do."

Brent nodded in understanding and left the room.

It was then that I checked the basket by the door which I had set up for letters to be put in my room.

There were more letters to me.

Bella from what we were able to find out, Tommy is not happy with the fact that your position is permanent now. He has reservations on what kind of leader you can be. There have been multiple conversations that he has had with Terrance and with Tobey who are both unwaveringly loyal to you. But he is still unconvinced. As far as Tina is concerned, we have not found any evidence on the matter either way. She is more concerned about making sure there is no corruption in the Council. As for Sarah Bradley and Tanya Diavecca. Sarah is against you because of what transpired with you and Tyronne. She doesn't believe what happened and seems to think that Tyeisha had hid something about what happened from her. She doesn't trust anyone well. As far as Tanya Diavecca, she has a thirst to get everyone to like her and to understand that she is not her sister, she wants to prove herself to others. It might be your best bet to get on her good side as soon as possible so you get on each other's good side. We will keep an eye on her, Sarah, and Tommy. Again, sorry about earlier at the meeting. – Miguel.

I folded up the letter and threw it in the fire in the fireplace in my room and laid on the bed in deep contemplation.

"Try not to worry about things that are out of your control, Bella," Midnight hooted as I nodded in understanding.

It was then that I put on my black robe, brought my sword and attached it to my side along with my pink and gold powder and I quietly left the room and locked the door behind me after putting the rest of the cards that I had and the envelopes that were in my basket in my pocket. I was able to sneak outside without being seen. I thought of the fountain and the walking path that was beside it and said, "Forlossem." Immediately I disappeared and was instantly on the walking path that ran next to the large water fountain and the lake. I was reading the cards; each one was like a cry for help to me. All of them were important. I looked over at the water as it peacefully streamed past me along the lake from the water fountain. Geese flocked around the water, carefreely enjoying the nice breeze that was flowing around the lake. As I looked ahead, I could see Tanya sitting on a bench looking out into the water not realizing I was there.

"You should go talk to her," Emrys said wisely as I remembered what I had read back at my room in the note from Miguel as I nodded thoughtfully.

"She has a thirst to get everyone to like her and to understand that she is not her sister and wants to prove herself to others. It might be your best bet to get on her good side as soon as possible."

"Well, hello there. I didn't expect to see you here of all places," I said smiling at Tanya who looked up at me and raised her eyebrows in surprise and then nodded and smiled at me.

"I like to come here to think about things and reflect on the day," Tanya said thoughtfully looking out onto the lake, seemingly undeterred by my presence.

"It is very nice and peaceful out here, it does make for some good thinking time, and exercise," I said smiling at her as she nodded seriously.

"I suppose so," Tanya said quietly and then looked up at me, "Bella, can I ask you something?"

"Yeah sure," I said smiling at her and then noticed her face was serious.

"What made you want to be on the Time Council?" she asked me.

"That is an interesting question," I said thoughtfully, "To be honest I was asked to be a member after what happened with Terry Kai my stepsister. I didn't want the position at first to be honest. I didn't give them an answer right away to be a temporary leader until after we found Brent's parents and closer to the election."

I paused for a moment in silence.

"But after I followed through with my word to Brent to find his parents. I along the way got to know my siblings for the most part. I got to see how they all work. I realized that they were the connection I was missing, and along the way I fell in love with Brent," I explained looking ahead into the water, "I didn't think I was fit for the job at first. I had doubts of being successful at it to be honest. It was a lot to handle, the lives of the city and then being couped up in the Tower, it wasn't what I wanted, to be locked up in a cage unable to see the City I was supposedly leading. I wanted to be able to get to know the people and know the situations that they were in firsthand. I only ended up deciding to join as long as I wasn't going to be locked away in the Tower forever. I wanted personal freedom to roam as I chose, like I am now. It helps me to clear my mind to have that change of scenery. But it was fear at first that stopped me from attempting the idea of even asking to be a Time Council Leader," I said to her as she looked up at me in disbelief.

"I had to understand that just because certain rules, and regulations and ideas are set in stone, it doesn't mean its not possible to affect change. By talking to the council to see if it was possible was the first wall to break down. To, with courage ask if it was possible. The worst case scenario would have been they say no, and already I thought this was the worst case," I explained.

There was a moment of silence.

I could tell she was scared, and it seemed to finally hit her that she was officially a Leader of the City now.

"Why is it people don't pursue their dreams? Why don't people do better than what they are doing, if they are capable of it? I think that most people don't do it or go to the next step to accomplishing their dream is because people don't know what they are supposed to do yet. Subconsciously, we don't believe that it could happen for us, or don't believe they deserve it. At the time, I had a limited lack of vision and self-esteem when Terrance first asked me to be a Time Council member. I couldn't see myself living beyond where I was at the time, I was living at David and Sharons. I didn't know I could be doing better than I was. I thought that that was it at the time. I realized though that fear kills dreams, fear kills hope, fear ages you because it puts your body under stress, and then here your timecard moves quicker. I have noticed this happens when we are stressed, as I see yours is moving quickly," I said to her noticing she was showing her timecard. She immediately hid it.

"Don't let your emotions control you. Where you are right now
doesn't determine where you are going to be. You need to keep growing and pushing yourself. Have the courage to fail and try again. Realize it's okay, even as a leader to make mistakes, we are not perfect. That's how we grow and

become better leaders. You have within you what it takes to become a great leader!" I said to her.

She nodded.

"Fear can hold you back from accomplishing the dreams that I know you can do! Fear can paralyze you if you let it, and what is the benefit of letting your fears consume you? Fear is an acronym for False Evidence Appearing Real, and it is a mindset that we automatically have that can be changed. Look at your life right now, whatever you have produced, it came out of you, because of your choices, now you are a leader! This is the person you have become today."

It was then that she started crying in my arms.

"I don't think I could handle this," Tanya said crying in my arms worriedly, "You should have read the cards I have. The department of the Housing Authority is a mess and now I understand why my sister felt like she had to drink all the time in her room. She couldn't handle it all."

"It's going to be okay," I said to Tanya, "Take it one card at a time. You need to start building yourself up. Sometimes the only good things you will hear about you are the things you say to yourself. Learn to be your own booster. Start saying I can do this! I can make this happen! When I started to convince myself and talk to myself it was better than the negativity around me. Get yourself together, you can manage this, you just haven't figured it out yet. This is your training period during the first few months. This is the tuition you must pay for what you don't know. Get people around you who can teach you things you don't know, change the way you see yourself. No one is going to take care of business better than you. Make the adjustments so you can do what you want to do successfully," I said to her encouragingly as she wiped her tears off her face.

"You have nothing to fear but fear itself. Turn off things that can contribute to your fear. Recondition your mind. If you don't take the plunge someone else will. You must be willing to get knocked down so you can learn how to fight and hold your position. Most people don't get into the arena of life because they don't want to fight. But I promise you Tanya, if you can keep pushing yourself, and stay positive, everything will be okay. Tanya, then you will become like a beautiful butterfly pushing herself out of the cocoon of the stresses of life and become stronger in the end. You will be a great leader! I see it within you!" I said to her, and she smiled and hugged me.

"Thank you, Bella, for being you!" Tanya said through tears, and she stood up and smiled, "Goodnight Bella."

Tanya walked away back towards the Time Tower.

"You did such a great job back there Bella," Emrys said in my mind as I smiled watching her walk away, "I am so proud of you."

I felt a warmth come over me as I continued to smile.

"I think people forget that sometimes we all need a little encouragement to get through life," I said nodding at what happened feeling a little better about my status with Tanya.

Chapter 34

The Discussion of Time

I had gone to bed that night feeling a lot less pressure in my shoulders as things were finally coming along the way that they should and was able to sleep soundly that night.

I woke up the next morning to a knocking at my guest bedroom door. I noticed that Brent didn't end up waking me up to come over to my guest room. I walked sleepily over to my door and opened it to see that It was Socrat and James.

"Good morning fellow Council Member!" Socrat said smiling widely as I noticed he and James were wearing their robes already.

"Do we have a meeting I wasn't aware of this morning?" I yawned asked them as they looked at me blankly.

"No, I don't think so," Socrat worriedly said thinking he forgot a memo.

"Oh okay, it's because normally we only wear robes when we leave the tower or have a meeting in the chambers," I explained as they nodded in understanding.

"Well, there is nothing like being prepared," James said smiling with his hands together in his robes seemingly keeping himself warm.

"I guess we are just excited for our first days being in our official roles as Time Council Members," Socrat said rubbing the back of his neck with his hand feeling slightly embarrassed for not knowing the protocol on the robes.

"It's okay, not everyone knows this yet," I said waiving off my comment, "Don't mind me, I am just tired."

"Don't you have a wedding to start preparing for?" Brent said from behind James and Socrat as they both jumped.

"Right," I said thinking about what I needed to do.

"It isn't until next week," Socrat said looking at James, "You both have plenty of time!"

"It's not coming soon enough, good morning my love," Brent said walking in past Socrat and James hugging me as I smiled at Brent.

"What are we all doing today?" James asked me and then looked at Brent who shrugged.

"I have three cards I want to get sorted out today," I said aloud to James, Brent, and Socrat.

I pulled them out and showed them.

"Bradley from Village of Ailes"

I know this may be of little meaning to you possibly, but I need to know what is going on in my Village. People are dying daily. There is a killer here. Time is not being taken from anyone, but someone is getting a thrill of killing others in the dead of night.

Last night we lost six people. The night before it was only four."

"Henrietta from the Port Village of Thalmia"
I know you may be busy, but I wanted to let you know that recently there was an oil spill here and people are not able to depend on fishing for making a living to get by anymore as much of the fish have died. We need help cleaning the spill.

Tweadle from the Village of Bingley
"I only have a month left to live and I was wondering if there was any chance the Time Council or the Night Hunters might have extra time to give or any way, we can earn extra time?"

There was silence for a few minutes as the three cards were passed around the room.

"Well, the two villages are right beside each other and then this last one is on the way there. I don't know what we can do for the last one," Brent said calmly.

"I think it is time to use my sword and then get the help from the Night Hunters to find the serial killer and the oil spill," I said thoughtfully, "Can the three of you meet me in the Night Hunter Chamber room?"

It was then that we all disappeared. And I called the meeting to the Chambers.

"Good morning, everyone," I said happily looking at everyone who replied good morning wearing their Night Hunter robes. "I would like some of you to go to the Village of Ailes and find out who is killing the various villagers. There is a serial killer there. And then I would like the others on this side of the room to go to the Port Village of Thalmia to help with the oil spill there. The people there need our help to clean it up. The secret five please stay behind," I said looking around the room, "Meeting adjourned."

"Your wish is our command Night Master," they all said and disappeared.

Brent, James, Michael, Socrat, and I were the only ones left. "I would like to see if you all would like to go on two adventures with me," I said looking at the four of them.

"I thought we were going to wait until after the wedding?" Brent said smiling

"I don't think these can wait after all," I said seriously.

I handed everyone the card from Tweadle.

"I was hoping to go and visit this village that is just past the Village of Pasqua," I said looking quickly at Michael and Socrat.

"Are you sure that you want to go there?" Michael asked nervously.

"Not even we have been back to the Village of Pasqua in the years since we left it," Socrat said looking at me in concern.

"It is time," I said simply and then looked down at the card that Brent handed back to me, "and if I can help a struggling village and give them time, I will."

"How?" Brent asked me curiously.

"There is a reason why we are called the City of Sandglass – Time," I said thoughtfully remembering David calling it that. "I was also told that we have the ability to give out time and take time as being a part of the council," I said going outside the door of the Night Hunters.

"Please go fetch Terrance for me," I told one of the timekeepers that was outside the door who nodded and disappeared.

Within seconds, Terrance appeared in the Night Hunters Chambers.

"Bella, to what do I owe this pleasure of being summoned?" Terrance asked with his eyes twinkling.

"I need to know how the Time Council handles time. The people that we take time from for disobedience, What happens to it? How can we give time back to people?" I asked cautiously.

"We don't just randomly just give time to everyone just because. If there is economic decline in some areas, we help where we can. Why?" Terrance asked looking at us.

After a moment of silence, I gave Terrance the card of someone asking for time since they only had a month left in that village.

"You intend to give only time to this gentleman?" Terrance asked me curiously.

"No, I wish to give time to multiple villages to help them out," I said calmly.

"Which ones?" he asked me.

"The Villages of Thalmia, Ailes, and Bingley and also if there are any survivors or people living in the Village of Pascua," I said looking at Terrance who's eyes were wide, "nothing extreme just everyone an extra 5 years each."

"Five years!? Do you realize how much that is? There at least five hundred villagers in each of these three villages and we don't know how much in the Village of Pasqua, now that you mention it," Terrance said to me shaking his head, "The Time Council would not approve of this randomly. That is a lot of moral responsibility."

"Let me ask you this, isn't it our moral responsibility to be giving it to them? Why would it hurt giving these Villages more time to live and utilize the time for things that they need. Especially when one village, they are suffering because of an oil spill and cannot earn a livelihood because they are a fishing port town. While the other village is dealing with a serial killer. Then the third village has a man who has plucked up the courage to ask for more time. He went out of his way to message us to ask for more time to live," I said pleadingly.

For a moment I seemed to convince him, and he seemed to be persuaded.

"We have not authorized this amount of time to be given out so freely before," Terrance said thoughtfully.

"Do I have this request from the only Night Hunters? Or am I to understand that Brent, Socrat and James, as your capacity as Time Council Members, you are all also requesting this as well, under agreement with Bella's request?" Terrance asked looking at them individually and they all nodded.

So, with me, Brent, Socrat, Michael, and you Bella that is 5 of the members of the 13 so you need two more to get approval for this before I can say yes," Terrance said calmly as my heart skipped two beats, "then you cannot be outvoted for this."

I then thought about how the secret five is, we needed to add a replacement for Kaide and maybe have it so there are seven secret members.

"I see what you are thinking Bella, but you must understand the secret six are not to only be made up of council members they are Night Hunters. You would have to induct two more council members to the Night Hunters if they are okay with that," Emrys said in my head seemingly following my train of thought.

"Okay Terrance, you will have two more members by the end of the day to approve of this," I said aloud confidently.

It was then that Brent and Socrat and James and Michael looked at me curiously.

Terrance left the room as quickly as he had appeared and I smiled.

"What are you up to?" Brent asked smiling at me

"I have two more members to add to our Secret Group," I said smiling.

It was then that I went outside the chambers again and asked the Timekeeper to summon Tobey Kai.

Within seconds, Tobey was in the room.

"What is it with you?" Tobey said in slight frustration and then noticed who else was in the room and said, "Yes, Bella How can I help you?"

"I need your permission to add Tanya and Hope to the Secret organization of the Night Hunters and more specifically my team," I said eyeing everyone in the room before looking at Tobey who looked very reluctant.

"I am not trying to rain on your parade here Bella, but we cannot add any more members from the Time Council to the Night Hunters organization because of conflict of interest.

Adding two more members from the Time Council will put us at 7 and then anything we ask would be approved without question and it would look like we have too much power. The Bear Claw Clan organization would not allow it," Tobey said calmly.

"Well, we need approval from two more Time Council members," I said in frustration.

"Well, I am one, what am I just second in command to you? Don't you forget, I am on the Time Council as well?" Tobey said in slight frustration.

"Well can you approve us to give out time?" Brent asked curiously.

"Give... Give. Give out t-time?" Tobey said in surprise, "The Council doesn't just give out time like that to random people. We haven't done that in hundreds of years! We are not a charity! It is not morally responsible for us to just be seen to be giving out time like that!"

"Well, wouldn't it be morally responsible for us to not just collect time from people yet not give it out back to the people?" I said to Tobey. He looked at me with his eyebrows raised.

He didn't have anything to say in return as he put his fingers to the bridge of his nose rubbing it in slight frustration and then asked, "How much time? To how many people?"

"The Villages of Thalmia, Ailes, and Bingley and if there are any survivors or people living in the Village of Pascua," I said looking at Terrance who's eyes were wide, "nothing extreme just everyone an extra 5 years each."

"Five years? To all those people?" Tobey said in surprise.

"What would you do if you honestly had an extra five years?" I asked him. "Why would it hurt giving these Villages more time to live and utilize the time for things that they need. Especially when one village, they are suffering because of an oil spill and cannot earn a livelihood because they are a fishing port town. The other is just dealing with a serial killer. Then the other, there is a man who went out of his way to message us to ask for more time to live," I said pleadingly, repeating what I said to Terrance to Tobey.

"You do make a very convincing argument," Tobey said smiling at me and shaking his head and saying out loud to himself, "What would Terry have said to see how far you have grown?" Tobey smiled and then was silent for a few minutes in contemplation.

"Very well, you have my vote," Tobey said then looked at me and the others, "You need one more vote and then you can go back to Terrance, "After all, he is in charge of the Health and Well Being Department."

We all nodded in agreement with him as he disappeared from the room.

"So, are you going to ask Hope or Tanya for help on the next vote?" Brent asked me as I was silent for a moment.

"Tanya," I said as Brent left the room and came back a few seconds later with Tanya in a puff of pink and Gold smoke.

"WOW! How did you do that!?" Socrat said majorly impressed as Tanya smiled.

"Maybe one day I will teach you child!" Tanya said smiling at him and then looked over at me seriously and then said in her southern accent, "What d'you want?"

"I would like your support," I said to her smiling in a pleading sort of way as I handed her the card from Tweadle, "I would like to give out time from the Council Storage.

Tanya opened her mouth as if I had just slapped her.

"The Council doesn't keep time, do they?" Tanya asked me and turned to the others in the room as they nodded,

"There is a reason we are The City of Sandglass -Time. We can give people time," James said, "It just isn't done as often as we should."

"How do you collect it or transfer it out of?" Tanya said in curiosity.

"The Council when punishing people of their time, it is drained into a central sandglass below the tower," James explained as I hadn't even known that, "It is guarded by a group of fairies down there and given every manner of immortal and mortal protection. Only a minimum of four Council Members can go down at a time. One represents the days, hours, minutes and then the other represents seconds on the timeclocks. It is also the number of members that the founders decided it would take for one of the others to break down. If this was illegally done, one of the four is most likely to tell on the other Council Members if they broken in due to guilt if ever there was an attempt to steal from the City of Sandglass -time."

"What do we intend to do with the time we have collected?" Tanya asked me and then looked down again at the note about the man from the Village who was about to die, "Are we just giving the time for him? Do you even know him? It seems like you are being selfish."

"The Time Council is supposed to delegate Time back to its people every few years but it has not been done in over a decade. The council in recent years has been quick to punish and taken time from our citizens but not so quick to give back," James explained.

"Tweadle is a stranger to me, but I intend to have faith in his intentions since he went out of his way to courageously ask for time," I explained.

I looked at her as my eyes started to tear up.

"Where else do you intend to give out time charitably?" Tanya asked.

"The Villages of Thalmia, Ailes, and Bingley and, if there are any survivors or people living in the Village of Pascua," I said looking at Tanya and then to James who added, "Nothing extreme just everyone an extra five years each."

Tanya remained silent.

"What would you do if you honestly had an extra five years?" I asked her. "Why would it hurt to give these Villages more time to live and utilize the time for things that they need. Especially when one village, they are all suffering because of an oil spill and cannot earn a livelihood because they are a fishing port town, and the other is just dealing with a serial killer, and then the other, there is a man who went out of his way to message us, and to ask for more time to live," I said pleadingly repeating what I said to Terrance and Tobey to Tanya.

Tanya seemed to remain quiet about this at first.

"Why not help the other people in this City too and give a stipend of time to have, as a gratitude from the Council for Voting for us all?" Tanya said smiling at her idea.

I smiled even wider.

"I knew there was a reason I'd love you, Tanya!" I said smiling at her, "Please follow us."

We went up the stairs, and down the hall to Terrance's room and knocked on the door. Terrance opened the door and saw me, Tanya, Brent, James, and Socrat all in the doorway smiling up at him and he opened the door, and we found Tobey sitting there looking up and then smiling as well noticing I was there.

"Now what?" Tobey said and then he looked at all of us in the room.

"Bellatrix Kai, what am I going to do with you now?" he said laughing standing up to hug everyone with Terrance.

"I suppose they have convinced you to allow for this?" Tobey said to Terrance and then to Tanya who nodded. Tanya held onto both her hands in front of her, and walked towards the fireplace in Terrance's room, which was full of Royal Blue and purples.

"They have joined me in another idea, slightly bigger," Tanya said smiling wider, and then looked at Terrance and Tobey who looked at Tanya and then looked at me and then said, "Well, let's have it."

"We want to give back to everyone in the City of Sandglass, and the surrounding villages around us. We want to thank everyone for voting for the people they did, and for participating and we are giving everyone a stipend as a thank you."

"Wait, to EVERYONE?" Terrance said through smiles, and Tobey looked like he was going to have a cow, "How much time are we giving out?"

"I think because of the amount of time we are giving out we can give everyone five years still," I said looking at Terrance who shook his head.

"I don't know what this would mean for the Council to say, they will want to vote on it formally at least because of the extent that we are doing this now at this point, we will vote this afternoon," Tobey said putting his foot forward in slight anger and then put his finger towards each of us, "I need you all to know this, I am not against this idea, understand me. This is something that needs to be voted on in agreement with the council."

We all nodded and bowed to Terrance and Tobey as we then left the room.

We all looked at each other silently outside of his room and I knew with a smile where we were all going.

I had said 'Follossem" and thought of my room.

But no one was there.

"Well, I don't know what everyone else was thinking but here I am," I said laughing to myself at what happened.

After a few hours of reading various notes left for me from the Timekeepers, I got the summons for the meeting happening in a few minutes for the Time Council. I had started to get my robes on and smiled at myself in the mirror after putting on the Time Council Silver pin, and walked downstairs.

In my excitement of the prospect of being able to make a difference in the City of Sandglass and the surrounding area, as a Time Council Leader, I realized I was the first one in the Time Council Chambers as I walked in and took my seat.

After a few minutes the doors to the Council Chambers opened as a few robed figures walked in.

"Where did you all end up going?" I asked Brent, Socrat, James, and Michael walked in and sat at their seats as they looked at Tanya and smiled.

"Back to our own rooms," Socrat said looking at James and Tanya and then to Brent smiling as if they were up to something.

Within minutes, slowly, the other Time Council members came into the Chamber, and took their seats as Terrance stood up and was the first to talk at his seat.

"It has been brought up to me that Bellatrix has something that she wants to ask for us to vote for. I ask that we all be open-mindedly and hear her out," Terrance said pointing towards me and then sat back down as all the council members looked up at me, "Bella, you have the floor."

I stood up as everyone silently looked up at me.

"It was brought to my attention in our last meeting three specific cards that I have been contemplating over for the last few days that I am asking for a vote from everyone here today," I started to explain.

"Now wait a minute," Tommy said firmly standing up and looking at me with flashing eyes, "the cards we get are for our departments, we don't need to be sharing them like we are having some sort of study session!"

"Now hold on Tommy," Taylor said putting up his hand and motioning for Tommy to sit down, "We should at least hear our sister out."

Tommy nodded quietly and sat back down.

"As I was starting to say, there were three cards that I have been having on the back of my mind that have been bugging me because I want to help. Two of which I have already organized the Night Hunters to handle but the third thing I want to do has something to do with a suggestion of Tanya here," I explained as I looked over at her as she nodded for me to continue.

It was then that I passed the cards around to the various Time Council Members.

"Please read these and remain silent as you pass them on until everyone has had a chance to read them," I asked.

"The Night Hunters are going to look for this killer, and some of them are going to help clean up the oil spill. Then as for the third issue, it is more than just this man asking for help. He went out of his way to courageously request time from the Time Council. It led me to realize that this man is not the only one who is suffering working from job time pay, to job time pay for the hours. It is everyone and everyone had voted for us. Originally, I was just going to ask for time for only the three villages. But then, with the suggestion of Tanya, I would like to allow this for all the surrounding villages and the City of Sandglass -Time. I want everyone to receive an additional five years to be added to their timecards. The reason is because I want people to spend more time enjoying life, and give to them this time out of gratitude for voting for us all."

"Five years? For everyone? That over hundreds of thousands of people," Hope said worriedly "Then the Time cost of everything will go up."

"I hope not," I said to myself thoughtfully.

"Do you know how much time that is?" Tina said in concern realizing what this meant.

"That's hundreds and thousands of times to give away," Tessa said looking over at us as we nodded.

"Well, we have enough time stored below for this," Tobey said looking at everyone, "We have not exactly been generous about giving out time to the community that voted for us in the past. Maybe we can start a new tradition?"

"Tradition?" said Tessa shaking her head and looked around, "This is the third council I have had the fortune to be elected under. The others before you would never have considered this was something pertinent to be managing."

"People are dying daily out there because they are barely making enough time working to barely cover their family for food etc. to maintain humane functionality and you are saying it's not pertinent enough?" Brent said angrily, "That is very rich of you to say, acting like you have an abundance of time yourself!"

There was talking and arguing amongst the council members at the surprise of Brent's outburst of anger, who then had calmed down and apologized.

"Members of the Time Council I am sorry about my outburst of anger just now. But might I give you another example of the issue of the struggle of time out in the City?" Brent said sadly as a few council members nodded.

"I remember years before my parents had gone missing, before meeting Bella, a friend of mine had passed away. He was older than me, but he would spend time with me at my parent's bookstore and we would play hide and seek amongst the shelves. We would spend time together, while my parents worked there. After his funeral, I was reflecting on how much time I had left. I saw that at the time I had about 90 years left but keep in mind over time since then, my time left has to be used to buy food throughout my life, and bills, etc.," Brent stopped and looked at me as I nodded in support, "I remember walking at the park reflecting on my friend, whose life was so promising and he wasn't that much older than I am now. I thought about all the things that he had said he was going to do. He never got around to do those things. I started thinking about my own life, and how much time I had left to do the things that I would like to do. I wasn't sure what my life's purpose was at that time. I was still figuring life out. I thought about it quite a lot. I had some ideas, but I wasn't convinced. I didn't feel worthy to think that I could do this kind of work that I am doing now as a council member. However, I believe, everyone here can explain only all too well how they know how fragile life is. I don't believe for a moment that anyone of you take time for granted. I hope you all realize how much of a treasure it is and especially how valuable time is to

people on the streets of our great city."

Brent teared up and said, "I think the five years each for everyone we could spare. We would see how much more positive people would be, and less stressed people would feel having that extra time in their life to work with."

There was a silence in the room.

"It is true, I saw it myself today walking into this meeting," Tina said sadly as the room got quiet, "A young mother of a child who was maybe around eight years old passed away on the street. She reminded me of my sister growing up who had passed away. My sister and her husband were living Time check by Time check to raise their daughter. Her husband died shortly after from the drink. I had to raise my niece on my own until she came of age. Of course, shortly after I became a Council Member myself. But I know what it's like out on those streets. I know what the people are going through, even before I was a council member couped up in this Time Tower. Since then, times have changed and more has been built around the City of Sandglass, but the same struggles are still here nonetheless."

There was a moment of silence and then Tina stood up.

"As representative Council Member and Head of Discipline of all Citizens and representative of the second-hour, vote to allow for five years of life to be given to all citizens," Tina said proudly.

"Alright, I second the motion," Tobey said smiling and nodding at Tina.

"All in favor raise your hands," Tina said.

Everyone raised their hands in the end.

"I hereby say that we for the first time in over a decade have a unanimous vote!" Tobey said smiling widely even more surprised, as everyone looked around at each other who had their hand raised and started to applaud.

"Send out the time chargers!" Terrance said happily, "We must ensure that they are all distributed to everyone in the household. To ensure this, I vote that we enact a curfew for everyone tomorrow. Then all timekeepers are to go house to house and building to building to pass out the time."

Brent nodded and said, "Don't worry I will ensure that this is managed with great organization."

"Meeting is now adjourned. Bella, and Terrance, please stay behind for further instructions. Socrat on your way out please call in Miguel the Head Timekeeper," Brent said to Socrat who nodded. Everyone filed out of the room. Terrance closed the door behind the Council who had left, and he smiled silently at both of us and then there was a knock at the door as Miguel was ushed into the chambers.

"Did you request my company Mr. Genuit?" Miguel asked Brent who nodded, "We are going to be going on a very important mission, and we are joining forces with the Night Hunters with this task," Brent said as I nodded in agreement. Terrance ushed for the three of us to sit at a table that he set up.

The three of us were silent waiting for Terrance to start talking.

"An extra-large carriage is going to be arriving from under the Tower and it will lift on the lift from below the Carriage courtyard tomorrow afternoon," Terrance explained as I sat paying attention to what Terrance was saying.

"We are setting up ten thousand Time Chargers that look like this," Terrance said taking out a white box from his robes and ushered Miguel to put out his arm, "They work like this. You put the rubber prongs up to the persons forearm like this and press start."

After pressing start and pressing the rubber prongs of the device up against Miguel's inner forearm/wrist area, the timecard on Miguel automatically appeared from a hidden view on his forehead and increased by five years."

"Whoa!" Miguel said after feeling the sensation go into his head from his forearm, "Everyone is getting one?"

Terrance nodded.

"It has just been decided that everyone in every family, young, or old, is all getting an additional five years as a gift from us for voting for us and to help everyone out who is struggling right now. Also, pricing for everything is not to go up because of this added income either," Terrance said putting his finger up at Brent, "You need to ensure that the Timekeepers all keep an eye out for price gouging at the market from owners. Brent nodded in serious agreement.

"All owners of the stores are to turn in current pricing for their products before being given time. When giving out the time, the machine will not work for someone who has already been giving the time," Terrance said attempting to give Miguel another shot of time from the charger and it beeped two low beeps back and turned red, "This will prevent any corruption and gang violence because someone stealing these from us will not be of any value to someone who already has gotten the time charge to them. Also, each of these boxes helps up to ten people so it has fifty years per charge box."

Miguel Brent and I nodded in understanding.

"To make it easier I can split up the forces with you, so we don't hit the same homes twice. For every home already hit our teams will mark the doors with white chalk. This way we know what homes have been distributed the time chargers to," Brent said smiling, "I am calling a Timekeepers meeting tonight."

"I will have my Night Hunters join," I said smiling as Miguel and Terrance nodded.

"Alright we will see you all tomorrow," Terrance said smiling at us as we left the Council Chambers.

Within hours there were sixty Timekeepers and over a hundred Night Hunters gathered in the great hall of the Time Towers. It was one of the largest gatherings held in the Time Tower ever recorded according to Tobey.

I stood in front of the large crowd and gave them the instructions for the next day.

"Tomorrow is not your typical day; we need to ensure every citizen is home by four pm tomorrow and all store owners are at their respective stores. We need lists from all merchants of the products that they are selling and their pricing as of tomorrow before you give them the five years of time charge. We also want to ensure we get every citizen their charge. All it takes is a single charge. You are to instruct them not to adjust pricing within the city," I said pulling out my arm, motioning for Brent to charge my arm."

It was then, that the charge hit my body as it glowed in reaction to charging it. Brent looked at my timecard which showed

31,325:10:15:10 after the 5 years was added and when he did with wide eyes as I looked at him sharply and squinted my eyes at him not to say anything as he noticed and nodded his head.

That night we all successfully charged everyone within the multiple villages and all the citizens within the City of Sandglass. We also posted signs around the town stating for them to come to the Time Tower or see their nearest Timekeeper to be taken to get their charge that they are owed as a one-time thing in case they were missed.

That night we went back to my room in silence, and I could tell Brent had a lot of questions noticing I had over 1,305 days to live. When I charged him, he had only 1,005:38:14:08 left after charging him. Thinking back to when I charged him. I closed my room door and pulled the messages that had come in into my white basket and looked at the messages which were not important and could be filed away. I looked up at Brent and he kept staring at my forehead where he saw the timecard and he remained silent as I ignored him and walked over to my desk as he continued to watch me.

"What Brent?" I said obviously knowing what is going through his mind but wanting him to tell me.

"How?" he asked me

"How what?" I asked

"How is it that you have that much time? Most people just have like three or four hundred years to work with for food etc. and you have so much," he asked me

"Not everyone when they come into this City has the same exact amount of time," I said trying to shrug it off not sure if I want to tell him about the sword.

"Come on," he said sitting up on the bed trying to get me to sit next to him, "You and I both know that you were born here. We didn't get any extra time, and you still buy food and books with your time too and you still have a lot of time left. It's not fair and you still got the five extra years."

I walked over to him with a smile noticing that he felt a little jealous of the amount of time I had left.

"Interesting thing about time," I said softly to him revealing my timecard with him, "When you have a lot of it, you don't appreciate it as much. But when it starts running out, you realize just how precious it truly is."

"You are right Bella," he said looking at his own time, "I never really thought of it like that before. It's easy to take time for granted until we are faced with its limitations."

"That is why we should make the most of every moment that we have together as it is a gift, and we should cherish it. Life is too short to waste it on things that don't bring us joy and fulfillment. There is a reason I have this much time and I plan

eventually to share the reason to you when I am ready."
Brent nodded and smiled.

"I love you," I said softly to him as he nodded.

"I love you too Bellatrix," he said smiling at me and then said, "Oh I forgot to tell you, Tweadle from the Village of Bingley, I got to go there in the end."

"Oh really?" I said looking at him as he nodded and looked away to the floor remembering what had happened as he described arriving there in the late evening with his group of Timekeepers.

"The Chief who oversaw the Village of Bingley was who I had originally talked to when we first got there. I told him it was because of the ShadowMaster you and a few of us Time Council members that voted to help and give back because of Tweadle's letter to you. I told him how influential Tweadle's letter to you was in making sure the Time Council gave back to the community that voted for us," Brent said smiling and then he looked at me, "Now Tweadle is considered a hero of the Village of Bingley. I got to personally give Tweadle his five years left."

I remained silent smiling through tears watching him explain.

"I wanted to thank you for convincing me to be on this Time Council. It is an amazing feat that we did. We made a difference in people's lives, and it's so amazing to be able to do this as a leader!" Brent said smiling through tears.

I nodded as we hugged each other on my bed and then went to sleep for the night.

Chapter 35

Wedding Preparations

I awoke the next morning sat up in bed and looked at the wall calendar to my right. I smiled at it as I crossed off yesterday's date and looked at the day circled on the calendar for tomorrow.

"Tomorrow is the big day," Brent said from behind me.

"Which means tonight you have to sleep in your own bed for once not in my guest bed," I said turning around to him and leaning over the bed to kiss him as he kissed me and grunted and hid under my blankets playfully as I smiled and laughed at him being cute.

"Today I have many preparations to do," I said looking around the room for a change of clothes.

"I have to check my to do list at my desk in my room. Everyone got their invitations, we have the flowers set up from the florist. My parents have the caterers all set up and everything else is prepared honey," Brent said getting out of bed as I put on my shirt and pants and he hugged me from behind and kissed my head, "You nervous about tomorrow?"

"No," I lied smiling at him turning around and kissing him on the lips.

"Tomorrow you are going to be Mrs. Bellatrix Marie Kai-

Genuit," Brent smiled at me as I nodded.

"I will be at the Bookstore getting things ready there. You stay here and don't worry about a thing!" Brent said smiling at me as I nodded.

"Don't forget you have Timekeepers to keep track of too," I said as I left to go to my room. I had just remembered on my desk I had to handout the weekly assignments for the Night Hunters.

Brent got ready and had left for the bookstore within minutes. I walked to my room and over to the window behind my desk to see various people walking the streets outside.

There was a knock at the door as I turned towards the door and walked over to it and opened it.

"Hello Bella," Terrance said as I smiled at him and opened the door to usher him inside.

"Hello Terrance," I said to him smiling, "How can I be of help to the Head of the Health and Wellbeing Department?"

"Well," Terrance said smiling at the notion of mine, "You can tell me how your health is doing."

"What do you mean?" I asked walking to my desk and sitting at it.

"There has been talk that a few people saw how much time you had on your timecard, and they have been raising questions as to how you got so much time," Terrance said.

"I don't know what you are talking about," I said avoiding the conversation, "People like to talk, what of it."

"I would like to see your timecard records," Terrance said calmly looking at me as I shook my head.

"I have rights too, and how much time I have and how I get time is not anyone else's business," I said standing up from the desk and walking to the window behind it.

"No, it isn't anyone else's business, but I need to stop talk before it spreads. and as Head of the Department of Health and Well Being, it is my business," Terrance said firmly putting his hand out for me to put my forearm out.

It was then that I put out my forearm and he said something under his breath and my timecard appeared as he looked at it 31,325:09:10:01 as it was counting down.

"How did you come by this amount of time?" he asked me seriously as he looked at the history and saw that time had been added slowly to my timecard over 30,000 hours over the last few years.

"What is going on?" Terrance asked me curiously

"This is a heavily guarded secret," I said looking at Terrance and then out the window and then thought about Taylor and then looked at her desk which is mine now.

"I suppose being that you knew her and you know me, I can

trust you with this information and I haven't even shared this with Brent yet," I smiled at him and decided to continue to explain, "I have in my possession a gift that was given to me a few years after I was brought into this City. David and Sharon before they passed away, they gave me this Sword called the Sword of Damascus. This is a powerful weapon and as I wear it slowly time flows in me. It was given to me to use as a protection, and it can give and take time from those it is wielded against or wielded by." I explained looking at Terrance who saw my sword at my side that I always wear.

"I won't say anything of this to anyone," Terrance said thoughtfully, "But I must warn you, never to reveal to anyone how much time you have left. For your safety and security as well as to avoid any talk from people."

I nodded silently as he bowed and left the room.

Chapter 36

The Wedding

It was the day of the wedding, and I woke up smiling realizing that within a few hours I was going to be Mrs. Bellatrix Marie Genuit -Kai. I looked outside and it was raining.

"That means it's good luck," Emrys said in my head as I smiled. "Congrats Bella," Midnight hooted happily as I said smiling to myself, "Thank you both of you!" in my head.

It was a surreal feeling that I have been anticipating for years. "I love Brent Genuit, and I realized it along the way while we were getting to know each other. I loved him even with his faults, and I knew that he loved me the same way with my faults. We are not the perfect couple by any means. He was the first to get upset when I was trying to push him to learn to walk again but eventually, he realized that I was only trying to help him. "Along the way we all bonded," I thought to myself. I then laughed just thinking about the time when he first met Michael and Socrat and they learned about the adventure we were going to research and embark on. It was so many years ago and yet looking back, it seemed like it was only yesterday. Just then there was a knock at the door of my room as I walked over to the door and opened it to find it was Hope standing in the doorway.

"Hello Bella," Hope said smiling in her dress, "I am here to help you get ready."

"Correction," came a voice from behind her, it was Brent's mom, "We are here to help you get ready."

I smiled as I opened the door and let them inside.

"I will help you with the makeup," Hope said smiling at me.

"I am helping you with your hair," Shawna said smiling at me, "Don't you worry Brent is getting help from my husband David and his grandfather right now."

I smiled and nodded.

"Benjamin Wheatley from the Underground is the officiant of the wedding for you both," Hope said smiling at me as she carefully put on my eyeliner, "He is so dreamy looking!"

"Now, now Hope, we need to focus on Bella right now," Shawna said smiling at her as Hope smiled and nodded silently.

It wasn't long that the final touches were put on me make up wise and I put on my dress, it weighed a ton. But I smiled at myself in the mirror. There was a knock at my door. It was Terrance dressed in a full tuxedo. His red hair was cut short and pulled back as I smiled and ushered him in and he closed the door behind him.

"Wow, you look beautiful," Terrance said smiling at me as I nodded and thanked him.

"You know originally, I thought you were kind of creepy but I realized it was because you were in love with Taylor. I know that you have not invested into idea of dating anyone since. But I think she would have wanted you to," I said to Terrance as he remained silent and smiled at me.

"As usual you are too kind and caring to me," Terrance said to me with a smile and then he was silent for a minute and then said, "I might think on that notion awhile."

I nodded at him and smiled.

"Afterall, we find love when we aren't looking for it," I said to him smiling as he nodded.

There was a knock at the door giving me the signal to get ready.

"Are you ready Bella?" Terrance asked me to hold out his arm as I held onto it. I smiled at him as we left the room.

The procession music started as I walked down the aisle behind the bridesmaids and the groomsman who were already ahead of me. Slowly I walked down the aisle in my beautiful white dress with the flower girls ahead of me. The petals were laying on the aisle floor, like a beautiful back drop of a painting as I smiled. The guests were all standing in their seats smiling as they saw me. I was looking at Brent the whole time since I had first caught a glimpse of him when I came halfway into the room.

"Yes, I feel like this was meant to be," I said to Terrance as he walked up next to me, and I started to tear up.

"I know you both are going to be so happy together," Terrance said smiling at me as I nodded.

There he was Brent Genuit, clean-shaven and smiling in his tuxedo looking at me with the happiest smile I had ever seen on him. He had tears rolling down his cheeks in pure happiness as he watched me approach him with Terrance holding onto my arm and eventually, he handed me off to Brent.

"Hello beautiful," he whispered to me as he kissed my cheek his eyes were glistening in happiness.

We walked up to the top of the altar and Benjamin Wheatley stood between us facing the crowd.

"Dearly beloved, we are gathered here today in the presence of family and friends to witness the union of Brent Genuit and Bellatrix Kai in marriage. This is a special moment in their lives, and we celebrate their love and commitment to one another," Benjamin Wheatley said smiling at everyone who then sat down. "Do you, Brent Genuit, take Bellatrix Kai to be your wedded spouse? To love and to cherish, in sickness and in health, for richer or for poorer, for better or for worse, forsaking all others, if you both shall live?"

"I do," Brent said smiling at me

"And do you, Bellatrix Kai, take Brent Genuit to be your wedded spouse? To love and to cherish, in sickness and in health, for richer or for poorer, for better or for worse, forsaking all others, if you both shall live?" Benjamin Wheatley said

"I do," I said

"Now, Brent Genuit and Bellatrix Kai will share their vows," Benjamin Wheatley said nodding to Brent to speak.

"Bellatrix, from the moment I met you, I knew that you were someone special. You showed me strength, determination, and love like I had never experienced before. Today, in front of our family and friends, I vow to always stand by your side, to support you in all that you do, and to love you unconditionally," Brent said to me through tears.

I looked at his mom and dad who were tearing up and I looked at Brent.

"Brent, you have shown me what true love is. You have been my rock, my protector, and my best friend. I promise to always be there for you as well. To lift you when you are down, and to love you with all my heart. I vow to cherish the time we have together, and our connection and always be honest and faithful to you. Today we pledge to continue to grow together." I said looking at him

"To laugh together and to create a life full of happiness and love," Brent said through tears smiling at me.

"No matter what, challenges come our way, we will face them together as a team," I said looking at Brent, "I love you more than words can express, and I am so grateful to have you as a partner in my life."

"I promise to never give up on us," Brent said holding my hands together with his, "and to always strive to make our love stronger each day. I am truly blessed to have you at my side too and I can't wait to spend the rest of our lives together too. I love you so much Bellatrix Kai now and forever."

"May I have the rings, please? These rings are a symbol of your love and commitment to one another," Benjamin Wheatley said as he held onto the rings and slowly handed them to Brent and then to me.

"As you place these rings on each other's fingers, repeat after me, with this ring, I thee wed," Benjamin Wheatley said Slowly Brent put the ring on my finger and said, "With this ring, I thee wed."

And then I took the ring from Benjamin and put it on Brent's fingers through tears and said, "With this ring, I thee wed."

"By the power vested in me, I now pronounce you husband and wife. You may kiss the bride," Benjamin Wheatley said smiling and looking at both of us.

Just then Brent kissed me on the lips and at that moment

everything was all and right and well in the world, and I knew I was going to be in eternal happiness sharing the rest of my life with Brent and his family. I looked over at his grandfather who was tearing up in the eyes and nodding at me as I smiled and then I looked at Brent's parents who were smiling after we kissed. Everyone stood up and applauded as Brent and I looked at each other smiling. We then walked down the aisle of benches hand in hand, and the groomsmen and bridesmaids followed us to the reception area on the other side of the room that Brent and his parent's had set up for the buffet style set up for dinner. We stood at the entryway to the other part of the room separated by a makeshift wall as everyone came in and gave their congratulations to us and they took their seats.

After a few minutes everyone was sitting at the tables at their labeled seats and were eating happily.

"Bella, we are so happy that you are a part of our family now!" Brent's dad said smiling at me, as I nodded happily tearing up.

"I can't believe we are finally married Brent," I said looking at him in agreement, "this is the happiest day of my life."

"I feel the same way Bella," Brent said smiling at me kissing my hand.

As the night progressed, I had noticed that Brent's parents, Mr., and Mrs. Genuit seemed to be acting strangely around me. They exchanged glances with my brother Tobey, and my other brother Taylor earlier in the evening which seemed to start to create an unsettling atmosphere. I could sense there was tension between the four of them, but I couldn't quite put my finger on what was wrong.

Brent's parents approached us at the reception.

"Congratulations, Brent and Bella, its wonderful seeing our families coming together like this," Mr. Genuit said smiling at his son and then to me.

"Thank you so much!" I said smiling at Brent who held onto my hand again, "I am so happy to be a part of your family now."

"Oh, we have known your brothers now for quite some time Bella," Mrs. Genuit said seemingly drunk, "In fact, now that you are a part of the family now, you might as well know that we have a little family secret that we have kept hidden for years, even our son doesn't even know."

"Really?" I said curiously looking at Brent who shrugged not sure what she was talking about.

Taylor and Tommy seemed to be overhearing the conversation and made there over towards us as the tension seemed to rise.

"What secret would you be talking about Mrs. Genuit?" Tommy asked.

"It's someth-thing that d-ddates back many dd-decades now, something that could change everything," Mrs. Genuit said seemingly stumbling with her words in a drunken stupor.

It was then that Mr. Genuit puffed up angrily, "Now Sharon there is no need to be talking about that right now."

"Yeah, perhaps you better not talk about that right now," Tommy said snaring at Mr. Genuit.

Suddenly, all hell broke loose, as an intense argument erupted between Brent's parents and my brothers. They were accusing each other of something that happened years ago between my parents and Brents parents. Accusations flew, and harsh words were exchanged, revealing a dark family secret that threatened to shatter the fragile peace of the evening.

"You and our Aunt and Uncle didn't get along, did you?" Taylor said in anger

"You played that dirty trick on them didn't you!" Tommy said as Mrs. Genuit smiled

"It wasn't a dirty trick, we just fell in love with each other even though we were dating them at the time, and look things still turned out because they seemed to fall in love with each other as well," Mr. Genuit said

"Wait, you were both dating our aunt and uncle?" I asked as Taylor nodded.

"Yeah, Aunt Beatrice and Uncle Bernard used to date them

before your mom dated your Uncle Kahn," Tommy said, and they both played our aunt and uncle like they were falling in love with them and played them on for years.

"Yeah, but that's over now," Brent said looking at them seriously, "You can't seriously be holding a grudge against my parent's because of that!"

"Aye, and what makes you think that I would do that to Bella?" Brent said looking at Bella and then to his parents, "I am not you; I am fully in love with her."

My heart pounded in my chest as I watched the drama unfold before my eyes. The revelation of the secret sent shockwaves through me, threatening the foundation of my new marriage with Brent. I felt a wave of panic wash over me as she struggled to process the truth that had been hidden from us. Many of the guests at the reception had already started to leave saying their goodbyes to us as they noticed how my brothers and Brent's parents were behaving.

"We left our gifts for you both on the table," Tina said to me as her and many of the other Time Council members left. It was then that more people started to leave.

"Thank you all for coming," I said smiling at them as they looked over at Tommy and Taylor and Brent's parents who were still arguing and then they left shaking their heads at the scene.

Chapter 37

A Difficult Loss

I looked up and I had seen Kahn Tucker sitting at a nearby guest table. He seemed to be overhearing what was being said. He then made a smirking face at what was being said and it triggered me when seeing him make that face.

"I remember that face," I said under my breath.

"What face? What are you talking about dear?" Brent asked me as I put my hands on my chest and stood up.

I felt my heart beating faster and faster. I started having issues breathing and felt like I was suffocating under pressure and anxiety which suddenly hit my chest all at once.

It was then that I remembered crouching in the tent. The vivid memory terrorizing me as if it were yesterday, it seemed like it would be forever engraved in my mind, it was now replaying. Kahn's laugh filled my ears of the vivid memory and that smirk, as he dug his sword down into the chest cavity of my father from his neck. I fell on the ground as I watched again as he did it to my mother. Her scream was never heard before by me in such pain and while she was in agony. It was the same smirk he had worn years ago. I started gasping for air, overwhelmed by the past colliding now with the present. I then got up and stumbled away from the group, seeking solace in a quiet corner. My mind was reeling with memories of the night my life changed forever. The weight of the trauma threatened to suffocate me as I struggled to regain control of my racing thoughts.

"I can't breathe!" I said worriedly looking around the room and holding onto my chest. I started wheezing and I felt like I was running a thousand miles an hour as Kahn's face again came into my mind.

"Bella! Bella! Are you okay!? What's wrong?" Brent asked me to catch my hand as my brothers continued to argue with Brent's parents not noticing me.

Brent's heart ached as he saw me in distress and followed me as I ran away with Brent closely behind me with concern etched on his face. I ran into the stairwell that lead from the kitchen to the wedding reception. But before he could reach me, a piercing scream echoed through the reception hall, shattering the uneasy silence.

I had screamed in terror again at what I saw.

Rushing to my side, I turned around in Brent's chest and held him tight as this was all too much for me. He saw that my eyes were wide in terror. He saw my distress and hugged me immediately in return and then he saw what I saw. His blood ran cold as the sight of his grandfather was lying motionless in the hallway.

"NOOOO!" Brent screamed in pain as he held me tighter, and then I released my hug from Brent as I knelt over his grandfather to see there was no pulse.

Tears rolled down my face as I looked at Brent's face which was in anguish.

We went back to the reception to contact Brent's parents who seemed to be enjoying themselves as if nothing happened. Tommy and Taylor were still mad at Brent's parents and saw them in the corner of my eye. Brent and I walked up to his parents and Brent with tears flooding his eyes again said, "Grandpa Grant is dead."

It was then that everyone in the room stopped and looked at us in shock. Even my brothers had stopped arguing and looked over to us.

"What?!" Brent's dad said in shock at what Brent had said.

"We found Grandpa dead on route to the kitchen," Brent said trying not to lie about the secret hallway but at the same time tell his parents what was going on."

"Come, you need to see," Brent said through tears as his father started to cry, and nodded.

Within minutes Brent's father and mother, Tommy, and Tobey, followed us out of the room and into the hallway where Grant Genuit's motionless body was.

"NOOO!! DAD!" Brent's father said in panic

"There is something you can do about that Bella," Terrance then inaudibly whispered from behind me. I knew he was talking about the sword. I had already known that Grant had told his grandson the last time they had given him time.
I shook my head and said, "I know but he wouldn't want us to anyway. He had already been given time from Brent before, and he felt like he owed Brent his life."
Terrance nodded and then motioned for Tommy and Tobey to quietly leave and they walked away from us as Brent's dad and his mom started to cry over Grant's body with Brent. Brent walked over to me and hugged me and was crying in my shoulders.
"He's gone, just like that Bella, on our wedding day, my grandfather is... I can't believe it! Why didn't he tell me he needed more time? Why didn't he tell us! He was just here celebrating the wedding with the rest of us!" Brent said in my shoulder his voice was trembling as he was staring down at his grandfather's lifeless body.
"I know, Brent. I'm so, so sorry. He was so strong, always so full of life. This doesn't feel real," I said through tears that were welling up, placing my hand gently on Brent's shoulder.
"It's not fair! He's been the one constant in my life. He was always there for me, especially after my parents... after they disappeared. He was like a father to me! I can't lose him too!"

Brent said in sadness shaking his head, and his eyes were brimming with tears.

"You haven't lost him, not really. He is still with you; in everything he has taught you in your life. From all the lessons that you have learned along the way to this point. He lives on through you. Whether you realize it or not he is living and breathing on through you and what you are putting onto others. He hasn't a chance to die from this world if those who remember him and keep his memory alive live on and remind people daily of him," I said softly in his ear trying to hold back tears, "he is still alive through all the love he gave you. He said you were the strongest person he knew."

"He believed in me more than I ever believed in myself. He was so happy being able to help me set up this wedding for us. I just wish I could have done more for him; you know? He deserved so much more than this, "Brent said as his voice was breaking.

"You were the one that gave him life, more time, do you remember what he had said when you gave it to him?" I asked him with tears rolling down my face, as he shook his head. "He said, "I am grateful for the time you have given me Brent, but please do not do this for me again. I believe that my time will come when it is my time. I will not deal or beg or bargain for my time."

Brent broke down in tears.

"Brent he was so proud of you, of the man you have become. Every time he and I were together, he would talk about how much you have grown, how much he admired you. You were his world. You have given him so much joy and happiness just being with him. He loved spending his time with you right to the very end. You gave him everything- your love, your time. He never doubted you for a second," I said in a gentle voice with tears streaming down my face.

"He wanted you and me to be happy Bella. He felt like he had a sense of purpose putting this wedding together for us," Brent's voice cracked, "He was always pushing me for us to work together, to build something strong. I don't even know if I will know how to do this without him guiding me anymore."

"Do you remember what he said that day that we were looking for your parents?" I asked him. "We were so frustrated, hitting dead ends trying to figure out what they were researching and where they were." I said wiping a tear from his cheek.

"He told us that our strength wasn't just in what we could do alone, but what we could accomplish together. He knew we would end up finding your parents Brent, he had faith in us," I said.

"Yeah, I remember," Brent said nodding as tearing will spilling down his cheeks, "He said that if we stayed together, we could face anything that our love would carry us through, even when things felt impossible."

"He believed in us, in this… in our future. He told me once privately that he knew that you and I were meant to be. He said that love like ours, built through trials would last forever, that's what he wanted for us. That is what he believed," I said in a voice filled with emotion.

"I can't believe that he is not here to see it," Brent said sobbing quietly holding me tighter. "to see us after marriage. He wanted this so much for us."

"He will be with us Brent. I know he will. Every step we take, every vow we made it was because of him. He's the reason we are stronger, this ready to build our life together. And I will never forget how he pushed us to love each other more deeply to never give up on us." I said to Brent holding him tightly in return as my voice was shaking.

"I miss him so much already. I don't even know how to imagine life without him here," Brent whispered, his voice heavy with grief.

"I know I miss him too," I said tearfully stroking his back, "But we will carry him with us, every single day. I our love, in our marriage, in the way we live our lives. He will always be a part of us."

"You are right," Brent said looking into my eyes, "He always said our love would be stronger than anything we faced. And he was right. If I have you, I will carry him with you. We will carry him together."

"Together Brent," I said nodding as my own tears were flowing freely, "Just like he wanted. We will honor him by making sure we live out everything he hoped for us."

"I love you Bella," Brent said squeezing my hand, with his voice filled with emotions, "I promise you; I am going to make sure that we have the kind of life that he always believed in for us. No matter what. I am going to keep going and improving myself and striving for better for me and for the both of us together!"

"I love you too Brent," I said smiling at him through tears, "You never cease to surprise me. I know we are going to be okay. We are going to make him proud together.

"You both are so remarkable," Brent's dad said through tears as he hugged us both. We brought Grant's body to the front of the store and the Timekeepers were called to help bring his body to the mortuary.

"It's getting late you two," Mrs. Genuit said looking at us and then looked at her son, "Maybe you both should get some rest. It's okay, we will clean up from here."

Brent nodded as we left the bookstore, and walked back to the Time Tower noticing that everyone else had already left. When we got to the Time Tower everyone seemed to be in their rooms or in bed for the night.

"Today was a rough day for the both of us," I started to say looking at Brent after closing the door to his room, "But I don't want you to forget that this was also one of the happiest days of my life too. I am filled with mixed emotions now losing our grandfather and our wedding today. Things always have a way of working out in the end, even if it's in a way that we least expect."

"Bella, I know that I am upset about my grandfather's passing but even with that, I want you to know that I am so happy that we got married and he got to see the ceremony at least of us," Brent said.

We kissed goodnight and I nodded and smiled, and we both went into bed and tried to go to sleep.

That night we both tried to sleep in his guest room together.

Chapter 38

The Night Terror

I closed my eyes for the night and after a few hours, my peaceful expression quickly turned into one of distress as I started to have clouds of darkness surround me in my dream. Kahn's laugh echoed and the memory of Kahn smirking at the wedding came to mind, as I mumbled in my sleep, tossing and turning. Kahn Tucker, the ruthless commander, wielding his sword to strike down my parents in front of me, their screams echoed in my mind as if it were yesterday. The smell of their blood filled my nostrils, and I started to tremble in fear and was overwhelmed by a sense of helplessness.

Brent woke up with a start, as he tried to reach out to me gently shaking me awake.

"No, no, no, don't kill me too! I swear! Please!" I shouted

"Bella, Bella, wake up," Brent said in worry and concern as he turned on the lights.

I sat up, breathing in and out heavily as I tried to calm down.

"It was just a dream Bella," Brent said trying to rub my back in comfort.

"Just a dream," I said, my voice trembling through tears, "I thought he was going to kill me that day."

"What happened? Do you want to talk about it?" Brent asked

me gently wrapping his arms around me.

I need some water," I said as Brent nodded and left the room to get me a glass of water.

My heart was pounding in my chest as if I were still back at that moment in my parent's tent watching them being murdered before my eyes. I held onto my knees in bed in a fetal position thinking about what had happened to them. Brent saw that I was visibly shaking struggling to cope. I was overwhelmed with emotions that were consuming me. I had tried to bury this pain for years, and it just unexpectedly resurfaced leaving me feeling raw and vulnerable.

"Bella," Brent said softly recovering and walking up to me with a glass of ice water. He got into bed and helped me sit up and lay against him as he gave me the glass of water to sip.

"It was a nightmare," Brent repeated putting the glass of water on his bedside table and holding me with an arm around me.

"No, it was real, it happened, I just relived it over and over again," I said softly in a state of shock now holding my knees.

"What happened?" Brent asked me as I looked at him with sorrowful eyes, "You were there for me during a time I needed you. Now it's my turn to be there for you. In sickness and in health my love."

I nodded silently thinking about it hesitantly.

"I never told you how I came into this City or what happened to me when I was a child. Now that you are married to me, I suppose that you should have already known about me ahead of time. The truth is, David and Sharon were never my parents. I was never even related to them."

Brent nodded his head knowingly.

"I was told that they adopted you, and I have seen that they had raised you like you were their daughter," Brent explained what he knew, "David had asked if you wanted an apology from him in that letter but you never read that part to me fully. What happened Bells?"

I smiled at the thought of the new nickname he had given me and then hesitated.

"I tried to bury this pain I have had for years, and it resurfaced so unexpectedly," I repeated my thoughts aloud, "I feel so vulnerable and raw right now."

"You are allowed to feel that way towards me, I am your husband now," Brent said trying to urge me to continue to explain, "You are safe with me in here. I would never hurt you or use this against you."

"I know that you feel that you should be some unbreakable spirit Bella, but you are human and its okay to feel broken at times and to let others help you to heal too," Midnight said softly in my mind, "I urge you that you need to be more open to Brent."

"He is the one person you can be vulnerable to," Emrys said wisely.

I nodded to myself in agreement.

"Midnight is right, I feel like I should be this unbreakable free spirit, and I should be stronger than I am about this especially after all these years, but I feel shattered, and lost in a sea of memories with my parents and these memories of what happened to them, its all drowning me inside," I said as I started tearing up.

"I am right here Bells; I am here for you to talk to and to tell me what happened and what is going on. I can't read your mind. How can I help you if you don't tell me?" Brent said as I nodded and took a deep breath.

"This is a tale that is not for the faint of heart and isn't a tale of a happy ending either," I said taking a deep breath and sniffling.

"I was about fifteen when we first met. But what happened to me happened five and a half to six years before we met. I was in my Village spending time with my mom and dad. They were outside talking and then there was screaming as I put my head out of our tent. My mom said for me to stay inside and that everything was going to be okay. She promised. After a few minutes Kahn and his unit arrived at our Village of Pasqua. They wanted to know what my parents knew about something it was a hushed conversation between him and my parents and then I heard my father say, "I'm sorry but this is all we have! We are only a small village, and this is all the food we have for the winter! "How will we survive the winter without provisions and supplies?"

I started to tear up and then said, "Kahn made that smirk, the same one he made on the wedding yesterday. It's the same face that he made the day he killed my parents. He drove his sword from my father's neck down his torso through the rib cage from the top and blood was everywhere. My mother looked at me in worry and screamed in agony as Kahn killed her next. All David did that day was say to Kahn, "You shouldn't have done that." Then Kahn gave the orders to kill everyone else in the Village of Pasqua to leave no survivors. I was scared for my life. I didn't want to die. I didn't want to be killed. I saw Kahn's bloody sword as he pulled it out of my mother and the snow was now crimson red and it smelled horrible. David smuggled me into the City of Sandglass from my village in a basket of Rice that they stole along with a bunch of other supplies from our village and David was given the free basket of rice, which was crouched in, and Sharon and David made the decision to adopt me as their own."

Brent looked at me in horror as I described the gruesome details to him as I continued to explain.

"To this day, I have told Kahn I have forgiven him, but I have never forgotten and will never fully trust him. Even if he is my uncle and my mother's lover growing up. Their screams, their pain, I felt all over yesterday on my wedding day when I saw Kahn make that smirk. It all happened in my mind again as if it were yesterday and these nightmares had stopped for a while and now, they seem to be back again and I don't know what to do with them," I said holding my knees to my chest holding them close to me as if for dear life. Brent then hugged me after he had listened to me intently the whole time.

There was silence for a while as Brent seemed to be struggling with what to say to me.

"I'm so sorry Bella," Brent said thinking about what I had been through and I looked at him and he seemed to admire me more for having the courage to talk about it and relive it so I could explain it to him, "You are such a brave and courageous woman. I can't imagine how hard this must have been for you. But I want you to know that I'm here for you, you are safe with me, and I'll do whatever I can to help you through this."

"Thank you Brent, it means a lot to me to know that you are here for me. I just feel so overwhelmed by all these emotions. It's been a lot for me."

"I understand my love, it's okay to feel overwhelmed. B ut remember you are not alone. I want to support you and help you to cope with these feelings. We will get through this together," Brent said to me smiling, holding my hands together.

"Thank you so much, Brent, I love you so much. I don't know what I would do without you by my side," I said smiling at him and looking at Brent in his eyes.

"We will get through this together Bella," he said to me reassuringly, "One step at a time. I love you too."

As the night stretched on, we stayed up talking and comforting each other through my nightmare and memories that haunt me. Brent held my hand and it reenforced my feelings of safety and security with him like a blanket keeping out the chilly air on a frosty winter night. I found it easy to talk about things with Brent and talk about our memories together and how we had gotten through the obstacle of how he learned to walk again.

"I didn't think that I would ever be able to talk again Bella," Brent said to me, "But you gave me the strength and the resilience and with your perseverance it gave me hope that I would and with work, I was able to again. I promise to be the rock that you were for me as we have faced so many challenges in the past and now, I am determined that we will get through any future ones together like this one, because we have grown to love and understand one another."

I nodded in silence.

"Though the scars of your past remain Bella, you are going to emerge from these dark shadows of your trauma with a newfound resilience and determination," Midnight said to me as Emrys seemed to spread a warmth throughout my body.

"Yes Bella, you are going to be simply fine. You faced the darkness within yourself, and now you have the courage to fight back as you are not alone to battle these demons of your past. If you take that step forward, your spirit will never be broken as easily again," Emrys said

I nodded again to myself and said, "Thank you Emrys and Midnight," in my mind smiling at Brent.

"Let's try to get some sleep," Brent said hugging Bella who nodded and smiled, "I love you my dear, Goodnight,"

"Goodnight Brent," I said hugging and kissing Brent smiling. After an hour Brent awoke and saw that Bella was fast asleep and he left the bedroom.

Chapter 39

Old Sins Cast Long Shadows

Brent left the Time Tower that night and he started to walk down the road. As he walked closer to the bridge, he saw a figure of someone standing there. They appeared to be looking out into the water, as it streamed out heading away from under the bridge. There was a small light breeze of chilly night air that nipped Brent's his nose as he walked up to the figure in the shadow of the building nearby.

"Who is that?" Brent asked himself to feel slightly uneasy as he wrapped his Time council robe tighter around himself.

"Easy there Brent," came the voice in Brent's head as he nearly jumped, "It's just me Vitani, your Lion Spirit animal. I think it's Socrat, because I feel that Wren that highly energetic and intelligent squirrel nearby."

Brent nodded and took in a deep breath of relief. He then felt a feeling of warmth in his chest, on his neck, and on his right shoulder as a feeling of courage seemed to empower him to walk faster up to the figure.

"Hey, Socrat!" Brent said smiling at the figure of Socrat who stepped into the streetlight looking surprised about Brent's seeming foreknowledge.

"How did you know it was me?" Socrat asked in surprise.

"You forgot we have these spirit animal guides," Brent said smiling

Socrat looked at Brent and said, "No, only every time I am near James, I hear and feel Wren getting all giddy with James's spirit animal."

"What do you mean? I thought he just has that blue and gold symbol tattoo called, Verity," Brent asked as James nodded.

"The truth speaks to James," Socrat said to Brent matter-of-factly, "Just because it isn't an animal doesn't mean that the spirit is a mute. Symbols and item tattoos have spirit's attached to them too, which have positive and negative energies to them."

"Oh okay," Brent said nodding in understanding.

"I can't get my spirit to stop talking," Socrat said smiling at Brent who shook his head as Socrat started smiling at Brent. There was a moment of silence as Socrat seemed to be struggling with conversation with Brent.

"So, you couldn't sleep on your wedding night huh? Why aren't you not with Bella?" Socrat asked curiously tilting his head at Brent.

"Socrat?" Brent asked looking out into the water leaning on the railing of the bridge, "A lot has happened. There is more to what I realized was wrong with Bella from when I first proposed to her. I am having problems processing it all."

"What is going on?" Socrat asked curiously looking at Brent, "I know that in the past we haven't been all that close, but I want to be there for you and Bella."

"You know Bella, she always smiles all the time, so it is hard to tell when something is bothering her. You never know what is going on behind her smile," Brent said as Socrat nodded in understanding.

"Can I ask you something?" Brent asked him.

"How have you and Michael been able to process the losses of those you knew in the Village of Pasqua?"

Seemingly not surprised by the question Socrat looked at Brent thoughtfully.

"I must tell you; my family and I were not close. I was in the closet for forever, It was meant to be so. You may not know this, but I had a crush on Michael for the longest time. The day that our Village was attacked. Michael and I were not there. We were playing out in the nearby woods where we had our own treehouse. Later that afternoon, we came back, and we saw death, decay, and destruction. The images of my parents and their bloody demise and everyone I once knew and loved, will forever be etched on my mind. But we had no control of what the result was. Michael and I have had to cope with survivors guilt. We realized that had we been there, we might have ended up dead, like the other children at the time who were our age. We saw there were no survivors and went back to our treehouse were we had supplies for a little while. In the end, we decided it would be best to move forward to the City of Sandglass -Time, where there were more people. We thought there might be a chance to resettle, and live better lives possibly," Socrat said sadly and then turned to Brent, and put his hand on his, "I must tell you. Wren is telling me to tell you that Michael's experience and my experience of what happened and the events that transpired are different from what Bella's are. She saw her parents being horrendously murdered right before her eyes by Kahn. Her own uncle. Then she was basically unofficially kidnapped and adopted by David and Sharon who took her in as their own. She has had to grow up quick, be strong for others around her. For the last fifteen years she has always had David and Sharon to help her and be there for her, but what were her parents like for her?"

"I am not sure," Brent said sadly, "She has never talked about them to me. I want to know what it was like for her growing up within the Village of Pasqua. But I have been too scared to ask her."

"No, you haven't been scared to ask her," Vitani said to Brent softly, "You don't want to hurt her feelings. As much as you yearn to know the one you love, you also respect her enough not to want to cause her anymore pain."

"According to Wren," Socrat said rolling his eyes, "You need to bring it up and talk to her about her parents. How they raise her to manage fear and loss, and spirituality may kind of help her cope with dealing with the grief."

"But it's not only grief that she is dealing with," Brent said through tears, "She isn't sleeping well. She is also dealing with night terrors. I want to help her and fix this."

Socrat put his hand on Brent's arm in understanding.

"After the wedding reception and learning of my grandfather's death, I was so absorbed in my own grief that I forgot about Bella. My Bella..." Brent continued with his voice trailing out through tears with the water as it passed under him.

"You must be brave Brent," Vitani said to him in a soft whisper as Brent nodded and Socrat nodded and smiled at Brent.

"What's going on?" came a voice from behind them as they both jumped. It was James who came up to Brent noticing he was crying.

"Bella is dealing with Night terrors," Brent said as Socrat nodded and looked at James who shook his head sadly as Brent sniffled looking out into the water.

"Brent was about to tell me what happened," Socrat said as James nodded and a warmth came over Brent from Vitani who was trying to encourage Brent to talk about it as Brent nodded.

"I was so wrapped up in my own grief I forgot about Bella. Bellatrix Kai, the woman who means so much to me. She has been there for me this whole time since coming to the City, she is so selfless. I am supposed to be her rock, and I literally forgot about her because my grandfather died. It was one slip up and I should have been there for her."

"Go on, tell us what happened," James said putting his hand on Brent and said, "Verity."

Suddenly Brent found it easier to talk about it as a blue aura came from James that blanketed him and seemed to calm him as he took a deep breath and nodded.

"I don't know if you remember but at the reception Bella's brothers and my parents were fighting," Brent said as James nodded.

"Who could forget?" Socrat said, "it made everyone uncomfortable and disperse so quickly."

"Socrat," James scolded as Socrat shrugged and nodded for Brent to continue.

"Bella, at the reception when she saw her two brothers fighting with my parents," Brent continued, "While this was going on, Kahn was seen making a smirking face."

"I am not familiar with this specific face but go on," James said nodding for Brent to continue.

"Well, this was the same face that Bella saw that fateful night, when he saw her kill her parents. It triggered her memory, and it had started to cause her great turmoil. I hadn't known this at the time, but she had left the group of people who were congratulating us on the marriage rather abruptly. When she left that's when she then found my grandfather, dead. She called for me and I came running and found him," Brent said as he started to cry.

James muttered, "Verity," under his breath. Then there was then a lighter blue light that coming from James that seemed to surround Brent again as he seemed to calm down.

"It was the one time that I should have been there for her," Brent said sobbing.

"But how could you? You didn't know Brent," Socrat said as James nodded encouragingly.

"That same face that he made when he killed her parents, that stupid smirk that he made. A simple face that he made. It reminded her of one of the darkest days of her life, on the day that was supposed to be the happiest day of her life!" Brent said in frustration.

"Who was it that wanted him to be there?" James asked curiously.

"Bella said that she wanted him there because he is her uncle," Brent said sadly, "I should have told her no. But again she selflessly thought of me and my feelings knowing that he was a part of David's unit and yet knowing full well that this could have been done to her. I hadn't known that she hadn't fully recovered from dealing with the death of her parents. Like she hasn't professionally talked to anyone."

"Wren wants me to tell you something," Socrat said closing his eyes and then his spirit animal came to life in the air in front of them.

"I know you are going through so much right now Brent, but you need to be there for Bella too. It is also important for you to remember something. You cannot "fix" Bella. In any relationship this is true. Just as James cannot fix Socrat. You are not a licensed professional. It is not your responsibility to change or control or "fix" her. Instead focus on communicating openly and honestly with her. Setting healthy boundaries and supporting her with their own personal growth and development. Encourage her to seek therapy or counseling if needed," Wren said as Socrat nodded and then interrupted.

"We have Terrance, he is in charge of the Health and Well Being Department," Socrat said smiling, "Maybe he has a counselor who can help her."

"Don't interrupt me young Socrat," Wren said scoldingly as Socrat nodded.

"Yes Sir," Socrat said apologetically as Wren nodded.

"That is quite all right, anyway, you should offer your understanding and empathy. Remember both people in a relationship are responsible for their own actions and choices. It is essential to work together as a team to address any issues or challenges that may arise," Wren said shaking his tail wily as he spoke intelligently.

"Wren is right, you can't "fix" Bella, but we can all be there for her," Socrat said in slight concern.

"This is not to say that you don't care about Bella," James said putting his hand on Brent's shoulder. But you can talk to her and be there to listen to her and what she is emotionally going through.

"So should I talk to Kahn to talk to her?" Brent asked looking at Socrat and James and then to Wren who all remained silent.

"It depends," Wren said, "Is this going to help her and bring her closure? Or do you think this will open the wounds that she has already tried to seal up once more?"

Brent remained silent and then Wren disappeared back into Socrat.

"Well, you do what you think is best Brent," James said looking at Socrat, "It is getting late, we should get some sleep."

Socrat nodded as he and James and gave Brent goodbye hugs and left back towards the Time Tower. Brent stayed on the bridge thinking.

"Brent, you and Bella are going to get through this," Vitani said soothingly as he nodded, "just give it time."

Brent started to walk back to the tower thinking about his options. Then he made his decision, and turned away from the tower as the sun seemed to have crept up on him.

"It's already early morning," Brent said thinking about how much time he had spent being concerned and thinking about Bella.

"You know you love her Brent. But you must also take care of you and get sleep hun," Vitani said urging him to go back home.

"I will but there is something I need to do first," Brent said determined.

He walked down the path into town and turned down a few roads to eventually find Kahn's house ahead.

"Well, there is no beating around the bush on this one," Brent said to himself.

Kahn was outside his home tending to his garden as Brent walked up to him.

"Hey Brent! How is the honeymoon going for you both?" Kahn asked smiling at him.

"Um, actually that is what I wanted to talk to you about," Brent said rather seriously, "Can I talk to you about something serious?"

"Sure, Brent, what's on your mind?" Kahn asked looking at Brent putting his head on top of his hands which were on the handle of a rake standing up from his garden area.

"Bella had a nightmare last night about you, and it really shook her up. She said she saw that same smirk you made before you killed her parents yesterday at the wedding and it seems to have triggered a lot of painful memories for her," Brent said in concern looking at Kahn who shrugged.

"That poor child has been through so much at my hands. I cannot ask her to forget even though she said she had forgiven me." Kahn said shaking his head, "I didn't know that she was still struggling with that. I never meant to cause her anymore pain than she has already gone through."

Kahn took a deep breath in.

"She has thick skin you know," Kahn said looking at Brent, "I know people who would have gone as far as to try to kill me and ask questions later if given the chance. That girl has a lot of character, and a strong personality. Don't let go of her that easily."

Brent nodded at Kahn and took a deep breath in and out.

"I wish you both nothing but happiness," Kahn said to him as he looked down.

"I know you didn't mean to stir up trouble for Bella, but I think maybe it would mean a lot to Bella if you could talk to her about it. Maybe offer her an apology or some kind of closure. She's been through so much already and I know she would appreciate your understanding," Brent said to Kahn.

"I understand," Kahn said looking at Brent nodding and putting his hand on Brent, "I'll talk to her and try to make things right. Thanks for letting me know, Brent. Bellatrix is my niece and even though I have caused her great pain in our past, I am trying my best to improve my relationship with her. I still want her to know that she means a lot to me, and that I want to do what I can to better support her."

"I am not able to speak for Bella, to know that for sure eventually things will get better, considering your actions. Though you were following orders, you did this without considering your conscience nor consequence to Bellatrix and others," Brent said to Kahn who put his head down in shame as he started to tear.

Kahn continued to look down and said through heartfelt regret, and tears, "I know my daughter, Taylor would have been so disappointed in me for what I had done without consideration of my conscience first. I wanted so much to impress the council."

"I appreciate you talking to Bella for me," Brent said looking at Kahn and putting his hand on Kahn, "I know Bella will too. I will talk to her and tell her that to this day you still regret what has transpired with her and your family. Thank you for being understanding still and willing to help her through these grim times."

"Of course, Brent. Bella's important to us both, I want to do what I can to help undo the transgressions I have caused. We need to be sure that she knows that she has our support through thick and thin going forward," Kahn said smiling to Brent who had nodded in agreement, "Thank you for taking the time to tell me about Bellatrix."

Brent nodded and Brent left to go back to the Time Tower.

"You satisfied now?" Vitani said slightly annoyed as Brent nodded, "Good now let's go home and get some sleep."

Brent laughed and yawned happily, "Look who is so grumpy in the morning!"

They made it back to the room as Bella was still fast asleep, and Brent went back to bed lying next to her feeling better now having talked about what was bugging him and he was able to get to sleep more soundly.

Chapter 40

The Titus Report

The next morning came less than an hour later for Brent as I arose trying to wake Brent up.

"Good Morning my husband!" I said as Brent smiled at that hearing me trying to wake him up, "What do you have planned for today?"

"Sleep," Brent said from under the comforter that was on the bed.

"But it's a new day, the sun is out, we have to wake up," I said smiling happily trying to hug Brent through the covers.

"I only went to sleep an hour ago roughly," Brent said as I looked at him in surprise.

"You didn't sleep?" I asked him in concern.

"I was up late thinking about things," Brent said to me as I nodded in understanding and decided to let him sleep.

I walked over to the door and picked up the various envelopes of messages that were left for me from various Night Hunters and Time Keepers. I walked over to my desk, and placed the small pile of them in front of me as I opened the first one. I had started reading the familiar scrawl of one of the Time Keepers. Finally, my long-awaited wait for answers paid off. The word on the top of the page read:

The Dossier of the deaths of Martha and Jeff Kai.

According to what I was able to find out Bellatrix, it seems like Council Member Tim had people report to him from the Timekeepers regarding your parents. He also wanted to research the history of how the Village of Pasqua was set up, and about your parents who oversaw the Village. Years ago, the Village of Pasqua was started because a few people from the City of Sandglass were not used to living City life in their former life on Earth. They wanted something similar so, they decided that they wanted to live in a small village, which they started and set up on their own. The Village was prosperous as it allowed people to feel a sense of freedom being able to leave the City whenever they wanted to visit the first village. The original leaders Jasmine and Mertkaw Kai were your mom's parents, Bella. They had two daughters Martha and Beatrice. Kahn, Kaide, and Jeff were brothers who lived in the city and would get together with your parents. Kahn had a brief relationship with Martha, and they had Terry. But then shortly after she was born, Kahn decided to leave Martha. It almost destroyed Martha losing Kahn. But had she realized that with him being a soldier in his unit, he had grown colder and was no longer the man she thought she loved. Kahn took his 5-year-old daughter at the time, and he and her left to the City of Sandglass to live with his parents, never to be heard from again. A few years later, Jeff, Kahn's brother and Martha started going out and eventually Jeff married Martha and had Tobey, Taylor, Tommy, and Bella. One Summer, Beatrice took the boys for a few weeks and raised them in the city when they were at a more malleable age. When they came back home to the Village, they were never the same. Martha told Beatrice that she didn't want her sons raised being conscious of time, and spirit tattoos. She wanted to shield them from knowing of the power of the influence of time that the City had on its people, but it was too late. Unable to get the boys to change, Martha sent them back to live with her sister Beatrice, to continue to raise. It in a way worked out since she and Bernard were never able to have kids. Determined not to have their only daughter, you, turn out like that, they decided to hide the existence of your siblings from you, until you were old enough to understand. There was also this letter behind this report I wanted you to read in your own mother's hand and Beatrice's Response. I looked at the two pages behind and read the short messages between the sisters and could sense the distaste of her sister from my own mother.

"Beatrice, though I respect your decision to raise my boys your way while within the city limits, I will not have their influence negatively affect our Bella. We intend to raise her without the knowledge of them until she is of age to understand the Time situation there. We in the Village of Pasqua do not show Time to others while here, and it is not shown to each other as one of our Village Rules. I am grateful that you and Bernard will continue to raise our boys, and I hope that they end up being successful.

Martha

"We respect your wishes regarding the boys, and we will continue to tell the boys about your daughter, Bella. It is our hope that she doesn't resent you for keeping the knowledge of her own brothers, aunt, and two uncles, and her stepsister in the City were living just a few miles away. I hope you are keeping our parents' home and village safe as you promised Dad.

    Love Beatrice

After reading the two letters I continued to read the message of the report.

Your parents were killed because Michael reported to Tim about a certain meeting that was going to happen. Apparently, it's not what you originally thought that the meeting was about. It wasn't going to be about the underground. It was a rouge. Your parents knew someone was going to betray them because they put it out as a false trail. They were going to report the Time Road to the Villagers to keep an eye out for people out of the ordinary traveling through the town or escaping through the Underground. Bella, your parents were going to tell the Time Council about the Underground Time Road, which is why Tim ordered Kahn to kill them. Tim didn't want the news of this Time Road nor the people behind it to be exposed when he was part of the ones who was behind it all. Titus had written in the report what he had researched through the Council archives and hidden records for me. I could tell the letters between my mom and my sister had the Time Council stamp on them. Someone thought that the record needed to be that they disliked each other.

I looked up at Brent who still seemed to be sleeping away. I knew why my mother was the way she was raising me like this. The ideas of Time that I recently learned about coming to the City of Sandglass was something that even me at my younger age would have had a tough time to understand. Much less the idea of a child having to understand the concept of time and how to use it. It's like instructing a child about the adult ways of needing to be an adult at 5 years old. My siblings would have been much too young to understand. But even at

10 when they were learning of such things that summer from my Aunt that might have been too much even for them at the time not knowing how to be a child and having to grow up quicker. I had still remembered my time as a child growing up and playing outside on the streets kicking a ball around and playing tag with Michael and Socrat when I was younger. I had wondered how much of a childhood my brothers had growing up.

I then folded up the report and placed it back into the envelope and went on to the next letter

It was a letter from the White Wall.

Bella, I am just writing to thank you for what you and your friends did to undo what was done and stop what could have been. Thinking of you all and hope you are well!" – Your friend.

I knew it was from the chief and it was nice to smile and read the letter from him.

"What are you smiling about?" Brent asked me from the bed noticing I was smiling at my desk.

"The Chief of the White Wall sends his regards," I said smiling up at him as he rolled his eyes.

 "Well, I am glad that someone out there seems to know that we got married," Brent said smiling at me as I shook my head.

"He was thanking us for doing what we did to undo what could have been," I said as his face changed into an aghast look.

"I can't believe he didn't know about our wedding," Brent said looking at as I nodded at him.

"I had the Night Hunters spread the notices out to everyone everywhere I told them. But that only covers the City of Sandglass – Time, the other Time Councils and then a few of the outer lying villages. Not in the Underground or past the trenches," Brent explained as I nodded thoughtfully looking at him sitting up at the edge of the bed and I yawned and stretched at my desk.

"We need to talk," Brent said as I nodded, and he walked up to
me as he hugged me while I was sitting at my desk.

He kissed my forehead, grabbed my hands, and pulled me out from behind the desk. I kept my eyes on him as he slowly backed up towards the bed and we sat down next to each other still holding onto each other's hands.

"I love you," he said to me as I pursed my lips together nodded and took in a deep breath, "You have known for years that no matter what we have been through, we end up making it to the other side. I want you to know that what you are going through right now, is what we are going through together. You are not alone."

"You aren't going to leave me because I have these night terrors?" I asked him worriedly.

Brent shook his head at me with a serious face.

"You are the same woman that I fell in love within my bedroom all those years ago," Brent said smiling at me, "I am not going to leave you just because you have night terrors. That would be like you leaving me because I have diabetes or Alzheimer's or a disease that I contracted that was out of my control. I fell in love with you. The woman of my life with a big, kind and loving and caring heart. The person that you are, today, who is the person that is continuously trying to improve herself better than she was yesterday. The woman who makes mistakes, owns up to them, and learns from them. You are the most stubborn woman I love who is not critical of others. The woman who knows she is imperfect, but still smiles and brings joy and smiles to those around her. I love you because of your stubbornness and your perseverance. Without you, I wouldn't be where I am today. I love you for never giving up on me. You kept trying to get me to walk when it seems everyone else around my grandfather would just say, your poor son, I am so sorry he will be bedridden for the rest of his life and yet my grandfather found hope in you like I did that you would help us through this. To this day, I am so proud to call you my wife, it makes me so happy that you are my other half. I intend to be there for you no matter what, just like you were for me. When you were trying to make me better and help me and you never gave up on me. So now, it is my turn, I won't give up on you. I want you to realize that my love for you has no boundaries. It doesn't dictate that you need to only be a certain way all the time, it doesn't discriminate. My love for you is pure and with good intentions for the betterment of our future together. I want you to know that I know that we are going to get through this, and we are going to end up being stronger in the end no matter what. No matter what you need me to do, I will do it for you. I want you to know that I love you so much, so deeply that it hurts when I am not with you. I need you to know that I just want to spend the rest of my life with you."

I had started to tear up and cry. He was so loving and kind. I could tell he worries about me constantly.

"I love you too Brent," I said wiping the tears in my eyes, "I just don't know what to do about how to manage these night terrors."

"What helped you before?" Brent asked me as I looked out.

"I had Sharon and David," I said sadly as Brent looked down.

Just then there was a knock at the door, and it was a timekeeper.

"Special delivery for you Bellatrix," the timekeeper said as he nodded at me seriously and handed me a sheet of paper that was folded in half. He then walked off as I closed the door and sat up against the door as I read the note.

Bellatrix Kai

I took a deep breath realizing who it was from...

I know I may be the last person that you want to hear from. But I wanted to tell you that I was told by Brent that you had night terrors last night. I want you to know that as your Uncle, I am sorry that I have brought back painful memories for you. I want you to know that I never wanted to cause you any more pain, especially yesterday of all days being your wedding day. I want you to know that what happened that day was not easy for me in the end to have to cope with in the end. As it hasn't been for you since you lost your parents, but I lost a brother, and I lost

a former lover and the mother of my daughter. I was just following orders, and it killed me inside to have to do what I did in the end, to this day, it's a regret with which I must live. Though they were not easy to have a good relationship with towards the end, I loved them so much! As your uncle, I want to be there for you now and help you get through this. I know that you said you forgive me for what I did. I feel I don't deserve it. But also, to say it and to follow through with it are two separate things. I am terribly sorry for what had happened. I hope you can find the time for us to get together so we can have some type of closure together and fix our relationship and be there for each other more. Afterall, we are family, and we are all we have left. I am here for you whenever you need me. Let's support each other and heal together.
With Love

Uncle Kahn

"WHAT IS THIS?!" I said angrily holding out the paper to Brent who's ears turned red and he avoided my eye contact, "What happened to us getting through this together?! You brought him of all people into this! How dare you!"

"I'm sorry Bella!" Brent said to me as I threw the letter on the ground and stormed out of the room.

Chapter 41
Stunned

I ran to the library in the Time Tower which was up to the fifth floor. Brent had run out of the room to chase after me, but he was running as if I left the building. I didn't bother letting him know he was going in the opposite direction from where I was going. I wasn't in the mood. I knew he wanted to resolve the issue without delay, but I needed to think about things. Now Kahn knew the one thing I didn't want him to know.

"How lame is it that here I am still not completely over the one thing that happened over 15 years ago and even though I say I forgave him, I still haven't been able to move forward," I thought to myself in frustration, *"and in the course of a night, all it took, one interaction with that man and now I am back to square one."*

"Now now Bella," came a stern deep voice in my head, "You are no martyr. Stop playing the victim. Stop being so hard on yourself. That man, Kahn, was extending an olive branch to you, and your husband was only trying to help you. There is no need to think about this, just feel them, and sometimes, it's okay to just, let things happen."

"Hey Bella," came a voice from behind the shelf as I turned around. It was Terrance.

"Hey," I said slightly moody.

"Already having our first post-marital argument already I see..." Terrance laughed lightly, "That is why, I would never get married."

"Easy for you to say, considering if it were my sister, you probably would be swooning over her right now," I said.

"Swooning? Hardly the term I would use to describe me being slightly clingy to her," Terrance said turning slightly pink.

"Ask him what is on your mind right now Bella," Midnight said urgently.

"I have a spiritual push to ask you something right now," I said seriously, "If you had the ability to bring people back, would you?"

"What do you mean?" Terrance asked in slight concern.

"If you have the ability to say, bring my sister back and David and Sharon, would you?" I asked him.

"Well, it's one thing to ask if I would, versus if it is allowed," Terrance said calmly.

"What do you mean?" I asked.

"Have you heard of something called the balance of time?" Terrance asked me as I shook my head. He nodded his head slowly and looked around us to ensure we weren't overheard.

"Follow me," Terrance said ushering me to follow him with his right fingers. I followed him to the far end of the floor and into the stairwell hallway that no one seemed to be in as Terrance looked down and up the spiral stairs and no one seemed to be there.

"People today on Earth outside of our realm value time they make decisions based on meaning VS money. They choose to do things because they want to, not because they must. Time is one of our scariest resources because the value is tangible here with the things we do and want, and yet, it is practically infinite here. But when it comes to bringing back people who have moved on, we are acting like the watch maker. Do you know who that is?"

I shook my head.

"The watchmaker is someone who created all this space here. They are the one that has the power over the Time Councils and the watch maker has only intervened when it has had to once in history. That was during WW2 and the deaths of hundreds of millions of people most recently. Some here to this day remember what their lives were like then in that war. Now some are here because of the deaths from WW3 and the causes of that unfathomable event. Some are fortunate to have been born here and could have the ability to be reborn on Earth outside of the timelines of the City's of Sandglass. If we were to "bring back" let's say hypothetically those three people you mentioned, you would be under intense scrutiny.

What makes you better or different to only have the loved ones that you want back. What about other's who have lost their loved ones here? You would come across as a bit selfish wouldn't you."

I then nodded silently but remained quiet noticing Terrance's demeanor was a little rigid, and cold and let him continue to talk.

"Now why would you think that you would have that much power of time?" Terrance said harshly to me, "You aren't that special my dear. You may be a time Council Member and in charge of the Night Hunters, but you are not above any of us." Terrance was glaring at me silently for a minute as I was taken aback by his sudden reaction to me.

"No one has that kind of power of time to bring back people who have died," Terrance said shaking his head, "Some of us are still hurting from coping with people we have lost so why would you even mention that? Don't you think I would want your sister back if I could? Don't let that power get to your head, you remember that."

"No Terrance that wasn't it at all, I was just asking if it's ever been done," I said hesitantly realizing that I may have offended Terrance. He just walked out of the stairwell angrily as I stood there stunned at what just happened.

Chapter 42

Overcoming

"What was that about?" Emrys asked in my head as I shrugged and shook my head putting my hands to my temples and massaging them as I noticed a headache was coming.

"I am not sure what to make of what just happened, maybe he is having a rough day," I said aloud.

"Bella, that sword, can it revive people?" Midnight hooted softly in my mind.

"I think so," I said calmly, "Thinking about what I was getting into."

"You know what I am thinking about doing," I said to Emrys and Midnight.

"You want to use the sword," Midnight said quietly

"uh-huh," I said calmly as I walked down the stairs and outside the library and towards David and Sharon's house.

"Yes, but how? And for who?" Emrys said, "You can't bring everyone back that you have lost. Everyone's bodies are buried, and they have been dead for days and for some weeks. Don't you think bringing them back would be very selfish of you? They all even said, "When it's our time, it's our time to go."

"Yes, but then why was I give this sword? Such an article of treasure should be able to be used," I thought in my head. "Ah," Midnight said, stopping me in my thoughts as I paid attention to what he was about to say, "Be careful of the treasures that you come across in your life, because sometimes even the most precious of things comes with their own burdens that the beholder must carry. The price of beholding such power or powerful object is responsibility. You must be careful that this sword doesn't get abused and or put in the wrong hands. *You were given this gift – NOT THE TIME COUNCIL.* Sometimes the burden of responsibility can be too much for the beholder to manage."

"Yes, I am aware. It is a responsibility that I must ensure that its protected, and that there may be consequences from reincarnating the dead back to life. But what would be the consequences of this? Everyone would be happy, and everything would be back to normal with David and Sharon back. They would still be able to be there for me just as Grant Genuit was there for Brent. Also, if we could bring them back, why not my sister and my parents?" I asked aloud.

"We know that you are in grief, but we must learn to let this go," Emrys agreed with Midnight. "You mustn't use the sword to bring back anyone from the dead."

"This grief, is a natural albatross that everyone must carry, but it doesn't have to be held up by only one person. Others can also help you get through this pain, and there is nothing wrong with asking for help now and again. Put your pride aside, and you must understand that it's too late for them to come back.

Also yes, as for Kahn, we all have regrets that we have made, which are mistakes now and again. We are not perfect, and Kahn is not too far gone to be able to be forgiven. No matter how many mistakes we have made in our lives, it is never too late. But this mistake would be one, if you choose to bring them all back. Just think if it weren't for their deaths things would not be the same for any of them, not even for you. Your parent's would want you to come back home, and they would be lonely in the Village of Pasqua since there is no one left. If they were to come back, they might even end up having survivors guilt. Then there is Brent's grandfather, he didn't want to come back remember, if it was his time, it was his time to go," Midnight logically tried to explain to me as I remained in contemplative silence.

"Yes, as for your sister, Tobey has her former position on the Time Council which she would want back. Kahn and you are still getting over the deaths of your sister and his daughter and your parent's deaths. In regards to the idea of bringing your sister too, Terrance is still grieving. James is also grieving his father, Kaide's death. People are trying to heal, bringing them back from their peace, would be a huge mistake and possibly catastrophic with consequences to everyone's mental health." Emrys explained as I nodded to myself.

"How does one get over these feelings though, I just feel so lost sometimes going day to day without David and Sharon," I said.

"Theodore is dealing with their deaths too but everyone grieves differently," Emrys said.

"David and Sharon were a great support to me when I lost my parents. They would talk to me and help me work through whatever I was going through at the time. They would help me to unpack things easier in my mind," I said.

"Well now, we are here," Midnight said to me as Emrys warmed me over my body. I thought about what Sharon had said to me whenever I had the Night Terror.

I thought back to last night when it happened. I was screaming and shouting in my sleep acting as if I ran up to Kahn and knocked him out with all my might after I had just seen him kill my father in my dream. I had relived Kahn killing my mother as if it was yesterday.

"NOOOO!" I had shouted and cried balling every time I heard his sword meet the bones of the bodies of my parents rubbing against his sword as he smirked doing it. I would wake up in sweats and my body shaking with fear and anger for not stopping it every time.

"It was just a dream Bella," Sharon would say calmly rubbing my back as I would take in a deep breath and let it out slowly trying to calm myself down so I could go back to sleep, "You cannot allow these emotions to control you. It's only natural to be emotional as we are emotional human beings but we cannot allow for them to control us and let it define who we are."

"She was right you know," Emrys said, "You know what she meant right?"

I nodded my head in silence.

"We can be angry at the situation because it happened and we can show that emotion, we have that permission to be that in the moment. However, that doesn't mean we need to "be that anger," all the time. You cannot allow that anger to flourish in you to the point where you are miserable all the time," Midnight said wisely.

"I just feel emotionally overwhelmed," I said to them, "Now Brent went to Kahn, and now I feel like an emotional nincompoop."

Midnight and Emrys laughed at me, "I am glad you both find me entertaining."

"Bella, we have been through a lot together, and we are not laughing at you, we are laughing at the fact that you think you are one," Emrys said trying to clarify the situation.

"We know that you are a strong and independent woman. You shouldn't feel the need to be like that all the time. It is okay to be vulnerable with us and to have imperfections. We couldn't dream of treating you any different. Just because you have had true traumas in your life. Traumas that others could scarcely imagine happening in front of them, you ought not to let them define who you are as a person. You will overcome this grief, because we have seen you do this before," Midnight said, "Its completely understandable to feel emotional during these night terrors, but remember we have the power to control our emotions, do not let this dictate your actions."

"Easier said than done when I feel so powerless because of what Kahn did. Now things are worse because he knows," I said to myself, "I cannot shake off this fear and anxiety no matter how hard I try."

I then remembered what Sharon had once told me, "It's all about finding coping mechanisms that work for you. Whether it's deep breathing exercises like you just did or visualizing you being able to have stopped Kahn to try to get over it. There are ways to help calm your mind and ground yourself during a night terror. It won't happen overnight for you to overcome this but with practice and persistence, you can start to gain control over your emotions again," I smiled at this memory of her holding me in a hug.

"You see now you are doing better," Midnight said hooting happily, "Maybe try visualizing Sharon hugging you during these night terrors holding you and protecting you from harm.

"That sounds like a good idea to try," I said to Midnight now smiling.

"Remember Bella, you are not alone in this. You have me and Midnight and Brent and Kahn to help you though this," Emrys said as I nodded through tears, "I miss Sharon and David, and I miss Kaide, and I miss my parents and Grant."

"Your feelings are valid, and you are allowed to feel his grief, but you need to move forward," Midnight said as I nodded, "Matter of fact you really shouldn't have treated Brent like that. He was only trying to help you. If I am not mistaken, he was trying to allow for you and Kahn to have closure. Closure is important for you to be able to move forward."

I took in a deep breath and reflected on Brent, and how he had tried to run after me after I had stormed out of the room. Emrys then whispered, "Midnight is right, he was only trying to help you have closure with Kahn, he wasn't trying to cause you anymore pain."

It was then that I nodded and walked back to my room, and I found Brent sitting outside my door.

"Your room was locked, I tried to chase after you Bells when you stormed out. When I left, I realized I locked myself out," Brent said sadly looking at me through tears, "I am so sorry Bells. I was just trying to help fix this."

"I know, I am sorry too Brent. You just needed to give me time to think about things and cool off," I said walking up to him and hugging him as I released the hug. I then unlocked my room door and let him in first and locked the door behind us. It was then that Midnight floated out of me and perched himself on the d0esk perch as I sat down at my desk.

Chapter 43

The Special Gift

There was a knock at the door and Brent opened it and there were several Timekeepers that were at the door and in their hands they all had wrapped gifts.

"The wedding gifts sir," said the timekeeper as Brent nodded and ushered them in.

"You can put them on the bed here," Brent said smiling at me, "You forgot about our gifts dear."

I smiled and shook my head as I saw Brent get giddy at the sight of all the gifts being placed on the bed as more and more of the timekeepers came into the room with handfuls of the gifts. After all the ten timekeepers came into the room with their handfuls of gifts from the wedding reception room. I paid them all with ten hours of time each as they looked wide eyed at me and smiled and bowed gratefully then they all left as Brent closed the door behind them and walked over to the bed.

"You are always so generous, come over here and help me out," Brent said smiling.

"I will write them all down," I said shaking my head, "Afterall, we will need to send out thank you cards for all these gifts."

Brent nodded and excitedly starting to unwrap various gifts from people from the wedding. Soon the room was filled with kitchen gifts, decorative things for our room and various gadgets and small home appliances.

"What do people think we are going to do, have a house in town as well?" Brent asked me as I thoughtfully looked at him. "No, you weren't thinking of that were you?" Brent asked me curiously putting down a toaster we had gotten.

"Well, the thought occurred to me that we will not be in charge of the Timekeepers and Night Hunters all our lives. Eventually we will need to be holding elections again to keep our Time Council spots," I said to him as he nodded.

"You wouldn't consider moving to another City of Sandglass, would you?" Brent asked me as I thought about things a little and shook my head.

"I don't know," I explained, "I guess it would depend on our situation, and where we are called to be."

It was then that Brent continued to look through more gifts and he unwrapped a baby bottle and binky and diapers.

"Really?" Brent said smiling widely, "Kids?"

"Oh my," I said smiling widely looking from the baby gift to Brent and then to the baby items again and started laughing, "That's a conversation we haven't even had yet."

Brent's ears turned pink.

"Eventually I would consider having a child," Brent said turning towards me.

I nodded in agreement but left it at that, as Brent opened the last gift which was an outfit for him to wear which he seemed to enjoy.

It was then that I was drawn to an already opened letter on my desk that was facing me.

It was labeled From the City of Sandglass – Time and thought about it.

"Unfinished business," I thought to myself, as I opened it and re-read it. I then stood up and walked around my desk to Brent who was still sitting on the bed and I looked at him and smiled.

"Come on Brent," I said as I grabbed his hand and pulled him off the bed and we walked out of my room and down the hall and went outside.

"Where are we going?" Brent asked me as I remained silent, "We have more gifts to open."

It was then that I handed him the letter from Kaide as he read it aloud, *"This is kaide, I know by now my son has made it to the Time Council. This was a prewritten message. I don't want you to think I am back. I instructed a dear friend of mine who is a Timekeeper to give this message to you at this exact moment. Firstly, I knew I was going to die soon, way before*

our original mission to the Trenches. I wanted to give myself a chance to enjoy being with you all and my son. I know James is going to ask for Socrat's hand in marriage soon. I whole heartedly give my permission. I want him to know and that when it happens, he will need to know that not only am so happy for him, but I am so proud of how he chose to live to be true to himself and not to try to live to please everyone else when it came to finding his partner. People need to learn to accept that love is love and no matter how you turn a relationship as long as it's not abusive, or toxic, and it's full of love and unconditional support, respect and trust of each other, that matters more.

I have one last bequest of you and Brent.

Within the Trenches, I have hidden a special artifact, that is ancient, and rare. You need to use the word "Goethe," and it will appear. You will find it in the wall above the table that is there along the path. This artifact is a special wedding gift for you and Brent. Use it to your will. Be careful in returning to the Trenches. I wish you and Brent all the love and support in the world - All my love and regards, Kaide."

Brent continued to follow me a few steps behind and then he stopped as he saw we were headed to hidden entrance to The Underground.

"But wait, why are we not bringing anyone else with us?" Brent asked as I turned around and glared at him.

"This is supposed to be something that you and me do," I said as he nodded and slowly continued to walk up to me with his hands still in his pockets.

"You are still mad at me aren't you," Brent asked me as I didn't react, "I feel guilty for telling Kahn, but he needed to know."

I shook my head silently and put my hand up to him to stop.

"No," I said to him, "I am not mad at you for that. I recognize that you did what you thought you needed to, in order to help me. This letter, I think there is more to this."

"What do you mean?" Brent asked me curiously.

"Why would Kaide send us all the way to The Trenches to find this when he could have just given it to us himself when he put it there or when we saw him?"

"We need to be on our guard," I said as we went through The Underground tunnels to the City in the cover of night. We walked through the city within a few hours and made it to the edge of town. The Trenches were darker looking than ever.

"We don't know who is going to be in there at this hour," Brent shuddered, "What if something happens to us?"

"I have faith we will be okay," I said calmly as I buttoned up my black Night Hunter Master Robe and Brent did the same with his Time Council Robes.

We walked on for what felt like hours through the narrow path.

"Bella, be careful," Brent said as we walked, and my foot got stuck in a root in the ground that was sticking up. Brent caught me as I started to fall forward.

"Thank you, Brent," I said gratefully as he nodded.

"Don't worry Bella, I got you always," he said smiling at me as I turned a slight pink and smiled. We rounded a corner and finally found the table that was mentioned in the letter.

I looked around us and couldn't see anyone around us.

"Do you think we should wait until morning?" Brent asked me nervously.

I then shook my head.

"No, this was left for us," I said calmly, "No one else knows we are here, and it's our wedding gift."

Brent smiled and nodded in understanding. I put my hand on the wall above the old ancient wooden table.

The wall above the table seemed as solid as a rock but I put my hand on the wall above the table and closed my eyes and said, *"Goethe."*

It was then that the wall pushed back and opened up a hollow space. Within the space there was a small old looking weathered wooden box and a letter.

Chapter 44

The Decision yet to be made

I reached for the box and placed it on the table in front of me and opened the letter. I looked over at Brent before reading it as I felt a surge of excitement ran through Brent and I. "Bella and Brent, you have done it, you have both found a secret and treasured gift above all others. Your love for each other. I know that at this moment you are probably wondering what is going on. It is my duty, no, this is a burden that is unfortunately meant to be passed down to you both," I read aloud and then looked at Brent who took in a deep breath of concern and breathed out nodding for me to continue and I nodded and took in a deep breath of concern myself before continuing.

"Your parents were the secret keepers of this box through the Bear Claw Society. That is until they passed away that I was the next in line to discover that I was next in line to inherit it. I was also told that you Bella would be the next one after me to inherit this," I continued to read and look up to Brent who nodded for me to continue.

"What you are about to open is a treasure above all others that I had mentioned before. This is the Watchmakers Watch.

Already I was told that you have the Sword of Damascus from Sharon and David and as you already know that this sword contains a lot of power. Specifically, the power of time. To be able to give and take life is an immense power in and of itself. Which in the wrong hands can lead to the destruction of everyone around it. The Watchmakers watch is also powerful. With it, you can use it to have a conversation with the watchmaker anytime. You can use it to go back in time and use the sword to ensure that someone doesn't die. In theory you could go back in time and give life to someone who has already passed away. Afterall the sword I am told has 5200 years in it. But when you do this, there are consequences to doing it. You must think carefully before doing so and perhaps a wise conversation with the watch maker first wouldn't be a bad idea. The wearer can use the watch to travel within their timeline back to the past and review events of the past or hold someone else's hand while wearing the watch and take that person to review your timeline or their timeline as the wearer's choosing. The watch can increase the ability to double the time when earning time for the wearer for normal deeds like sleeping for example, The wearer will gain 16 hours for sleeping for 8 hours instead of only gaining eight hours. Over the centuries many have searched for this watch. It has also been called the Time Flex Watch and it's extremely powerful. To use the watch, you must place it on your wrist pull out the pin on the side and turn the dial to seven. When you push it back in it will stop time and allow you to talk to the Watchmaker. Fair warning, the Watchmaker is not a patient person. Time is particularly important to them. They will send you back to this moment after you are done having conversation with them. Personally, I want you to know that I do not want to be brought back to life. You might find that a commonality among those who have passed away when you attempt to bring them back. The persons spirit must also be willing to come back as well for you to have them come back."

I looked up at Brent who nodded, and I finished reading the last of the letter.

"I want you to both know that it has been the view of many watch keepers before me that they have wanted all the councils not to know who has the watch and nor allow the councils to have such power over the people of the various City's of Sandglass. I am so happy that you both found each other and continue to be strengthened in your relationship after everything that you continue to go through. I am so sorry to place this secret upon you both but this needs to be kept secret. If you wish to use this watch and bring back people with the sword, I advise that you both figure out a way to explain how the person you bring back is alive. Knowing that you have had the sword this whole time has been a burden on me as I would have loved to have my own parents come back but it would have been selfish of me to ask and then figure out how to explain to the council and various people that knew them how they came back to life. Giving yourselves more time or more time to others around you is different than bringing someone who has already lived through their time to come back to life. This is a burden to figure out if you wish to take advantage of or not. This is entirely up to you. I am told that when you are almost out of time yourselves, ensure to entrust the secret of the watch and the sword to someone who would be able to keep it a secret from the Time Council's and ensure to be inconspicuous. I love you both, Kaide."

I finished reading the letter folded it up and then slowly opened the box. It looked like an oversized watch box and in it was another box which was glowing. I opened the inner box within the box, and it revealed a silver watch with a golden face and two blue light stripes along its band.

"So, are you going to use it?" Brent asked me curiously, "I mean you could use it and bring someone back from the dead and place them in one of the other City's of Sandglass and we could move out of course pending approval."

I thought carefully about what I was going to do as I looked at the watch that was glowing in the box.

"Bella, do you know what you are going to do in the end?" Emrys asked me in my mind as I remained silent. It was then that I thought about the lives of David and Sharon and Theodore's reaction to their deaths. I thought about Brent and his reaction on the day of our wedding of his grandfather's death and I thought about James and Kaide and how Kaide didn't want to come back. Then I thought about Kahn and my stepsister and how much grief it had caused between them and how much a second chance would mean to Kahn. Finally, images came to my mind of my ultimate thoughts of the lives of my parents Martha and Jeff Kai, "Oh how I miss them," I thought to myself. "Bella," Brent said turning to me and grabbing my hands as the box was sitting on the table wide open in front of us, "Do you know what you want to do? Either way, I want you to know, I love you and support whatever decision you make."

I nodded and silently contemplated what I was going to say.

****

City of Sandglass Volume 3 - The Time Turner's Watch

Coming Soon November 2025

City of Sandglass: Time, Time Council

Hour Representing	Name of Council Member	Responsibility to Run
1	Tim McKobe	Head of the Safety and Security Department
2	Tina Marrowe	Head of Discipline for all Citizens
3	Tobey Kai	Head of the Night Hunters/Spies
4	Tommy Kai	Head of the Financial Department
5	Tyeisha Bradley	Head of Education and Civil Resources Department
6	Tyrone Mattley	Head of Natural Resources Department
7	Tanya Fidel	Head of Job Security and Placement
8	Terrance Kindle	Head of Health and Well Being Department
9	Taylor Kai	Head of Security Department / Financial Department, second in command
10	Terry Kai	Second in Command of the Night Hunters Department and Special Projects
11	Tessa Stormberg	Head of Social Injustices Department and Judge for Social and Criminal Cases
12	Theresa Diavecca	Head of Housing Authority Department
13	Theodore Johnson	Duties Unknown

From the Author of Grey Matter Book Series....

City of Sandglass Volume 2:
Beyond the Trenches and the Damascus Sword

Written By:
Anthony S Parker

The City of Sandglass Volume 2 – Beyond the Trenches and the Sword of Damascus

Bellatrix Kai now a woman coming of age has grown so much over the years and yet seemingly she still struggles with the pains and horrors of her past. Those around her try to support and help her as she struggles with gaining power. Gaining a lot of wisdom along the way, she gets through grief from the loss of those she once knew and loved and with those who are suffering from grief around her. Attempting to be strong-willed and persevere through these life struggles she only becomes stronger as the bonds of friendship are reinforced, and she learns of more secrets while going on adventures with those she loves.